MW00488332

2/27/09

RAVENHEART

K. A. Thomas

Comfort PUBLISHING

Copyright © 2008 by K. A. Thomas.

All rights reserved. No part of this book may be reproduced, stored in a retrieval system or transmitted in any form or by any means without the prior written permission of the publishers, except by a reviewer who may quote brief passages in a review to be printed in a newspaper, magazine or journal. The author guarantees all contents are original and do not infringe upon the legal right of any other person or work. The views expressed in this book are not necessarily those of the publisher.

First printing.

Cover design by Colin L. Kernes

Library of Congress Control Number: 2008935569
ISBN 978-0-9802051-5-2

PUBLISHED BY COMFORT PUBLISHING, LLC
www.comfortpublishing.com
Printed in the United States of America

›

For Chris
My Starshine

"I am my beloved's and my beloved is mine..."

PROLOGUE

KEEPER KELVIN LOOKED WESTWARD from the white sandy beach over the great expanse of ocean that now separated him and his people from their former home. After six days of sailing, they could no longer see the pillar of smoke rising over what had been a prosperous island nation. Kelvin could only assume that the island had finally been swallowed up by the ocean after the flames from the mountain had left it barren. This had been the prophecy, after all. For many years, the keepers on the island had known that the final day could come at any moment. Still, Keeper Kelvin marveled that it was he who would see his people into the next age of their existence.

The morning sun was rising behind the keeper and a cool breeze came off the ocean, lifting his priestly robes and twirling them about. Kelvin turned away from the west and let his attention fall to the sandy shore where men were pulling the longboats onto the dry land, women and children still bundled up inside the sturdy crafts.

There were only four boats that escaped the island and survived the six day journey to this new land. Kelvin could not count the crafts the evening they departed. The situation was far too desperate for counting. All he knew were the reports provided by the other keepers. Keeper Granvor had reported to him the loss of two ships shortly after they had departed the docks. Granvor had seen the ship's sails catch fire when the showers of soot and cinders from the mountain blew into their path. There was no turning back to save the three or four hundred folk who went into the water. The danger from the mountain was too great. Two other keepers also reported losses but had not wrung their hearts to explain what exactly had occurred. Kelvin, too, had seen his own burning ship and was grateful for their lack of detail.

The population of the island had to have been upwards of fifty-thousand people.

With only four boats left containing no more that four hundred souls a piece, the death toll was painfully clear.

Kelvin imagined that most of the islanders had died in the first few minutes of the disaster as a cloud of thick ash rushed towards them in a whirling wind of death. Cities were wiped out in seconds and there was little time for escape. Those that had made it to the ocean, into the safety of the boats, had little with them. Only the most valuable or most sacred of possessions had been saved. There was little food and fresh water. After three days of hard sailing, they had found no other land. All they had ever known was their island. The people murmured that they would find no other land, that the Creator God had doomed them to a watery death.

On the morning of the fourth day they spotted birds. By mid-day, they could see land in the distance, a tiny speck of mountain top rising out of the cool waters. The people had shouted, hugged each other, and they sang their praises to the Creator God louder than ever before. The people came to Keeper Kelvin and kissed the ends of his robes.

"Surely, Keeper, the blessing of the Creator God will return now! Surely his power will come back!"

Kelvin touched a blue stone pendant around his neck, remembering their joy. The stone had not been warm with magic for weeks, nor did a hint of power return with the sighting of land. The blessing of the Creator God was gone. Kelvin knew that it would be many years before the blessing would return. Still, he could not bear to disappoint the people who had only just found their hope. He said nothing.

Keeper Kelvin looked across the water to the furthest boat being pulled onto the beach of the mysterious land before them. A tall man in long red robes stood in the water directing the ship's path toward land. This was another keeper, the Keeper of Time. Kelvin felt anger and sadness stir in his heart. His long years as a servant of the Creator God told him to repress such feelings, but he could not find the strength. The man's selfish pride had destroyed them all.

Kelvin looked for the red pendant around the man's neck but did not find it. The evil red stone, the sister stone of Kelvin's pendant, was not in its usual place. Kelvin scanned the boat and sure enough, found the man's youngest daughter sitting quite forlornly with a small gold box resting on her lap. She stroked the box, almost unconsciously it seemed, with affection.

Since the disaster on the island, two surviving keepers had come to look upon Kelvin as their leader. Only the third keeper with the red robes, Keeper Talfor, showed him any disrespect. It made some sense. Kelvin was the Keeper of Creation and by nature, time destroys everything that is created. It had been Kelvin's idea to put one keeper on each boat. After all, the people had looked to them for leadership on the island and now they were the only leaders the people had. Their king and his entire family had been wiped out in the first cloud of ash from the mountain.

The last boat was now being pulled ashore, and Kelvin watched closely.

"Keeper Wadro, keep your boat in line!" he shouted as gently as possible to the short, balding man trying to direct the other survivors in their endeavor to get the boat ashore. Wadro had fallen behind or come close to ramming the other boats many times on their journey. Kelvin was relieved to have found their salvation if it meant only that he did not have to keep track of Wadro's boat. The man was an excellent keeper but a depressingly bad seaman.

Finally, the boats were unloaded and the people could not resist shouting for joy as the last mother and child stepped onto dry land. It was an amazing moment, and as Kelvin stood with the other keepers, he felt for the first time that they might actually be able to begin anew.

This new land was different than their old home. The air was decidedly cooler than the people were used to, and the trees were taller and more numerous. Above the shoreline Kelvin could see a thick spread of brilliantly green grassland bordered by an evergreen forest. Beyond the trees, gray mountains rose out of the earth like jagged teeth cutting across the landscape.

Kelvin could find no signs of people in his view. It would be foolish, however, to assume the land to be uninhabited. Though their island nation was isolated, it did trade with many independent fishermen who spoke of villages and tribes inhabiting a vast mainland.

Wadro and Granvor set about organizing groups to look for berries and fruit while Kelvin gathered the surviving fishermen and had them set about making nets. Later, they would begin transforming one of the longboats into an efficient fishing vessel.

As night began to approach, the shoreline where they had landed seemed to have transformed in the course of one day into a tiny, rudimentary village. Torches were set up to break through the darkness and women set about boiling water and looking for herbs that might be growing nearby. Men were returning from the surrounding trees with rabbits and other small game for roasting. Children worked to turn blankets into small tents and had their first meal in days.

Kelvin looked over the encampment with relief as he waited for the other keepers to join him by a small campfire. But it was not a keeper who next greeted him. As he watched, a beautiful woman made her way through the tents and slowly approached. She carried a small wooden bowl. Her auburn hair was pulled back behind her back and her simple white robes were stained from her work that evening. She knelt in front of the keeper, offering the bowl up to him.

"Keeper, the priestesses and I insist on you eating. It has been many days and . . ."

"Have you and the others eaten?" he interrupted.

She nodded, "We have, sir."

He took the bowl from her hands and drank the broth inside. He was hungry, but it was his duty to make sure those around him were fed first. "Stand up, Priestess. What is your name?"

"I'm Luna, a priestess that served the king in his temple to the Creator God."

"And how did you survive?" he questioned, grateful that yet another servant of the Creator God had survived the blast. "The temple was destroyed within moments."

She frowned, remembering the tragedy, "I was away, on the coast visiting my sister." She gestured back toward another camp fire. Here there was a circle of women including one who looked remarkably like Luna. "I beg your forgiveness, sir," she bowed slightly. "My sister serves the spirit Kal, the one who had proclaimed herself the Goddess of Time."

"And you?" he asked. "Who do you serve?"

"I am loyal only to the God who creates." She looked up at him and smiled. "I'm glad to see you here, sir. It gives me hope."

He could not help but return her smile. "It's good to be hopeful, priestess."

She bowed once more and made her way back to the little fire where her sister and some of the other priestesses had gathered. She glanced back once, offering him another smile. It brought him a sense of joy he had never allowed himself to feel before. Keepers were not allowed to love women. Perhaps in this new world some things would change.

The arrival of the other keepers turned his thoughts away from the priestess. There they were standing before him, waiting for direction: Talfor, Wadro, and Granvor. They all bowed to each other in recognition and respect of each other's titles and then Kelvin began.

"Keepers, the disaster that has befallen us is grave. The power of the Creator God has left us." He touched his pendant. "And the spirits that were sent to us for guidance have betrayed or left us." Kelvin eyed Talfor who shifted uncomfortably, and then he continued, "It is my belief that we should destroy or bury the red pendant that very likely caused our world to crumble. We should then build a temple here to the Creator God and seek his appeasement."

Talfor huffed, "Seek the appeasement of the God that deserted us, left us to die in fire and ash?!"

Wadro banged his staff on the ground. "You have no right to contradict anything that is said, Keeper. It was the foolishness of your daughter that caused all of this!"

"Silence!" Granvor, the oldest among them shouted. "We will get nowhere lifting our voices. Keeper Kelvin is wise and he, more than all of us, has the right to lead."

No one spoke for a moment. Then Kelvin began again, "The red pendant was never meant to be. It's very powerful and dangerous. We know, Keeper Talfor, that you were not responsible for its creation and therefore, we will not hold you responsible for what it was used for. However, now it is in your possession and it is dangerous. It must be destroyed."

He nodded, "It is very powerful, I agree. But perhaps in the right hands..."

"There are no right hands for this pendant. It was created by Kal and can only be used to destroy. I've seen its nature and so have you."

Wadro nodded in agreement, "Destroy it. You have my support."

"And mine." Granvor stepped to Kelvin's side. "All the remnants of Kal should have perished on the island as far as I'm concerned."

"Then we are in the majority. Keeper Talfor? Will you follow this decision?" Keeper Kelvin regarded the man with as much compassion as he could muster.

After a moment, Keeper Talfor nodded, "I will bring the pendant to you in the morning."

"Very well." Kelvin looked at each of the keepers. "We will destroy the pendant in front of all the people as an example of what can happen when the quest for power rules a life."

Talfor said nothing more. He turned abruptly to leave, his face contorted in a disgusted frown. Granvor stopped him, taking his arm. "You would do well to listen to Kelvin's wisdom."

Talfor only pulled away, unable to look at them. His steps were heavy and angry as he made his way through the people to his daughter's side. Kelvin watched Talfor as the keeper whispered to the girl. Finally, Kelvin turned and spoke to the others, "Let him go. He's angry and tired. In time, he will see the rightness of our decision."

The men went their separate ways into the darkness. Kelvin stood for a long time in front of the fire thinking about the future. He said a short prayer to himself, hoping that the Creator God would send them a sign of where to go and what to do. Would they ever be a great society again?

The morning would bring even more questions. Keeper Talfor was missing and with him, more than three hundred of the island's survivors. The red pendant was gone and there was no way to get it back. Confronting Keeper Talfor could mean a skirmish and no one wanted to see more lives lost. Kelvin took comfort in the fact that the pendant was powerless for now, only able to be brought back to life when and if the Creator's Pendant came to power again. That time would be many years in the future, perhaps centuries. Kelvin could only hope that then, the red pendant would be destroyed. Only time and prophecy would tell.

As he looked for hope over the field that stretched in front of them and in the forest that lay to the north, a woman made her way toward him. As she stepped up beside him, she took his hand.

"My sister and the other priestesses are gone. I feel as though I am alone."

Kelvin squeezed Luna's hand. "You are not alone."

It was in that moment that his eyes caught sight of something white and beautiful running across the plains before them. Out of instinct, he reached for the bow slung over his back.

Chapter 1

OTTO WENT WALKING IN THE woods every day. His life was routine, marked by a rhythm that not even drums could mimic. Sunrise was a quick breakfast in the town square where all the old widowers took their meals. Then it was off to help his friend, Jasper, tend to his garden. After his lunch, he worked on the furniture he made for the town's wealthy inhabitants. In the best part of the day, after the evening meal, when the sun was just about to scuttle off behind the horizon, he walked in the woods.

It was not a social life but it was an ordinary one for an old dwarf like himself. In his younger years he had been quite a popular fellow, the most handsome and charming dwarf in the town. He married the town beauty and he loved her with a fire that would make a blacksmith blush. Everything seemed perfect until the following year when she prepared to give birth to their first child. Being male, he was not allowed into the small birthing room of their home. His wife was attended by several birthing mistresses who assured Otto that all would be well. But soon, the birthing mistresses sent for more aid and after just a few hours had summoned the herb mistress, the most skilled of the dwarf healing tradition. Long hours passed before Otto finally heard the soft cry of a baby.

But his joy was not to last. No sooner had they put the baby in his arms than the birthing mistresses informed him of his wife's condition. Otto had barely enough time to say goodbye before his darling closed her eyes and journeyed into the great abyss of the unknown. It was only a week later that the little child Otto loved so dearly followed his mother in death. He had been tiny and suffered greatly from a congestion the herb mistress could not understand. Otto sobbed, too heartbroken to assist, as he watched his friends place the carefully bundled child into the cold ground. It was many months before the dwarf emerged from his house to once again sell his furniture at the market.

By tradition and law, dwarfs marry only once. So at a very young age, Otto joined the ranks of the widows and widowers who took their meals together and distanced themselves from the rest of the township. They provided each other with comfort and friendship in hopes of forgetting what they had all lost.

However, Otto missed the constant companionship of a wife. It was not in any dwarf's nature to be shy or withdrawn, and he longed for company, some constant chatter as he worked to keep himself from thinking about his wife and child. In an effort to assuage his loneliness, he adopted a small kitten which he named Jack. He and Jack were instant friends, and Otto enjoyed caring for the small animal. But the old dwarf still felt a longing in his heart for something more.

It was then that he endeavored not to think of what he had lost. Otto buried himself in his little cat and his work and his long evening walks. He sorted out the days passing with diligence and planned for what the next day might bring, keeping his mind filled with thoughts of work and his simple life.

On this chilly fall day, he thought of the chairs he had left to make and how he might carve a table from one solid oak trunk. Otto thought of his friend, the weaver, who he could ask to make him a warm coat for the approaching winter. Maybe he could also trade a few solid wood chairs to one of the farmers to pay his portion of the cost to feed the widowers.

As he was thinking, he watched a cold wind scatter leaves across the forest floor. It seemed to carry them gracefully, like fairies dancing in the air. But the breeze also carried something else: a queer, soft sound. Otto quieted his thoughts and listened carefully as the cry came again. Memories from many years before were suddenly dancing in his head. Even though he was a father only briefly, he knew the sound of a child in distress.

Otto calmed himself and told his uneasy thoughts that it might be a bleating kid who had lost its mother nanny goat or maybe a calf crying in the evening air. But when he heard it for a third time, his heart quickened. This could be nothing other than a child.

He followed the cries to the edge of a stream, and there, he saw a baby wrapped carefully against the cold in warm fleece blankets and nestled in the long grass under a tree. It looked as if the child had been placed there with care, as if a mother and father might reappear at any moment.

When the child saw Otto, its soft crying stopped and it looked at him with wonder. The child could not have been more than a few months old and was clearly human from her shape. The border of the human kingdom was only a three-day ride by pony down the steep mountainside and so it was reasonable that a child could get lost in the woods. However, here was a child too young to walk and humans never came this close to the dwarf villages. The peoples preferred to keep to themselves for their own reasons.

Otto looked at the child and the child looked at Otto. For long moments he stood there contemplating what to do.

"Hello?" he called in a low voice to the trees. "Is anyone around?"

It was a silly question, but somehow Otto needed to ask it. Did he honestly expect the child's parents to suddenly appear from behind a tree? No one was in sight and if someone had been anywhere around, Otto would have heard the break of a branch or the sound of footsteps on pine needles. It was not an easy thing to hide in the forest.

Carefully, he approached the bundle and held out his hand, feeling of the soft wrappings. He let out a cry and stepped back as he felt the fierce tug of a tiny hand only a little smaller than his own take hold of his beard and give it a swift yank.

The child laughed at his outburst, a long, gleeful baby laugh, and its fat lips smiled at him.

"You are a strong one, aren't you?" He smiled, sensing a dimly familiar emotion gripping his chest. He had felt this way when he held his own sick child in his arms.

He sighed. There was nothing to do now but take the human baby home for he certainly couldn't leave it to a cold fall night.

Heaving the bundle into his arms, he made his way carefully back to the village, the baby cooing and laughing the entire way.

Otto was unsure of exactly what to do with the child so he brought it to the village square where he knew many of the other widows and widowers gathered after the evening meal to talk and make merry before nightfall.

When he approached them carrying the baby, he was immediately greeted by a fanfare of widows, young and old. They bombarded him with questions and marveled over the child in his arms.

"A baby! A human baby. Where did you find it? How can this be? Is it a boy or a girl? So large…"

So Otto sat down on one of their benches and, holding the child protectively in his arms, he told of how he had found it hidden in the grass beside the stream.

"The stream's too low even in this time of year to carry such a burden. Someone must have placed her there," one of the women said after he finished his tale.

"How do you know it's a girl?" one of the men asked.

The woman only chuckled. It was Girda, and she had given birth to ten children. Her husband had died only the previous year, and had he not, no one doubted that she would be giving birth to her eleventh child.

"Check under the wrappings if you will, but that's a girl's laugh if I ever heard one. Let me hold her, Otto, you poor man, heaving her all this way."

Otto handed the child to Girda but moved to sit next to them, keeping a protective eye on his forest find. Had the child been a dwarf and smaller, he would not have given her up at all.

The group talked amongst themselves for almost an hour before deciding they should call the town chief to the square for his wise judgment on the matter. Someone went to fetch him, and the others stood around, gawking at the baby.

"What should we call her?" Girda asked. "It's not right for a child to go without a name even if we only keep her for a few days."

"For a few days?" Otto felt a stab as he said it.

"Certainly. Surely her parents will be found or some sign of how she was lost." She cuddled the child closer. "Poor dear."

The others murmured softly around them as Otto looked into the child's eyes. She was looking back at him much as she had when he first saw her in the forest. Her eyes were the color of the richest forest leaves. They burned like emeralds in the deepest caverns of the earth.

"Ayla," he said, "because I found her under an oak tree. And her eyes, they're. . .they're the color of spring leaves."

Ayla meant oak tree in the old dwarf tongue. Girda shook her head, "You men and your professions. Have to give them a name for what you work. Can't be Bonnie or Liana, has to be named for an old tree."

Otto smiled, remembering that Girda's husband had been an iron worker and all of her children had the names of the metals he labored over. Long ago, Otto had named his own weak son Pafe, for a tree that grew along the river bank and was just as weak and sad to look at as that small babe. Girda was right.

When the town chief, Justra, arrived at the square he had already been told what the messenger knew about Otto's encounter, but he asked that the widower relay it again. He listened with a keen and interested ear.

"Girda and I had just decided to call her Ayla when you arrived," Otto finished, waiting for the chief's reply.

Chief Justra's brows furrowed with an air of concern, "This human child could mean much trouble for us, Otto. What if her parents only lost her in the woods and we have humans coming into the village to search for her. Or even worse, what if a human comes here looking for her and accuses us of taking her by force?"

The crowd murmured. The thought of humans coming into their town was not a pleasant one. They did not even deal with the creatures in matters of trade and few dwarfs had even seen one up close. They knew of them from books and drawings but little else was known. It was rumored that they were mistrusting and war-like, eager to fight any battle that they thought they could win.

"But what shall we do with her?" Otto asked, eagerly awaiting the chief's judgment. In a dwarf town, a chief's pronouncement was as good as a human lord or kings. Dwarfs existed in towns and villages, but not as a nation. It was for each community to decide how it wished to act. Only occasionally did the chiefs of every town and village gather to decide matters of trade.

Chief Justra nodded, satisfied with his decision, "We will send a message into the human kingdom with the next market trader that passes along the forest road. We will say what we have found and ask that someone comes to claim her."

"And if no one comes?" Otto asked.

"Then," said Justra, "we will take her to the nearest human village and leave her with someone who knows how to care for her rightly."

Another murmur passed through the gathering of dwarfs and Otto stood up, "Sir, if no one comes to claim the child, I would like to keep her for a companion in my old age." There arose a startled cry from the crowd around him. Otto continued, raising his voice above the crowd, "As you know my own wife and child died many years ago, and I have been alone all this time. It would be comforting to have someone to care for and to look after."

Chief Justra shook his head, "Otto, we don't know the first thing about caring for a human child. . ." he hesitated and then added, "I know you're alone, Otto, but a human child is not a cat. . ."

"It can't be all that different from a dwarf child and I learned much about that in the week before I lost my own son." He faltered a bit, his voice cracking, "Sir, I found this babe in the woods and I feel. . .I feel I should care for her."

There was silence as all awaited the Chief's response. He looked from the widower in front of him, old, fingering his hat and graying beard, to the child in Girda's arms. After a moment, he let out a tired sigh.

"If no one claims her, you may care for her."

Otto smiled broadly, "Thank you, sir. Thank you."

Chief Justra held up a halting hand, "But I fully expect her to be claimed, and if someone comes into this town looking for her, I expect no fuss in giving her up."

Otto nodded, "No fuss. None at all."

Chief Justra left them and the group of old and young widows and widowers gathered around the child again, cooing and talking in high tones to the little girl who was already almost half the size of Otto.

Chapter 2

THE WHOLE TOWN WAS BUSY preparing for the festivities. It was the beginning of spring and in just a few hours, the annual Matchmaking Ball would take place. All boys and girls who had lived through at least fifteen summers were required by both tradition and law to participate.

This would be Ayla's second year to go.

The ball took place in the town's center square, boys gathering on one side and girls gathering on the other. After the Chief announced the start of the festivities with the crowning of the Matchmaking Ball Prince and Princess, the two parties came together, took dance partners, and paraded around the square in a lively choreographed dance. The prince and princess were chosen by all the younger children who would vote the week before the ball. After being announced and crowned with rings of flowers, the prince and princess generally led the choreographed dancing throughout the ball.

Ayla knew the dance well though she had never danced it in the square.

Those boys or girls left without partners gathered with their parents on the sides of the square and waited. Many were asked to dance soon after the first lively parade. A few were not asked to dance at all.

The boys and girls would dance constantly through the evening, twirling and spinning with great laughter and excitement. The girls wore their hair down and decorated their tangled locks with flowers. The boys wore their best frocks and groomed their beards. Sometime just after midnight, the chief would appear and announce the final dance.

This time, each boy would choose a girl to be his final partner and he would lead her to the floor. Weddings were celebrated in the days that followed.

The girls who weren't chosen or the boys who refused to choose went back to their families for another year to await the next Matchmaking Ball. Children only became adults after they were married or after they had lived eighteen summers. Past that age, a child was no longer allowed to participate in the Matchmaking Ball and would join the ranks of widows, widowers, and orphans who cared for each other in their own way.

Ayla sat on the floor of her father's home and tried not the think about what was to come. Girda stood behind her, brushing her long dark hair and twirling the strands into braids.

"You have such beautiful locks, my darling," Girda cooed to her, knowing she was nervous about the night that lay before her.

Ayla knew that she was different. She was not a dwarf and there was no boy in this town who would ever choose her to be his bride. Who wanted to marry a girl that was at the very least a head taller than the tallest standing boy?

Last year, she had been the only girl to leave unmatched. She watched as the dwarf families shook their heads and turned away from her either in pity or in shame. She saw her best friends, Coren and Amber, married that year. Since they started their own families, they had not made time to speak with her. Not that they had really ever been her friends. More than once she caught them giggling with the other children about her size and there were many times that she was not invited to play in their games.

"It doesn't matter that my locks are beautiful, Girda. I'm tall and I'm ugly. No one will pick me." Ayla leaned forward, resting her head in her hands as Girda began to adorn her braids with flowers.

"There's nothing wrong with being an herb mistress or a teacher at the academy, you know."

Girda was trying to make her feel better. By tradition, though not law, women who became teachers or herb mistresses did not marry. A married woman's primary concern should always be her husband, and the jobs were much too time-consuming for women burdened with children.

But Ayla did not want to be an herb mistress or a teacher. A part of her wanted a normal dwarf life with children and a family. But there was also something else. It was a desire she couldn't name, just a feeling that lived on the edge of her heart telling her there might be something special waiting for her in the world.

However, Ayla knew she might never discover her true desire. Girda and Otto had been talking to an herb mistress since the previous spring, trying to get her to accept Ayla as an apprentice. Otto had recently insisted that Ayla include the names of all the principal herbs in her studies. It seemed to Ayla that her days of dreaming were nearly over. Soon enough, she would find herself under the watchful eye of a lonely widow, learning about plants and weeding gardens.

"There," Girda said, slipping the last flower into her hair. "Don't you look beautiful, my dear."

Ayla loved the way Girda called her dear. The woman had always been like a mother to her even though she had five other daughters to look after. As those daughters grew up and took husbands, it seemed the woman was ever closer to Ayla.

But Ayla wondered why Girda insisted on calling her beautiful when she was so very obviously a tall, ugly thing. The dwarfs valued women who were small and had bodies thick around the hips, good for child bearing. Long blonde or red hair twisted into thick braids was considered charming for an unmarried girl of Ayla's age. Ayla had none of these features to distinguish her. She was tall and slender with unruly black hair that could never, even under Girda's strong hands, be forced into a braid. Her face was thought plain and too thin looking, its complexion wanting for a color which the sun seemed never to be able to provide. Indeed, it was widely agreed upon by all of dwarf community that Ayla's only beautiful feature could be found in her namesake. Her green eyes were deep and knowing, a look that many an old dwarf recognized as a blessing from the Creator God.

The front door of the little house shut with a soft thud and both turned in the direction of the noise. Girda kissed her cheek, "That would be your father returning. I must have words with him. I'll send him to have a look at you in a moment."

Girda shuffled out of Ayla's room and closed the door, showing the girl a broad smile that Ayla could tell was for show. The woman was tired and her mind was preoccupied with something serious.

Ayla crawled on her hands and knees to the door. She was used to the position as it was the only way for her to get around the tiny dwarf houses. She leaned her head against the cracks in the door and listened.

"What do you mean? Do you want to send her away?" her father was saying in a hushed voice.

"Well, isn't it time the girl got to know her own people? She dreams of a dwarf life here with us."

"She is a dwarf girl! There's not one reason why she shouldn't…"

"Otto, listen to yourself! She may have been raised a dwarf, but she'll never be one. She can't be one, and no boy will pick her tonight, you know that."

Ayla knew it was true but to hear it spoken by Girda – she felt a piece of her heart break off and rise as a lump in her throat.

"So she'll be an herb mistress or a good teacher…"

"That's not what she wants. She wants to lead a normal life with the hope of love and…"

Otto's voice was rising. Ayla had never heard him speak in more than just a firm voice, even when she was being scolded. "We all wanted that, Girda. We all wanted it at some point, but some of us can't have it!"

There was silence between the two adults for a moment before Girda spoke. "Don't condemn that girl to a life of loneliness, Otto. You have done a fine job of raising her and she's beautiful and wonderful. She deserves to go back to her own people. It's time to send her home."

Ayla heard the front door slam and quickly, she crawled back to her space in front of the mirror before her father entered. She pretended not to have heard and tugged at one of the flowers in her hair.

"Hello, daughter," her father said softly.

"Hello, father," she said in calm reply. It was tradition for children to always greet their father's return home from the day's labor with such a greeting.

Otto took a few steps toward her and rested both his hands on her shoulders. She looked down at her lap, realizing that only when she was sitting were his shoulders even with hers.

"I know you too well," he said. "You have been perched behind that door listening to Girda and me argue. Am I right?"

She could only nod. Children were forbidden to lie outright to their parents.

Ayla would not even consider deceiving him. She felt an unwanted tear stream down her face.

"Ayla," said her father's calm voice. "You tell me what you want, and I will make it happen."

She turned and looked back at him. "I want ... to stay."

It was all she managed before a small sob began, and she put her face into her hands.

He stroked her hair careful of the flowers and hummed a sweet melody that his wife dreamed of singing to their own child many years ago.

"Daughter," he said, "would you be content to be an herb mistress or to teach at the academy?"

She shook her head, trying to fight the tears, "No.... but maybe I'll grow to like it. ..maybe I'll..." She stopped. She could not imagine ever learning to love working with plants or with the tiny dwarf children who stared at her when she walked into the town's markets. Still, they seemed less horrifying than the thought of being sent away from all she had ever known. As much as she wanted something more, she didn't feel strong enough to seize the opportunity to seek it out. "Don't make me go."

"I'll not make you go anywhere. But I want you to be happy." He stopped and thought for a moment. "When no one came from the human kingdom to claim you, I knew that the Creator God had given me a great gift. You are a dwarf to me and to Girda, and we will love you always." He looked into her crying green eyes, "You are so beautiful. Let us not speak of such sad chances, eh? Maybe a boy will take you away tonight. And if not, you have one year yet."

He smiled at her and she could not help but smile back. She knew that there was no chance of anyone picking her at the dance tonight, but she felt a small winged hope flutter in her chest.

That day, Otto and Ayla did not take their supper with the widows and widowers in the square. It was custom for each family to take in a few of the widows and orphans and provide them with a meal on the night of the Matchmaking Ball. It was all a part of the spring tradition. Ayla and her father, however, preferred to use the occasion as an opportunity to dine together in their small house. Otto made a fine bean pudding and Ayla was able to get some strips of ham, dried and salted, left over from winter storage. It was quaint for a spring feast but Ayla didn't care. She would rather dine with her father than any other company in the world.

The sun's pink glow just on the tops of the trees signaled that it was time. As soon as evening lapsed into night, the children would begin their dance.

Ayla looked at her plain brown boots the entire way to the town square. She had never got used to the stares of the other children, and she did not want to see any of them on her way to being left out once again.

Despite knowing that she would not be picked for any dances tonight, she reviewed the steps in her mind and clicked the beat of that first song with her tongue. The memory of trying to learn that dance was seared into her mind.

Unlike the other children, Ayla had never gone to school. Her father had taught her everything she needed to know and the chief conceded that it was probably best she learn at home. But when it came time to learn the matchmaking dance, Otto insisted she join the other children.

"You'll make friends," he told her. "Besides, I could only teach you to dance like a man."

It was a miserable two weeks.

None of the boys wanted to be her partner and the girls shot her laughing eyes and whispered to each other. She ended up bent over and dancing with quite possibly the stupidest boy she had ever met. She vowed never to forget the dance if only to prevent her from ever having to learn it again.

It was one of those dreadful days when she had run home and asked her father if he could saw off the bottom half of her legs.

"I'll wear my shoes where my knees are and no one will notice how tall I am!" She was sobbing and laughing as she said it, trying to put on a brave face but wishing also that her father could understand what it felt like to be different.

He only sat next to her, patting her shoulder comfortingly, "No, no, you are exactly how you are supposed to be. If they don't like you just because you are tall, then they are silly and stupid and they are missing out on the most wonderful person I know." He grinned at her and then added, "And besides, your shoes wouldn't fit on your knees."

She loved the way he always managed to make her laugh even when she felt like sobbing. Otto was her father as far as she was concerned and perhaps never having her own family wouldn't be that bad. She could take care of him as he got older and perhaps even take up his trade one day instead of being a teacher or a herb mistress.

As she arrived at the town square, she looked up and saw that many of the girls were already there. She walked to the right side and stood on the very corner of the stone square. Perhaps no one will notice that I don't get picked, she thought. Maybe if I just stand here all night...

She raised her eyes from her boots and watched the girls and boys gather around her. She was very aware that she stood at least a head and a half taller than anyone around her. Her cheeks went a rose color and she sat down. Maybe then even fewer dwarfs would notice her.

Golda and Jem were lining up next to her. They were Girda's twin daughters, her youngest, and this would be their first year to participate in the festival. They had been eligible the previous year, but both girls had come down with illnesses and could not attend the dance. Consequently, the two boys who had plans to pick them had not picked at all the previous year. Ayla looked across the square and saw the boys waving.

"Golda," Ayla said, getting the girl's attention, "those boys are waving..."

"We see them!" The petite blonde dwarf snapped and waved back to the boys. Her sister followed her lead and the two of them took a few steps away from Ayla.

Golda and Jem were nothing like their mother. In fact, Girda's children had not lived with their mother in the sixteen years she had been a widow. It was custom for any unmarried children of a widow or widower to go to a married aunt or uncle to be raised. Only in the case of there being no living or no fit relative to take the children was a parent allowed to raise a child alone. Girda spent time with her children every day, but they were the responsibility of Girda's older sister and her husband. Ayla had met Girda's sister only once and could not remember her name. In a moment of self-righteousness she decided the woman's name wasn't worth remembering. She had been pig-headed and rude.

Ayla shifted to sit on her knees and looked over to the small platform that sat on the edge of the square. Some of the older men were gathering there now with their lutes and fiddles. The sun had disappeared over the horizon, and Ayla could feel the day turning to night. Torches were lit and the chief took to the center of the platform.

"Welcome, all you people of Glendon Town, to the annual Matchmaking Ball!"

There arose a number of cheers from the crowd and everyone clapped excitedly. Ayla managed to put her hands together a few times.

"Tonight we will give away many of our girls and boys to be brides and grooms in the coming week. Here, they will pass the threshold into adulthood and we, as parents, will watch them come into fresh, beautiful lives of their own."

'Not me,' thought Ayla, as she found her eyes straying back to her boots again, 'It won't happen to me.'

Another man stepped onto the platform and handed the chief a small piece of paper. The chief cleared his throat and offered a small grin to the crowd, "And now the time has come to announce the prince and princess of the Matchmaking Ball." He unfolded the paper. His grin turned into a frown. He called the other man over to look at it and after a confirming nod, the chief cleared his throat.

"The prince will be Gustave Yurison."

There was a small gasp from the surrounding adults and confused looks. The children covered their mouths to hide their laughter as Gustave took the stage and was crowned. It was the boy Ayla had learned to dance with. She felt a knot growing in her stomach.

'They're making fun of him,' she thought.

The chief clapped as the flowers were put on Gustave. The boy stood there grinning like a happy cat. Ayla realized he didn't know he was the brunt of some awful joke.

"The princess will be Ayla Ottodaughter."

She gasped when she heard her name and felt her heart beating horribly fast in her chest.

Golda punched her shoulder, "Well, get up there, princess!" Then she laughed.

Ayla stood up, and amidst the shushed laughter of the children and the hushed whispers of their parents, she made her way to the platform. Unwanted tears were streaking down her face. All this time she thought the other children were at least kind enough not to notice her. She thought they would at least leave her alone in her isolation and misery, but now it appeared that was not the case. They had condemned her to public humiliation, leading the dances as a mockery of what she was – a dwarf in human skin. Worse – some girl had given up her privilege to be Ball Princess so that they could shame Ayla for everything she was but did not want to be.

When she got to the platform, she stood there looking at her feet for a moment before she realized no one was putting a crown of flowers on her head. She looked down, and the chief was standing there holding the crown unable to reach. Embarrassed, she took the crown and placed it on herself. There was more laughter from the children and even some from their parents this time.

She forced herself to look out at the gathered group as the chief continued with the more formal announcement of the ball.

"Ye common folk of Glendon Town

Time to make merry and do not frown..."

They were staring at her. Every single pair of eyes on the square and around it was locked on her. They were not friendly eyes.

"This night youth will dance

This night they'll romance..."

She could see them smiling and whispering to one another. She knew they were gawking at how tall she was and congratulating themselves on such a brilliant plan. They were not sorry for her at all.

"A Matchmakers Ball

It will match them all..."

'Not me,' she thought. 'Not me. No one will ever marry me.'

"The child has grown

To go away from home..."

After the next verse, Gustave and she were supposed to begin the dancing. She turned to face him, trying to look happy, trying not to cry. Just because she knew what was going on did not mean she had to spoil his ignorance by revealing the joke. She wanted to just do the first dance and get it over with. Then she could hide along the corners of the square for the rest of the night.

"One story ends

Where a new one begins!"

Ayla heard the music and saw Gustave put out his hands to her. She tried not to think about what the other children were saying. She tried to forget that this was all a joke. As she tried to push out how horrible and embarrassed she was, she caught Golda sneering at her from the corner of the square. Her defenses came crumbling down and she stepped back from Gustave, shaking her head and crying.

"I'm sorry!" she said. "I can't. I just can't!"

She turned and fled the town square, sobbing and apologizing as she went.

CHAPTER 3

AYLA RAN. ONE BOOT AFTER the other hit the ground as she made her way through the houses and cobblestone streets. She passed her own house and then her father's workshop where he was sitting outside smoking his pipe.

When he saw her, he sat up. "Ayla?" he called, "Ayla, what's wrong?"

She did not dare stop. She did not want to disappoint her father by telling him what had happened. This night seemed to confirm that she was unable to live a normal dwarf life.

She passed the widows' huts and turned onto the path that would take her into the woods where she had been found. The path she followed slowly turned into the tangled web of forest debris and before long, she was pushing through the tree limbs and new growth of spring as she made her way to the stream.

When she arrived there, she stood by its banks, the trickling of the water offering her little comfort. She was exhausted from running and shaking from her tears. There was nothing left to do but clench her fists and howl at the wind.

"Curse you!" she yelled to no one, her fury finally bursting forth. "Curse you for leaving me here!" She kicked a nearby tree and quickly regretted it. She stumbled over, her foot feeling a sharp pain. She pulled her knees to her and put her head down, unable to find any more tears and too tired and hurt to stand up again.

Voices suddenly carried on the wind.

She sat up, listening. Her worst fear was that someone from the dance had followed her here and now they were going to torment her even further. Soft footsteps made their way through the underbrush. She heard the voices again.

"She'll be out here somewhere. She always goes running to that stream ..." it was her father's voice.

Then came the voice of the weaver, one of her father's good friends. "It wasn't right, what those young folks did to her, but I still don't see why the chief let her go at all."

"By law, all dwarf boys and girls must attend when. . ."

"Yes, yes, I know," said the weaver, "but I'm sorry, Otto, she's not a dwarf girl and she never will be!"

Their voices were getting closer. Ayla did not want her father to find her like this, afraid and hiding in the woods. She crawled a few paces away from the tree and carefully stepped into the stream. Her father had taught her years ago that the woods refused to conceal the steps of man or beast, but if one walked very carefully in the stream and only let the water run over his ankles, he could get away without being heard.

'I can always follow the stream back,' she reasoned to herself, and she slowly began to walk. She, like all the dwarfs in the village, had never been downstream before. There always seemed to be an unspoken danger there, a strange fear of the rest of the world. Ayla was afraid of that world, too, but the shame of encountering her father as a disgrace kept her from turning back. Step by step, she made her way through the cold water careful never to let the stream run too far over her boots.

The voices of the weaver and Otto disappeared in the trickling of the stream.

She walked for another hour, gripping her shoulders against the chilly night air. The moon was rising, but Ayla could barely make it out. A thick cover of clouds was rapidly gathering in the sky hiding the small half-moon for minutes at a time. A very dark night lay ahead of her. The tall brown rocks that rose out of the stream were turning into threatening black shadows, and the water seemed to swirl around her feet at a faster pace. Her toes were wet and cold, and one foot still throbbed slightly from kicking the tree. It was time to go home and face her father. She knew he would only try to comfort her, but inside, his heart would be breaking.

She stepped onto the bank and shook her feet to free them of as much water as possible. The leather was completely soaked and her skirt was brown around the hem. These were her best clothes. Maybe Girda could wash them clean again.

A lumbering through the woods caught her attention and she looked up, frozen in the faint moonlight. The sound of something heavy was moving through the trees just a few steps in front of her. She held her breath as the outline of the beast took shape.

It was a bear.

Most of the forest animals the dwarfs feared took to their heels when Ayla approached. A few red foxes could easily overpower a dwarf hunter, but they would flee from Ayla even when she was a child. Badgers and raccoons also presented a challenge for the dwarfs. Wild dogs were perhaps the worst, killing at least a few dwarf men every spring. Still, they all ran from Ayla.

But bears were an exception.

An encounter with a bear was a story few dwarfs lived to tell. It could take more than a dozen dwarf arrows to take down the massive beasts which made them impossible to hunt. They were terribly aggressive, and Ayla had been warned many times that bears often attacked unprovoked. One spring, a group of dwarf men traveling to another village for a rare gathering had stumbled upon a bear and her cub. Only one made it to the village. He spent several months there, recovering from his wounds.

Carefully, Ayla stepped back into the stream cautious of her every sound. Her footstep made a small splash and she stopped, looking towards the bear.

The animal stood on his hind legs and let out a soft snort. He was sniffing at the air.

Ayla didn't care who or what heard her. In her fear, she fled downstream as fast as she could, unaware of how deep the water was or where her feet were stepping. She was sure the bear was going to give chase, and her heart beat like a horrible dancing rhythm in her chest. Her wet skirts were slowing her down as the water got deeper, climbing from her ankles to half way up her shins and then to her knees. She felt like she was dragging her legs through the water as she struggled to get away.

A sharp stone on the bottom of the stream betrayed her, and she fell on her face in the cold water. She was up again in moments and chanced a look behind her. In the distance, she could see the outline of the bear sitting in the middle of the water. Ayla froze, unable to take her eyes off the massive creature. His paw was diving in and out of the water and to his mouth.

Fishing. The bear was picking out small fish and minnows. He didn't seem interested in Ayla anymore. She couldn't stifle a small thankful laugh as she took a few deep relieving breaths. The bear's fishing, she told herself. It's okay. You can go home.

She stood up, feeling the cold air strike her soaked body, and she shivered. As she regained her footing, she took one unconscious step backwards, downstream, and felt her foot slide out from under her. She hit the water again, and this time felt it pull her back, into a deeper pool. When she tried to put her feet on the bottom again, she realized she was caught up in a fast moving current, and it was pulling her further downstream and through a torrent of water. Her feet would only scrape the rock bed and she was barely keeping her head above the fast moving flow. Dwarfs had no occasion to learn how to swim.

She thrashed her arms about violently looking for anything to grab onto.

"Help!" She choked out a scream, forgetting about the bear. She knew she must be miles from the town of Glendon by now. Her head went under and she felt the current lift the crown of flowers from her hair. She struggled to the surface once more and let out another scream. "Please! Please, someone help me!"

An old dead tree was hanging over the river, its limbs dragging the water just inches away. She stretched out her hands in desperation.

"Please!" she cried again and felt her hands touch the tiniest branch. She gripped it and risked a sharp pull. Soon she was holding onto a thicker branch.

Thank you, tree, she cried in her mind.

But the tree was rotting and the branch couldn't support her weight. It broke, sending her and the tree limb spinning back into the current.

I'm sorry. She almost heard the tree cry to her. Your time has come.

Ayla held onto the branch, too exhausted to fight the current and too relieved to have something to hold onto. She pulled her head above the water as much as she could and wrapped her arms around the limb. Her eyes closed in a faint sleep as the cold water whisked her away from everything she had ever known.

Chapter 4

AYLA FELT HERSELF DRIFT IN and out of sleep as the water carried her further downstream. Once she felt herself dropping and pulled even closer to the branch, her eyes tightly shut. Both she and the wood went under the water for a moment and then they were afloat again, spinning in the current of a small waterfall.

Soon after, the rush of the water slowed and she felt herself drifting, the water gently lapping at her sides. She slept easier after that, letting the water take her where it willed.

She woke up with the sun in her eyes and her arms still clinging to the branch. At first, she wasn't sure where she was, and she blinked wildly trying to get used to the light.

She moved her right hand to grip the branch and with her left, felt the water around her. She wasn't moving, and there was a soft muddy surface at her back. She put her feet down and felt the murky bottom of the river just a few feet below. Cautiously, she stood up, still shielding the light from her eyes.

She was standing in a shallow part of the river. Just ahead of her, the water flowed under a bridge. The stone crossing had two large culverts to let water through, but was low enough to the river that Ayla and her branch had become wedged against the shoreline. It was rather lucky. Ayla could hear the rush of water downstream and knew that it meant a large waterfall was nearby.

She took a step onto the bank and sat down. How far from home was she? Reasonably, all she would have to do was follow the river upstream until she came to a section she recognized. However, the river could move faster than anyone on foot. The journey could take a week or more, and Ayla had no provisions, only a wet, tattered dress and soaked leather boots. She looked down at the flowing water and followed the river to its source with her eyes. A mountain rose above her, and she wondered if her town was on the other side. She knew she had to be close to the human border, and she shuddered at the thought. How would she explain to others like herself that she was really a dwarf?

Hoof beats on the road near the bridge caught her attention, and she quickly hid herself in the brush alongside the river. Wherever she was, she didn't want to be discovered yet. Still, curiosity got the better of her. She had never seen another human before and perhaps the travelers were only friendly merchants. A tall oak growing near the road provided just the right footing, and in a moment she had slung herself into its arms, climbing into the cover of its leaf laden branches. She found herself a comfortable, hidden spot on a branch that hung just over the road. She watched the road eagerly, holding her breath.

She knew the travelers were not merchants as soon as they came into sight, but who they were, she could not tell. It was a procession of what had to be at least fifty horsemen. Each man wore silver armor etched in gold forming the shape of a bear with its claws outstretched, ready for attack. A sword hung at each man's side and gleaming shields danced up and down on their arms. Ayla thought that this must be the most remarkable scene she had ever witnessed. She leaned out further on her branch.

The armored soldiers were led by two men who wore only light chain mail and red tunics which were also emblazoned with the clawing bear. One wore a robe lined with gold and sat very high on his horse. His blond hair was pulled back and Ayla thought it was quite odd to see a man wearing his hair like that of a woman. His face was handsome but awkwardly shaped, thin and pointed. Ayla thought he looked like a hawk made into a man.

The soldier that rode by the blonde haired man's side sat very tensely, his eyes glancing all about and his hand on his sword hilt. He wore a rather simple red cape and in dark contrast to the other man, had nearly black hair. It was pulled back in a similar fashion as the other, only it was not quite the length. As Ayla watched the men parade toward her, she thought her heart would burst. A new found sense of both dread and excitement was spinning a knot in her stomach.

The soldiers continued down the road until they reached the bridge. It was then that the dark haired lead man held up his hand and in a moment, the entire troop came to a halt.

The lead riders were right under Ayla's tree.

"We'll stop here and water the horses," the man said, putting his hand back on his sword and dismounting. His voice was young but laced with authority as well as an accent Ayla had never heard before.

The troop of soldiers quickly dismounted and led their horses down to the river below the bridge. Ayla could see why they would choose this spot. The bank was wide and flat before sloping up to the road. The horses made their way down to the water easily.

Two of the soldiers took the horses of the leading riders to the river's edge to drink and soon the dark haired man and the blonde were standing side by side under Ayla's tree, supervising the soldiers on the riverbank.

"How far to the nearest village? I'm ready to be home." The blonde spoke for the first time, crossing his arms.

"Not long now, Crown Prince. Halforton is another day yet. From there it's only four days more until we reach the capital."

They took a few steps away from her tree, and Ayla had to lean out onto the branch a bit more in order to hear them.

"I'm glad to be done with this war," the one called the crown prince said. "Our borders stretch as far as Greenwood Lake now, and if my father doesn't bother with diplomacy, we could fully conquer the kingdom by the year's end. What do you think of that?"

The other man took a deep breath, "I think it means more bloodshed."

"Are you getting soft again, Roderick?" The crown prince laughed.

"No, I was merely thinking of all the young men who were killed in this war." Ayla detected a hint of very solemn disdain in his voice. "How many more would we take for yet another campaign? There won't be any young men left to work the farms or apprentice the artisans."

"You're wrong," said the crown prince. "Because of my father's wars, the black-smiths have weapons to make and horses to shoe. There are fewer mouths to feed from the farms and in the new parts of Talforland, roads and towns will need to be built. No, no, no. . .the wars are only making us richer and stronger."

Ayla couldn't hear what the other man said in response. They were moving away again, toward the other side of the road. She inched out on her branch to try to hear them again. As she did, she heard a snap behind her and looked back. The limb was cracking near the trunk of the tree. Any second she would fall onto the path in plain sight of those below her. She looked up and grabbed the limb just above her head.

There was a louder snap and the limb she was sitting on fell to the ground. It was a long drop and now she was hanging by a branch further up in the tree, one that looked weaker than the one she had been sitting on.

Below her, the soldiers were gathering and pointing. Some laughed and she realized that they could probably see the bloomers beneath her skirt. She tried to pull herself up but could not find the strength.

"Ho there!" She heard a voice below her, "Spying from a tree, are we?"

She looked down and saw the crown prince standing in the middle of the crowd of soldiers, a broad smile on his face.

"Please!" she cried in a panic. "Please, help me!"

The soldiers only laughed more.

"What were you going to do?" the crown prince yelled again. "Drop a branch on my head?"

She looked down and for the first time noticed the one called Roderick standing at the crown prince's side. His look was grave, drawn with a frown so serious Ayla imagined that he never laughed. Roderick said something to the prince she couldn't hear.

"Fine. Alrigh,." the prince said in reply. "Get her out of there."

Roderick was already stripping the light chain mail from his arms and before long he was climbing the tree, one boot after the other. It took him only moments to reach the branch where Ayla was hanging. Gripping the trunk with one hand, he stretched out the other to her.

"Take my hand," he said. "You're going to have to trust me and let go."

The rabble below her was laughing again. Ayla winced as her hands slipped slightly against the rough skin of the tree. "How do I know I can trust you?"

"I don't think you have a lot of options."

Ayla made sure she had a tight grip with her left hand. Carefully, she extended her other hand towards him, straining to reach. Roderick slid forward and took hold of her wrist.

"I have you!" he said. "Now, let go and swing towards me."

She looked up at her other hand, "I can't."

"It's alright," he said. "I won't let you fall."

Ayla looked desperately towards the man who held tightly to her wrist. She had never even touched another human. How could she be expected to trust one so soon?

Ayla's hand slipped again and she let out a short cry. Her right hand instinctively tried to pull away from Roderick but he held her fast. She didn't have much time left to think about her decision.

Ayla took a deep breath and released the branch, swinging towards Roderick as she felt her weight pulled toward the ground. For a moment, she thought she was indeed falling. Then he had her; both Roderick's hands were firmly on her wrists and pulling her into the tree alongside him.

The soldiers below them laughed and jeered, the prince included.

"Come on," Roderick said to her quietly. "It's alright."

Slowly, he helped her climb down the tree. As she felt both feet hit the solid ground, she breathed a sigh of relief. But the relief was not to last long. When she turned around, she knew she would be facing a horde of soldiers who seemed to want only to laugh and point. It would be like the Matchmaking Ball all over again. But there was no running away this time.

As she turned, she felt a sharp pain to her head and realized too late that one of the soldiers had seized her by the hair and was pushing her to the ground.

"On your knees, peasant!" the soldier growled, and she tumbled into the dirt.

When she looked up, the crown prince was standing in front of her wearing a mischievous half smile and regarding her like freshly killed game.

"Must think she's a princess, this one. I was willing to forgive it when you were in the tree, but such a blatant show of disloyalty on the ground can't go unpunished."

The surrounding soldiers chuckled and Ayla saw Roderick step from behind her to the prince's side. "Oh, let her go, your highness. She's obviously just a lost peasant girl who came to the path to see your passing, that's all."

"Have you no humor, Roderick?" The prince was not going to let her go so easily. "She'd make a fine little maid at the palace, don't you think? I'd quite enjoy looking at her every day."

There were crude remarks from the soldiers and Ayla felt her stomach might leap right out of her mouth at any moment. Now she was sure she wanted to go home, provisions or not.

"Please!" she managed. "Chief, sir, Crown Prince...." she stammered, not knowing how to address this man properly. "I'm only lost. I fell into the river last night, and I only woke up here this morning. I'm just lost. I didn't mean to do any harm. Please, I'll just be on my way."

The men were quiet, as was the crown prince. He regarded her with a curious look, "That's a strange accent you have, girl."

A murmur went through the soldiers as Ayla continued, "I live in a dwarf town, sir, and I believe it must be miles from here. I just want to go home. Please." She felt herself starting to cry as she choked out the last words.

The men continued to whisper amongst themselves. Some made strange signs with their hands. The prince gripped Roderick on the shoulder. "Do you think she's..."

Roderick just shook his head, "I don't believe in witches."

The prince shook his head, "And I didn't believe in dwarfs but this is..."

Ayla's heart beat faster, "I'm no witch. I just want to go home. Please just let me go. I just want to go home."

The prince took a step towards her, "You say you come from the mountain, upstream?"

She shook her head yes, hoping it was the right thing to do. The prince just nodded and then said, "Bind her up and throw her in the back of one of the supply carts. We'll sort this out when I get home."

"No!" Ayla cried out but it was too late. The men had seized her and were dragging her across the road.

"Sire, if she's a witch...." she heard one of the men start.

The prince was already walking away, Roderick keeping pace next to him. "Do whatever you must."

The next thing Ayla knew was pain and darkness.

CHAPTER 5

AYLA WOKE UP TO THE SOUND of horse's hooves beating steadily against a dirt and stone road. Wheels scraped along the gravel of the road beneath her. It was a noise not unlike the scraping of her father's tools against rough, unwilling wood, and for a moment, she thought she might open her eyes to see him standing before her, ready to chide her for falling asleep in the workshop.

She could see the workshop well in her mind's eyes, having spent much of her childhood sitting on a stool next to her father studying her lessons. Like her own house or the square where the widows gathered and gossiped, it was one of the few places Ayla felt comfortable. Sometimes her father would give her a break from her lessons and would show her how to carve scrap wood into intricate, miniature figures. She made a little cat using their calico Jack as a model and some birds in flight. After Otto discovered the creations sold well in the marketplace, he let her take more time to make them. Sometimes she would sit up at night and perfect the details of her animals with her knife. She found it difficult to stop carving until her figurine was complete. Otto would often find her asleep on the floor of the workshop the next day if he left her to finish to her work. He had started to insist that she go to her bed before him just so he could be sure she was getting her rest.

The grinding of the wheels on the gravel slowly came to a halt, and Ayla opened her eyes. All at once, visions of a river and being carried off by soldiers flooded her memory. This was not the workshop and her father was not nearby. Ayla quickly tried to sit up but found her hands and feet were bound with a heavy rope. She rolled onto her back and looked up, searching her surroundings.

She was in a cloth covered wagon. There were wooden barrels and cloth sacks on every side of her marked with what she assumed was writing. The words were unfamiliar but she thought the barrels might contain food. It made sense that a group such as this would need to carry a mass of supplies. The cloth covering that kept the supplies safe and dry fell in front of her and was ripped from top to bottom for an opening, a sort of door. The strips of fabric fluttered slightly as a cool evening breeze intruded into Ayla's space. The light beyond the cloth entrance to the wagon was pale, and Ayla knew that the daylight was fading outside. How strange it was to wake up in the morning, only to have slept through the day.

Ayla rubbed her forehead. It was throbbing where the soldier had hit her that morning. She was also very aware of the hunger that burned in her stomach. The last time she had eaten was with her father, Otto, before the Matchmaking Ball.

Men were now moving and shouting to one another around the wagon. Their words were only a series of commands, ordering the troops to spread out to different sides of the road. The party was making camp for the night.

The shadows of two soldiers suddenly appeared outside the wagon, and after a moment, they raised the cloth door to peer inside.

"Well, well, well, our little witch girl is awake."

One of them held a sharp knife and wore a grin of rotted teeth on his face. The other stood by and watched her, his arms crossed indifferently. Ayla pushed herself back with her feet, sliding out of the men's reach.

"Don't try any witchy stuff or I might have to poke you!"

Ayla shook her head.

The two men climbed into the wagon and took out a barrel and a sack. "Better be glad we spotted you at the end of this journey or we wouldn't of had any room for you back here. Would have had to drag you behind."

The man with the rotted teeth laughed, and they carried away the barrel and sack leaving her alone again. It was some time later that she heard men's voices and the sound of laughter.

The sun set, and the only flickering of light she could make out was from a fire quite a distance from the wagon. The light made eerie shadows on the covering, and she closed her eyes, trying to shut them out. She caught the heavenly scent of meat cooking over a fire and wondered if the soldiers would think to feed her.

An hour passed or maybe it was longer. She sat waiting, wondering if they had forgotten about her and if she should say something or scream out loud. She thought about the man called Roderick who had helped her from the tree. She wondered who he was and if she could trust him. Would he help her get back to her town or was she now destined to stay with these humans forever? If this was any example of what humanity was, she wanted no part in it.

She was so lost in thought that she didn't hear the men approaching and was surprised when the cloth door was opened again. It was the same two soldiers as before, only now they had two others with them.

"Yeah, she's awake."

Two soldiers crawled into the cart and one lifted a small knife to her chin. Ayla let out a cry.

"Don't worry, witch girl. We're only cutting your feet free, see?"

He cut the bonds holding her feet together and the soldiers pulled her out of the cart.

"Now, we'd hate to drag you so pick up your feet."

Ayla obeyed as they led her to the light of a camp fire burning a short distance away from her cart. There on a stone sat the prince, still richly dressed and peeling an apple with his dagger. At his side was Roderick. A few others also sat around the fire but not as many as had witnessed her fall from the tree.

"Well, now," said the prince. "A great doom hasn't befallen us so I guess you aren't a witch unless you'd like to call fire down from heaven and free yourself now, hmm?"

There was a round of chuckling. Ayla looked at Roderick. The man did not wear a smile and his gaze was steady, piercing.

"Tell us, now, where you come from and I promise you'll only get a light punishment for spying."

She took a breath. All she knew to tell was the truth. Anything else would be a lie and a worthless, ill-formed one at that.

"I come from a dwarf village. I fell into that river and was swept downstream to. . ." Ayla stopped; the men were looking at each other and chuckling.

"A nice bedtime story," the prince interjected. "Fairies and dwarfs. Aren't you a little old for that nonsense?"

"It's the truth," she mumbled, looking at her feet once more.

"And what do they call you, little dwarf girl?" the prince asked.

"Ayla," she said, noticing that her voice sounded smaller and more insignificant than ever.

The prince sneered as the soldiers around him laughed again. Roderick was still silent, his expression like stone.

"Let us teach you a proper introduction," the prince said. "I am Crown Prince Noland Proudheart of Talforland, heir to the thrones of Granland, Kelvinor, and now Wadroland. As you can see, my father's empire is now quite vast." He gestured to Roderick, "Your turn, Roderick."

Roderick stood up. "I am Roderick Strongheart of Kelvinor, chief guard to his highness the Crown Prince of the Talforland Empire and captain to this rank of men which is sworn to protect him."

Roderick sat down on the rocks again and crossed his arms, still frowning. Prince Noland laughed, "He also forgot to mention that he has no sense of humor. Now you, girl. Try again."

Ayla was confused. Dwarfs did not have a second name but for their fathers or mothers. That was only used on formal occasions or when signing agreements. Mentioning where you were from seemed quite pointless unless you were, by chance, in another town or village. But dwarfs rarely left their hometown for any reason.

"I am. . ." she stuttered, "Ayla Ottodaughter of Glendontown."

The prince raised an eyebrow. "What a strange name. Where is this Glendontown?"

Ayla thought for a moment. She had never had to wonder where her town was. She knew it was next to a stream and that it must be by the mountain she had seen or beyond. She had no occasion to leave Glendon and had never wondered where it might lie according to the rest of the world.

"Well, speak up, girl."

She felt her words, weak and useless, tumble from her mouth. "I don't know."

"You don't know where your village is?"

She shook her head and looked at her feet. "I. . .I had never considered it."

The prince laughed out right and the soldiers followed suit as if unable to decide whether the comment was funny without the prince's permission.

"Such a simple mind!" he cried. "Gentleman, I believe we've stumbled across a village idiot. Roderick!"

Roderick stood again.

"You said we will ride through Halforton in the morning and that's the nearest village to where we found this prize, yes?"

Roderick only nodded.

"Then we'll prop her up on a horse and see if anyone claims her. She's bound to have family there."

Ayla was suddenly reminded of how she was found, how the town had sent word to the nearest human village that they had found a child, and could someone please come and claim her.

No one came.

This village of Halforton must be that settlement, and Ayla wondered if they would remember a sixteen-year-old message. Maybe someone could at least tell the prince that she wasn't lying. She had come from a dwarf settlement in the mountains.

Her stomach was rumbling and the smell of cooked meat hung in the air around the fire. She looked to the prince beseechingly, "Please, sir. May I ask…"

"You may ask nothing!" the prince said. "A peasant such as you are. And you will address me with the proper respect." He stood, taking a few steps toward her, looking like a hound on the foxes trail. "We'll undo your bonds if you promise not to run away. You have my assurances that if you do run away, you will be caught and rather than kill you, I'll cut out your eyes so you can stumble about blindly in the forest. Would you like that, little Ayla?"

She could only shake her head.

"Good then. We have an arrangement. Take her back to her cart and cut her bonds, but see that two guards are placed there, Roderick. She is never to be left alone. If she escapes, anyone posted on that watch will be disbanded and live as a marked man."

The prince was so close Ayla could smell the wine and digesting beef on his breath. He leaned in even closer and whispered so that only she could hear, "You are very pretty, little Ayla. I think I should like to keep you for awhile. If we do find your keepers … well, they will be paid in full."

Two of the soldiers took her by her arms and drug her back to the wagon. They didn't even give her a chance to find her footing before they tossed her inside and took the watch to guard her.

As she sat up from the hard wooden floor, tears began to streak down her face. Mad thoughts of escape were running through her head and yet she knew it was useless. She was trapped with no way out. Never mind that she would never have the courage to enact a plan, could she think of one.

She pulled her knees to her chest and wrapped her arms around her legs. There was nothing to do but wait for morning and at least the promise of being free from the wagon. The prince had said he would sit her up on a horse. Dwarfs only used horses for pulling carts and most of the animals used were ponies. The giant horses she had seen the soldiers riding were proud, high stepping beasts. The prospect of riding one caused a bit of excitement to twirl in her stomach. Of course, the burning sensation of a whole day without a meal was also resting there.

Food, she thought. She was in a supply wagon surrounded by barrels and sacks of food, and yet, she feared to touch anything. Her stomach groaned again and she put a calming hand over it.

Hours passed and sleep did not come. She heard the guards change watches and watched the shadows play against the covering. Two soldiers she hadn't seen before peered inside to make sure she was there. They said nothing and Ayla longed for the comforting words of her father.

It was an hour after the second watch was posted that Ayla heard footsteps approaching and then Roderick's voice. "How goes it?"

"All's well, Captain. The girl's not made a sound."

"I'll keep the watch a while. I would rather you lads get some rest. The prince is eager to get home and won't tolerate any slow riders."

The soldiers did not complain, and Ayla heard them stalk off into the night. She sat up and watched the opening expectantly. After a few moments, she saw the shadow of Roderick flickering in the firelight back up against the torn wagon opening. Through the opening came his hand, and in it was an apple.

Ayla had never been so happy to see an apple in all her life. She crawled to the opening and took it.

"Thank you," she managed, taking a bite. "Thank you. I don't know how to address you properly, but you have all the thanks I have to give."

"My name is Roderick, and you have no need to call me anything more," he whispered. "I would like to speak with you, but be still and wait a moment longer."

Ayla nodded though she knew he could not see her. A moment later his hand slipped back through the opening holding a bit of bread and dried meat. She took it eagerly, gobbling it down. Her hunger would not allow her to think of manners though she found herself strangely conscious of Roderick's presence outside the wagon. She was happy he could not see her ferocious feasting.

Soon after, Roderick lifted up a corner of the opening and sat on the back of the wagon.

"Ayla," he began, "is everything you told the prince true, about being from the mountain and living with the dwarfs?"

"Yes." She nodded simply, wiping a crumb from her mouth with her sleeve.

"Have no fear in telling me otherwise. I'll tell the prince nothing if you are from another village or were just pretending?"

"What I spoke was the truth," she said, slightly frustrated and feeling a bit more confident with Roderick. "I was found as a baby along the stream and taken in. The dwarfs sent word into the human kingdom, but no one ever came to claim me."

Roderick nodded. Through the moonlight, Ayla could see a bit of uneasiness in his eyes as he asked another question, "And how old are you?"

"I've lived through sixteen summers now."

Roderick looked away, into the encampment and took a deep breath. "Then it's true. You are who I thought you might be."

The thought that anyone might know better than she who she might be was quite strange, but given all the events of the previous day, she was willing to accept it. Roderick, it seemed, held some mysterious key to where she had come from and how, at such a young age, she had arrived beside a steam near a dwarf village.

Ayla leaned toward him, "Who am I?"

But Roderick was not yet ready to reveal the mystery. He turned toward her and looked her directly in the eyes, "Can you be brave for me?"

The question startled her. "I'm not very brave but … yes, I … I think so."

"You must be," he said with urgency. "And you must trust me. Can you do that?"

She felt now that he might be the only one she could trust. "Yes. I do trust you."

"Good," he said, letting out a breath. "We must get you to the palace in Jade City. I hate to put you at such a risk, but it's the only way…" He stopped, realizing she wasn't following. "Ayla, you are very special, more precious to this kingdom than I can tell you right now. You must say nothing more to the prince, and if he asks you again who you are, say only that you were cast out of your village and must find a new place to live. I think he will take you to the palace, and once we are there, I will come to you and tell you more. Can you be patient and trust me?"

She nodded, her head spinning with questions, "I think I can."

"Say nothing of this to the prince," Roderick warned her again. "He is not to be trusted. Now, you must get some rest. You'll have to ride tomorrow. I'll keep the watch a while longer."

He stood up to close the opening, but she reached out and took his hand, "Wait!"

He stopped and looked back at her.

"Why are you telling me all of this? Aren't you the captain of the prince's guard?"

For the first time, Roderick smiled at her. "I am not what I appear to be. You are not the only one with a secret, my lady."

CHAPTER 6

SLEEP CAME EASIER FOR AYLA AFTER speaking with Roderick, but her dreams were merciless. She felt once like she might be drowning and awoke with a start only to return to a dream of being chased by golden bears. Her skirt was weighted with lead, and she couldn't run fast enough to escape.

She was pulled from her sleep by two soldiers early the next morning and placed on the saddle of a brown mare. They led her to the front of the line where she could see both the prince and Roderick waiting as their horses were saddled as well.

"Be glad we lost a cart to a broken wheel earlier this week, girl," a young soldier growled to her as he put the bridle on her horse, "or you'd have had to ride on one of our warhorses."

Then his voice changed. It softened, and he spoke in a whisper that only she could hear. "This one's used to pulling carts and she may walk a bit funny with a lady on her back, but she's as gentle as a kitten." He actually smiled at her and Ayla had to smile back, relieved by his sudden change in tone.

"I'm Landon Openheart," he said. "The captain told us not to speak with you like this, my lady, but I couldn't help it. I just wanted to tell you some of us are on your side."

Ayla was astounded. She didn't know anything and least of all did she know whose side she might be on. What could it mean that some were on her side? If some were on her side, then someone must be on another side. The side of the prince, she reasoned.

"I have to go, but I do have one message for you," he whispered as he tightened her saddle, looking around to make sure others weren't listening. "Don't deny anything in the village. Say it's all true."

He gave her one last boyish grin before frowning again and heading into the crowd of soldiers. She looked after him, glad to have at least two friends.

The prince's voice startled her. "Well, girl, are you ready for your audience? Halforton is only ten minute's march away. We would have stayed in a tavern last night, but the captain here thought it might be dangerous. I don't mingle with peasants, anyway." His eyes narrowed on her, "Oh, but you're a pretty exception."

Ayla felt herself shudder as the prince and Roderick started the procession towards the village. She was grateful the horse seemed to know where to go. She had no idea how she might lead the animal. She simply let the reins hang loose in her hands and hoped that the mare would find her way.

A few minutes of riding later, Ayla saw a small girl along the path ahead of them. She was picking wildflowers and when she saw them, she turned and ran, dropping the bundle. Ayla thought she heard the girl shouting for her mother as she ran away from them.

They passed a cottage after that and Ayla realized that it must belong to the little girl and her family. A woman was standing outside of the house, her head bowed, looking at the ground. She was surrounded by at least ten children of varying ages, the little girl among them. They all had downcast faces.

As they drew closer to the village, more little houses appeared along the road on the right and left. More people were gathered outside their doors with a look that reminded Ayla of defeat. No one would look up at them.

They passed through the whole village like this, the people gathering everywhere, their faces downcast. Before long they had passed through an eerie, silent town square and were leaving the village behind.

It was just outside of the town's remaining houses that the prince suddenly called for them to halt. Without words, Roderick took the reins of Ayla's horse and the three of them rode along the side of the procession until they reached the very end of the line. Ayla almost gasped at what she saw.

The entire village had gathered behind them, following the procession with the same downcast eyes.

"People of Halforton, I give you permission to humbly look up at me."

The people slowly raised their heads and looked very cautiously from Roderick, to the prince, to Ayla. None of them spoke. There was not even a hushed whisper from the crowd of people.

"This one was found a day southeast of here and will only tell us lies about where she is from. Does anyone here claim her? I command you to speak now."

There was only silence and Roderick turned to the prince. "Perhaps if you offer them payment?"

The prince nodded, speaking again to the crowd. "As I am pleased by the look of this girl, I intend to make her a servant to myself and my father. I assure you, we only seek to pay the party responsible for her and do not wish to punish you for her lies."

A man stepped forward from the front of the line and kneeled before them. Ayla caught him stealing a glance up at her. His eyes were a bright blue, shining with youth, though his manner was quiet and humble and his beard was long and gray. He was filthy, looking like a wandering peddler more than a villager.

"You may speak," the prince commanded.

"Sire, this girl is my daughter, Ayla."

Ayla flinched at the sound of her name coming from this unfamiliar man. If he did know her, how would he know her name? The dwarfs had named her.

"She was cast out of our village a week ago for refusing to serve the lord mayor here. We didn't mean for her to lie to you, Sire. She has on occasion told some strange stories to us as well."

The prince looked at Ayla, "Is this true, girl?"

Ayla looked at Roderick and then to the man. Neither seemed to give her any clue or hint as to what to do. She could only think of Landon's words.

"Yes," she stammered. "I .. It's true."

She expected the prince to say more, but he only looked back to the man, "You did not teach your daughter to respect the crown so I will pay you less than the fare share. Roderick, give the man twelve gold pieces."

Roderick untied a pouch from his waist and counted out the gold. A moment later he tossed the coins on the ground in front of the man.

"Good, then," the prince said, nodding to Ayla and Roderick. "Shall we?"

They rode back to the front of the line, Roderick leading her horse again. The procession continued, and Ayla wondered how far the villagers would follow them.

She could not see or hear them since they were at the very back of the troop.

"Roderick." She heard the prince's voice in front of her. "If we are going to be riding with this girl all the way to the capital, I desire that she look . . . and smell. . . pleasing. You will ride back to the village and retrieve a dress. I expect you should catch up with us by nightfall."

"Sire," Roderick replied, "I am the captain of your guard and it might be best if we sent. . ."

"I desire that you go," the prince said sharply. "I and the fifty men you leave behind can look after me."

Roderick nodded and shot Ayla a long glance before riding back towards the village. Ayla found herself strangely unsettled by his absence.

"Girl," the prince said to her as soon as Roderick disappeared. "I desire your company. Ride next to me."

Ayla would have done exactly as he asked but her horse was moving of its own accord, and she didn't know how to make it change its pace to ride along the prince's side.

"I can't, sir," she said quietly. "I don't know how to make my horse move there."

Prince Noland chuckled to himself, "Of course. Simple minds."

He slowed his horse and brought it alongside her. He studied her for a long moment before turning his gaze back to the path. "Those were some horrible lies you told in the forest. Like dwarf and fairy stories, do you? My men thought you might be the Freeland Witch."

"Freeland Witch?" she asked, feeling like she should respond.

"Do you not know the stories?" He looked at her again, this time with very true amusement. "My. . . You are either quite daft or quite sheltered. Well, since you like a good story so much, I'll tell you."

He cleared his throat with great show and began, "There once was a woman who lived on that mountain which, of course, was covered with all sorts of things like dwarfs and fairies. She learned from them how to do magic. Played all sorts of tricks and jokes on the nearby villages. Then one day, a great party of them went up the mountain and slew her in her own home." He laughed for a moment and drew a finger across his throat. "Since that time, anyone who has gone up that mountain has not returned. We even sent up a party of soldiers once to see if there were villages there. We did not hear from them for months. The village of Halforton finally sent a message saying they had found bodies in the river.

"Since then, my father has been scared silly by stories of that witch and has sworn to leave the mountain be," he sneered. "He's a religious old fool, and what the keepers tell him, he believes. When I'm king, I shall send a thousand soldiers, and we shall see if there is any witch!"

Ayla stared silently at the road in front of her as the prince babbled on. If there was a witch anywhere near her town, she certainly had heard nothing of it. She was also quite confused by the human response to her speaking of dwarfs. None of them had seen the dwarf villages so they obviously assumed they didn't exist. It seemed a silly thing to not believe in something simply because it had never been seen. She had never seen another human, but she knew from her books and father's lessons that they were real. You couldn't really see the wind, but it blew quite freely through the trees. Plenty of things existed that you couldn't see.

"I wish to speak with you," the prince said, his voice sounding very boyish for a change, "like you are a lady. Do you like games?" Ayla nodded. "Good then, we shall play a game. I will speak to you as a lady and address you as Lady Ayla and you will call me Lord Noland."

The prince was indeed being quite boyish and when Ayla regarded him again, she realized that he was barely a man at all. He could not have been but a few summers older than her, perhaps twenty.

"What does your father do, Lady Ayla?"

'Which one?' Ayla thought to herself, 'the father in the village they just passed or her real father in Glendontown?

"He makes furniture, Lord Noland."

"Fine wood tables and chairs, no doubt. I shall have to send for some."

Ayla thought fast, "I doubt my father's furniture would please you."

"Oh," said the prince, thinking. "But you are the daughter of a duke in my game, and he would make fine furniture as a hobby."

"Oh, yes," Ayla said, catching on. "Fine wood furniture, sir. From the tallest and strongest oaks."

It seemed strange to be pretending something that was true. Her father did make furniture for the wealthiest dwarf families in Glendon, and he would only use the best wood. She was sure that no one could match Otto's craftsmanship.

The prince's voice changed from being boyish to his more serious tone, "Why do you call me sir? It is an improper salutation for one as high ranking as I."

"I'm sorry," she said cautiously. "In my town, that's what we use to show respect. I don't know what else to call you."

"And your accent? Your father didn't speak that way."

Knowing Roderick would want her to protect the lie, Ayla thought quickly. "My mother spoke this way. I don't know where she was from. She died."

The prince nodded, seemingly satisfied. "Lady Ayla," he began again, "it occurs to me that you have not eaten since coming to us. Are you hungry?"

"Yes. . .um. . .Lord Noland." She was not as hungry as she would have been had Roderick not brought her something to eat the night before.

He reached into his saddlebag and pulled out a bit of dried beef. "You may have this." He handed it to her with a great flourish, "But only because we are pretending."

She took the meat and thought about what a strange boy the prince was. When she had first met him, he was strong and intimidating. Now, he was playing games that were more fitting for a person of thirteen summers or so.

"Thank you, sir."

"It is not 'sir,' " the prince said, "unless you wish me to be a knight. You may say 'your majesty' or 'your royal highness.' Perhaps 'sire' if you prefer something shorter."

The names did not sound to Ayla like names she would ever want to use. She had heard that kings and queens of other lands had strange customs and titles. "Yes. . .. Your Royal Highness."

"Very good. Now, tell me Lady Ayla do you have a beau in your village?"

"A beau?"

"You know," he said, "a young lad who follows you around and gives you flowers. That sort of thing."

Ayla remembered the Matchmaking Ball, "No, Sire."

"Good," he continued, "then I shall not have anyone contesting my claim to you. Do you want to live in the palace with me, Lady Ayla?"

She looked at him for a long moment and then turned her eyes back toward the road. She remembered what Roderick had said. It was important that she get to the palace. She didn't know why. Ayla did know that she was not interested in spending more time with the prince than absolutely necessary. Roderick was the captain of the prince's guard. Might he be trying to gain her trust on behalf of the prince?

She chose her words carefully. "That depends on what I would be doing at the palace, Lord Noland."

The prince laughed merrily, "Oh, you would be serving, no doubt. I should love to see you bringing me my breakfast every morning. You are very beautiful, you know. I am surprised that even with your lack of scruples some foolish boy is not following you around."

It was not the first time the prince had called her pretty, and Ayla found her mind dwelling on his statement. Was she really as beautiful as he seemed to think she was?

The prince said no more and after a moment, kicked his horse's side and galloped too far forward for them to speak.

Their game was over for the time being.

Chapter 7

AYLA'S LEGS AND BOTTOM were sore. They had been riding the entire day without rest and now that the sun was disappearing from the sky, had finally decided to make camp for the night.

The prince shouted to Ayla as he dismounted and tossed his reins flippantly to a waiting soldier, "You can sleep in your cart again, girl." He stomped by her horse, once again becoming the intimidating figure Ayla had first met by the river. Ayla flinched.

Landon came to see her back to the wagon. Though he said nothing and escorted her with a soldier like frown, she was relieved. She reminded herself that he and Roderick were her friends. At least, she hoped they were. Before Landon saw her into the cart, she stole a look across the troop of soldiers. Roderick was nowhere to be seen.

Ayla crawled to the back of the wagon and leaned her head against a barrel. She wondered if she would see Roderick again that night.

A few hours passed. The two men she had seen the day before retrieved yet another barrel and sack but did not speak to her and did not offer her any supper. After the sun went down, Ayla watched the light of the many campfires dance across the cloth covering of the wagon. She wondered what they might be cooking this evening but dared not peek beyond the fabric. It was clear from the two looming shadows that the prince had not neglected to post guards outside her cart.

Her eyes were starting to close with sleep when the flap opened and there was Landon, carrying a small roll and a clay bowl filled with something steaming. She sat up.

"Crown Prince Noland gave us orders to see that you were fed."

He sat the meal down and disappeared from the opening. The dish contained rice, beans, and something green she didn't recognize. She ate slowly, scooping out the soup with pieces of the roll. It didn't taste pleasant at all, but she was grateful to have been remembered.

Time passed slowly and it must have been another hour before the noise of the soldiers talking and laughing outside quieted. The guard changed, and she saw Landon in the opening for the third time that night. This time he was wearing a friendly smile.

"Are you alright, my lady?" he whispered.

She nodded, afraid to make a sound. He was whispering, and she knew that he couldn't be seen speaking with her.

"Do you need anything?"

"Water," she whispered. She was thankful to be fed, but she had not had a drink in days. Her thirst was starting to make her head pound.

Landon pulled a soft leather pouch from his side and handed it to her. The opening of the pouch was tightly bound with another bit of leather. She quickly untied it and took a drink. The lukewarm liquid felt refreshing to her parched mouth. She rewrapped the opening as tightly as she could and handed the pouch back to him.

"Has your captain returned?" she asked.

Landon nodded, "He will be with you later tonight. Jovan is here on guard with me, and he's your friend as well. We'll watch you until the captain arrives; you needn't worry."

She could not see Jovan's face, but she was glad to know she had another friend.

Landon returned to his guard position, but for Ayla, there was nothing to do but wait. Soon, the quiet talking from the many campfires died down, and she was surrounded by the gentle sounds of night. She heard crickets chirping in the woods nearby and not too far away, frogs began to croak. Together, they filled the night with a powerful bedtime song. She began to feel herself drifting off to sleep.

When Roderick opened the cloth flap sometime later, he startled her, and she jumped, suddenly awake.

"I'm sorry," he said. "I didn't mean to scare you." He held out his hand, "Come with me."

She took it and he helped her out of the wagon. "Where are we going?"

"The prince has asked that you look presentable and that you bathe. There's a pond nearby." He led her down a path into the surrounding forest. "It's not far. I have a dress for you and some oils."

"Aren't you afraid I'll run away?" she asked.

He stopped and turned to her, "Should I be afraid, my lady?"

She smiled. "Do you trust me?"

"Yes," he said, still looking at her.

"Then I say I shall not run away."

Roderick led her off the road and down a narrow forest trail shrouded by trees. Soon the light of the moon was completely absent. Roderick offered her his arm and she took it.

"I used to walk this trail as a boy. I know it well."

"You said you were from Kelvinor when you introduced yourself to me on the prince's command. Is that where we are?" she asked.

"This was Kelvinor a little over fifteen years ago. It is now merely a providence of the Talforland Empire." His voice seemed to change when he mentioned Talforland. It did not have the pleasant tone it usually held when he spoke to her.

"Talforland. That's where the prince said he was from?"

Roderick nodded, "Over a decade ago, the King of Talforland claimed that Kelvinor was sending raiding parties through villages along the border. It was an excuse to declare war. Kelvinor was quickly conquered. The king, with the blessing of his brooding keepers, then set his sights on every other kingdom, determined to create an empire that reached the Eastern Sea. So far, he's enjoyed great military success at the expense of the common folk."

"Keepers?" Ayla asked.

"Priests," Roderick explained. "Talforland worships many dark gods and the keepers supposedly hear them. They only encourage the king to wage more wars."

"But if you're from Kelvinor. . .and now you are working with the Prince of Talforland? I don't. . ." Ayla paused as Roderick helped her around a thorn bush. He interrupted her before she could begin again.

"Things are not always as they seem. I serve the prince, but my allegiance is to Kelvinor."

"If we're in Kelvinor now, is the prince taking me to Talforland?"

Roderick brushed some low hanging tree limbs out of her way, "Thank goodness, no. After Talforland conquered Kelvinor, it became more of an advantage to set up a capital here. Noland's sister watches over Talforland while the king himself stays in the old capital of Kelvinor, Jade City. Oh, here we are."

Ayla could see the moon reflecting off of a small pond in front of them. The water looked cold and stale, strangely inviting. She was very dirty from her two day journey and her body itched. The dress she had worn to the Matchmaking Ball was in tatters and patches of dirt had collected on the skirt. She smelled like horse.

"The dress and the oils," Roderick said, handing her the bundle. "I'll go back up the path, and you can call me when you're ready."

"Don't go too far, please," she said suddenly, surprising herself.

He smiled, "I won't."

Ayla removed the tattered remains of the party dress and set aside her underclothes. She wanted to rinse them, but the thought of wearing them wet was too uncomfortable for her to bear.

The dress Roderick had brought from the village was made of a material Ayla had never seen before. It shone in the moonlight and was soft to the touch, like spun cotton with a glassy surface. The dwarfs used some cotton for summer wear but mostly wool and skins for their clothes. Her best party dress had been made with wool and the vest from sheep skin. It was a dull color but typical of what every dwarf wore. This new dress was bright blue and so light that she was afraid she might feel naked.

Ayla set the dress aside and slowly stepped into the water. She wrapped her arms around her body, shivering. It felt almost as icy as the mountain stream near her town. Ayla knew she would get used to the cold soon enough and waded out into the lake until it was deep enough for her to dive under the surface. As the water covered her body, she felt the icy coldness start to melt away. When she emerged, she rubbed the oils into her hair and face and relaxed a bit as the aroma of lilac filled the air. She thought of Roderick and Prince Noland. Her mind lingered on Roderick. He had a strong, handsome face that was marked by the trial of long wars. He was young, though he had to be older than the prince. Maybe he only looked older because he always seemed to be wearing the same serious frown.

But he didn't wear it with her. At least, most of the time he didn't. She felt her heart suddenly pick up pace, and she ducked her head into the water hoping to calm it. The darkness felt very close just now, and she was eager to finish with her bath.

Ayla climbed out of the pond and put on her bloomers and underclothes. She picked up the dress Roderick had left her and looked it over, suddenly realizing she had no idea how to put it on. The back of it laced up in an odd zigzag, and there was a white tunic with it which she didn't know how to wear. Guessing, she slipped the tunic on and pulled the skirt of the dress up to her waist. She found the armholes and pulled the top over the tunic. Only the back, with the lace, was left undone.

Embarrassed, but not knowing what else to do, she called to Roderick.

"Are you done, my lady?" His voice called back to her from the woods.

"Yes," she answered. "But I don't know how to get the back of this dress on."

There was a long pause, then Roderick's voice came again. "You don't know how to tie the lacing?"

"Yes," she said, turning red.

There was a pause again, "Well, do you have the rest of it on."

She couldn't help but give a laugh. "Yes!"

"Hold on, then. I'm coming."

She heard his footfalls on the path and a moment later he appeared. Roderick took a short look at her and immediately turned around.

"My lady," he said. "Your ankles are showing."

Ayla looked down at her feet. She had not yet put on her boots, but she didn't see how that was important. Dwarf women went barefoot all the time.

"Roderick, is that improper?"

He cleared his throat, "Yes, my lady."

"I'm sorry," she said, finding a rock to sit on and pulling on her stockings and boots. "Dwarf women don't have to keep their ankles covered."

He let out a soft chuckle. "And how do the dwarf men respond to this?"

"It's quite natural," Ayla explained. "So no one is angered by it or…well, you know what I mean." She blushed. "There, my ankles are covered, Captain."

Roderick turned and Ayla could see that he was blushing, too. She smiled.

"Turn around," he said, and she did.

She felt a tug at the dress. Roderick was lacing up the back of the vest. "Where did you get this dress?" she asked.

"From a woman in the village. It was the best thing she owned."

She didn't say anything, but he seemed to know she was waiting for an explanation.

"I sent a message to the village last night explaining what to do. They simply went along with it."

"And why would they do that?"

"Well, there are two reasons. The village of Halforton is. . .a sort of refuge for those loyal to Kelvinor. Because of that..." He paused, thinking. "We will speak of this more later. For now, know that the villagers knew the prince would be obligated to pay for you, and that meant more gold to see them through the next winter." He said it so casually. Ayla could not imagine people being bartered for like animals.

"Does that happen often? People buying people?"

Roderick shrugged, "Since Talforland invaded, yes. If you break the law, you can be sold. If you owe a dept, you can be sold. If your father doesn't like the look of you, you can be sold. These are evil times, my lady."

He finished pulling the last thread tight and tied the top in a knotted bow.

"Why do you call me 'my lady'?" she asked. "What does it mean?"

"It's a title," he said. "It means I respect you and wish to honor you."

"Would you just call me Ayla if I asked you to?"

He thought for a moment, "If you asked me to, I would."

She smiled, "Then please, Roderick. Just call me Ayla."

The dress was quite magnificent compared to anything Ayla had ever seen. It was light and cool, and she felt rather like a chief's daughter wearing it.

"Is this a fine dress?" she asked, wondering if it stood as an example of what was worn in the capital.

Roderick shrugged, "It's a peasant's party dress and quite fine for one of that class. The ladies in the palace are covered with more silk and gauze than one could ever want." He smiled, "It looks quite fine on you, my lady . . . Ayla."

Roderick offered her his arm and began to lead them back to the encampment.

"Why did the prince send you away today?" she asked as they walked. "You are his chief guard?"

"Yes," he nodded, "and the captain of this regiment. But as the prince gets older, he desires my company less and less. I suspect it makes him feel as though he is a child."

"Is he a child?"

Roderick scoffed, "Perhaps he still behaves as one. In any case, the law prohibits him to travel without my company until he has reached the age of twenty. He is nineteen now."

It was as Ayla thought, though he had appeared older when she first saw him. She imagined that here you were a child longer. It seemed to make sense to her in a strange way since she had heard dwarfs had shorter lives than humans. A dwarf who lived past sixty was a rarity. Yet her books had told her humans could live as long as a century or more.

Roderick continued, "I have served Prince Noland for nine years now. When I was fifteen I won the right in a tournament. Since then, I have hardly left his side."

Ayla had a thousand questions for Roderick but something seemed to tell her this was not the correct time to ask. She stayed silent the rest of the way back, hoping that when they did arrive at the palace, everything would be explained to her.

When they arrived at the encampment, Roderick helped her back into the wagon and posted himself outside the opening. "Don't worry; I'll stand the watch for awhile. Soon you will have a bit more than a wagon. We'll reach Jade City in three days."

She wondered how long he would keep the watch tonight. She slept easier knowing he was just outside, but dreams of any kind did not come.

CHAPTER 8

THEY DID INDEED REACH the outer edges of the sprawling city just after noon on the third day. Ayla was still riding her gentle brown mare and sleeping in the cart on the hard wood every night. Her back ached, and the prince found excuses to send Roderick away almost every day. Once he simply commanded the captain to bring up the rear of the line. When Roderick returned, the prince sent him to check on different ones of the soldiers and assigned him idle tasks unfitting of his title. As soon as Roderick left, Ayla would find herself the victim of yet another one of the prince's games.

Quite often the games were silly and unproductive but now and again she would pick up bits of information she needed. She learned that Talforland had conquered two other regions and was preparing to make war on a third. She learned that women who were not nobility were considered of less value than men of the same class. She also learned a lot about the different classes.

There were six in all. The highest class was that of the royalty and it included the king and anyone related to him. Prince Noland felt that he had to constantly remind her he was of the highest class and blood.

Then there was the nobility. This included the ladies at court who Roderick had said were covered with silk and gauze. It also included men of high rank in the army. Many counselors and advisors to the king were of this rank.

Under them were the keepers. Talforland worshiped many gods, the prince told her. There was a god for everyone and everything and the king did very little without consulting them. It was the god of war, he claimed, that told his father to leave the mountain and the Freeland Witch alone. Ayla thought it might be confusing to have many gods. One was all the dwarfs ever needed.

Next in line was the soldier class. Many peasants, of the lowest rank, volunteered to serve in the army just to escape the position they were born in to. They had more rights than the lowest classes but were still considered of little value.

Shopkeepers, merchants, fishermen, bakers and others who earned their living under a certain trade made up the guild class. This, the prince told her, was another way that peasants tried to escape the hardship of their birth. Sometimes a guildsman would take on a peasant apprentice. Once the peasant girl or boy became a member of the trade's guild, they and their family would be considered a member of the guild class.

Peasants, farmers, and peddlers made up the sods, the lowest class. Ayla thought it was quite foolish to give the people who supplied your country's food and labor the least amount of value. After all, what work could a king really do if given a rake and told to make plants grow?

Prince Noland informed her that you weren't allowed to speak to anyone of a higher class than yourself without permission. A peasant who spoke out of turn to nobility or royalty could find himself slated for execution or at the very least, a year's stay in prison. Another common punishment was to assign the offending sod to work for the noble until a dept of five-hundred gold pieces was paid. Of course, the prince laughed, after the noble charged the sod for food and shelter, there was perhaps only a single gold piece earned at the end of a month. The sod quickly found himself an indentured servant for life.

The whole system seemed quite foolish to Ayla. Dwarfs of all positions and wealth considered themselves to be of the same value. Each seemed to know that their position relied on the help of others. Even the chief, who everyone treated with respect, did not consider his role to be of more importance. Though sometimes the different groups didn't mingle, they didn't necessarily think they were better than anyone else.

It was truly frustrating to be riding with the prince for three days straight. The only relief she found was at night when Landon came to stand the watch or even later when Roderick would come. She didn't know what to expect from Jade City but she found herself relieved to be there.

"We'll reach the castle by nightfall," Roderick announced as he rejoined them, returning from one of his lesser tasks. Ayla knew the prince would not send him away again. Roderick had told her it would look bad to the king if the captain was not riding with the prince when they arrived.

They turned a corner on the road and Ayla could see a city sprawling in front of them in the center of what seemed to be a vast valley. In the center of the valley rested a white stone castle. Four towers rose into the sky around it, and one great tower rose from its center. It was nothing to like Ayla had ever seen before, and she found herself staring, her eyes wide and mouth slightly open.

"Impressed?" Prince Noland sneered. "The palace in Talforland is three times the size of this quaint little fortress. My sister has the whole castle to herself while father and I are away. Oh, but she's not running things. Kingdoms can't be left in the hands of women."

Ayla couldn't imagine a palace bigger than the one before her. They were still miles away and yet it rose out of the ground like a beacon in their path.

The houses they were passing on the outskirts of the city looked like little dirt hovels the dwarf children sometimes made as playhouses. The people standing in front of them mirrored their homes: Men and woman with knotted hair and dirty faces, the sound and smell of farm animals everywhere, children wearing nothing but ragged tunics with ties around their middle. Some were skin and bone, and Ayla suddenly felt guilty for feeling so hungry earlier. These people looked as if they hadn't been well fed in years.

"These are the poorest districts," Roderick said. "Some herdsmen, but lowly servants and beggars mostly."

"Sods," the prince scoffed, spitting in the dirt.

Ayla was amazed. No one lived in such poor conditions where she was from. It just wasn't acceptable. Those who had nothing were cared for by the widows or widowers. Work and generosity kept everyone fed and well clothed at the very least.

Next they passed through a small area of wooden houses where the people looked a bit more presentable. The children wore little jumpers and looked tidy but still resembled scarecrows. These people were farmers. Ayla could tell by the men's broad hats and their worn hands.

As they drew closer to the castle, the houses began to improve. They finally turned onto a cobblestone street, and Ayla could see that most of the buildings were shops with the people living on the second story. These people wore well stitched clothing, and their cheeks were rosy. They did not seem to mind as much the passing of the procession. Though their heads were bowed, they did not have the look of disdain or defeat. They looked only impatient and eager to get back to work in their shops.

"This is Jade City's biggest marketplace," Roderick said, pointing ahead of her.

A moment later they were passing through a massive square lined with carts. The carts were filled with everything Ayla could imagine. She saw fruits and bread, toys and fabrics. People were everywhere and she imagined it would have been quite a noisy place except that all the people were turned towards the procession, their heads bowed in silence.

It took them a few minutes to make their way through the marketplace, and then they were riding towards a huge stone gate. There was a wall surrounding the next section of the city. Ayla could see strange scorch marks on the wall and chains and long metal spikes adorned each watch tower. Through the scorched marks, Ayla could see patches of the clean stone. This wall had once been white. She imagined that it must have been quite different then, less brutal and perhaps even welcoming. The image before her now left her only with an ominous sense of foreboding.

"The nobility live beyond this gate," Roderick explained. "They prefer to remain separated and protected from the general populace."

The guards at the gate kneeled as they approached, and Ayla noticed that they weren't dressed in the heavy armor of the prince's procession. They were dressed more like Roderick, in a simple tunic and chain mail. However, they all wore swords and their hands seemed ever ready to grasp the hilts. The tunics were the same shade of red that all the men wore and had the same golden bears sewn into the front of the tunics.

The nobility lived in houses like Ayla had never seen. As they approached the castle, each house was grander than the next. They were several stories high and all made of white or gray stone. Some had elaborate balconies where Ayla could see people watching them. These men and woman did not bow their heads. In fact, some of them even waved and called out to the prince. There were several ladies who did so, but Prince Noland merely acknowledged them by lifting his hand and tilting his head slightly. The ladies were dressed in long, flowing dresses of extraordinary colors. Their fabrics seemed to shine in the sunlight, and Ayla was reminded of what Roderick had told her: Silk and gauze. She thought it might be uncomfortable to have to carry around so much fabric and for a moment was reminded of running from the bear in the river.

They followed a winding path through this district before reaching another high gate. Through the iron slats, Ayla could see a long courtyard dotted with gardens and fountains. There were pavilions with statues and the ruins of statues. In some places, Ayla could tell that there had been a whole structure, and now there were only white columns and marble slabs. Beyond all of this was the castle, rising in perfect condition out of the ruins.

A guard greeted them at the gate. "Your Majesty. Captain. Welcome home. The king requests your presence immediately." His eyes were straying off and on to Ayla as he spoke.

Prince Noland and Roderick dismounted, handing their horses off to the guards. "We should go now," Ayla heard the captain say to the prince. "We shouldn't keep your father waiting."

The prince nodded and then pointed to Ayla, "We'll take the girl with us. She'll make an interesting story for my father at the very least!"

"Please, Sire," Roderick frowned, "I am sure your father will only want to hear of the war's progress and will not be amused by this simple peasant girl."

"I insist, Captain," was all the prince replied, turning toward the castle.

As soon as the prince turned his back, Roderick was helping her off the horse.

"I'm sorry," he said quietly as they rushed to catch up with the prince. "I had hoped he would send you off immediately."

The prince walked with long, swift strides across the great expanse of gardens and courtyards. Ayla struggled to keep up and wondered why they could not have ridden the distance. Her legs throbbed from four days of riding, but walking was even worse. She had been sleeping on the floor of a wooden cart and her back seemed to ache with every step.

Finally they reached an outdoor corridor of columns which at one time could have been roofed. Ayla thought that perhaps it had been a covered walkway where royalty would walk about the gardens even when it rained. This led into a small pavilion. Smooth marble etched with strange drawings made up the floor stones and in the center stood a blackened statue. The prince stopped and sat down on the edge of the pavilion, muttering something about being too tired to see his father today and wanting supper and a soft bed.

Roderick turned to her. "The king will meet us here," he said and went to sit near the prince.

Ayla continued to look around the pavilion. She walked to one side to get a better look at the etchings. Many different images were carved into the stone, but there seemed to be no single thought or idea behind the complete mural. She could make out clouds and a flying dragon fighting with three griffins. There was a knight and a woman raising a small object into the sky. There was a unicorn to one side and a flying horse on the other. Then to one side she saw something that completely took her aback. There was an etching of a dwarf. He was of the same small stature as an older male dwarf and wore a long beard and plain wool clothes exactly like the kind her father would have worn in his workshop. It was a perfect depiction. She resisted the urge to kneel and touch the image.

Instead, she turned to the statue in the center of the pavilion. It was not made of black stone but seemed to have been scorched by fire, like the wall they had passed. The sculpture was of an archer, his bow drawn back, and ready to fire at the rising sun. He wore an expression as if in deep thought, as if his very life rested on where the arrow he fired fell. He was so brilliantly chiseled that he seemed alive and only trapped in the stone. For some reason, the statue moved her. She wanted to cry and wash away the blackness with her tears.

"Admiring the statue?" the prince said. He was watching her with interest. Ayla just nodded.

"That statue was burned like that after the war with Kelvinor. My father left it as a symbol of what we'd taken."

Ayla walked all the way around it, wondering what it might mean. As she reached the right-hand side, she noticed a small plaque with an inscription. She bent down to give it a closer look.

"That's written in runes," she heard the prince say. "No one can read it anymore."

But Ayla could read it quite well. It was written in an old form of rune that her father had her study as a child. The dwarfs wrote in runes, though in a slightly different way than this plaque read. Ayla read it to herself:

Here is Kelvin, Founder and Lord of Kelvinor. Where his arrow fell, so the city was built.

Ayla looked to where the prince and Roderick were sitting. The captain was watching her with interest while the prince studied his fingernails. Ayla looked away, sensing it might be important to keep her understanding of the runes secret for the time being.

Ayla looked off towards the palace where she saw a small group of people walking toward them. They were still a long way off.

"My father," said the prince, standing and walking toward Ayla to get a better look. "With some of the keepers. No doubt they'll have some omen or prophecy to share. I'll bet you a gold piece, Roderick, bad news for us!"

For once Ayla saw Roderick give the prince a smile. It appeared they both held a similar opinion of the keepers. "I'll take that bet, but only because we have good news to bring them. Perhaps they won't be so forlorn as usual."

As the party of men got closer, Roderick reminded Ayla that she should kneel and look down until called upon to speak. She was grateful for the reminder as she had grown quite a bit more comfortable speaking with the prince in the past few days. He had given her permission to bypass the formalities.

Ayla kneeled and waited.

When the king and his entourage finally entered the pavilion, all she could see of him were his flowing red robes and black leather boots. She could tell he had a heavy step, weighted with authority. Remembering what the prince had told her about offending peasants, Ayla did not look up.

"My son! My son! Home at last, I see." The king's jolly voice sounded above her as he embraced Prince Noland. "We heard news of your coming only days ago. How goes the war?"

"It goes well, Sire," the prince said. "We have taken all the land to Greenwood Lake, and the army has only a few small villages to march through before reaching the Eastern Sea. We have only weeks before we can declare official victory."

"It is as we predicted," came a raspy voice. "The bear brings a raven!"

There was a hushed murmur, and Ayla suddenly felt that all eyes were on her. She chanced a glance to the priest's feet and saw only simple brown slippers and the ends of green robes lined in fur.

"What do you mean?" It was Roderick's voice. "This girl?"

"Yes!" the raspy one began again. "You see the prince of Talforland whose sign is the great bear. He brings this girl with hair like that of a raven's wings. It is a sign!"

The keepers murmured to one another again. They all seemed to agree that it was a sign of something. Ayla could see the bears on everyone's clothes and she did have black hair but what it had to do with a raven, she could only guess.

"And where did this child come from?" the king asked seriously.

Ayla could tell from the prince's voice that he was regretting bringing her to his father. "We found her a few days ago hiding in a tree to get a better look at the passing army. Her village claimed she had been thrown out for refusing to serve the governing lord there. I paid a fair price and brought her with us, that's all."

"Her name is Ayla," Roderick added.

Ayla was grateful the prince did not mention her tale of dwarfs or the Freeland Witch. She feared it might bring another round of questions.

"A vision was had in the great temple but a few days ago," the priest exclaimed, a heightened bit of excitement in his voice. "A bear bore on its back a raven, and it flew to this very statue. Obviously, it was a sign of this girl's coming."

"Ayla," the king spoke, "look up at me."

Ayla did as asked and in a moment she was looking into the eyes of a large man with a piercing gaze. Father and son had the same eyes, she thought. He was covered in a full beard which might have looked dwarfish except for its length. The hair was well trimmed and completely white, like the hair on his head. He seemed old, and yet, he wore his age with dignity and fierceness. A solid gold ring rested on his head, and Ayla wondered if he didn't have a grander crown for more stately affairs.

"She certainly is a very pretty young thing, Keeper Nevin. But what could the vision mean?"

A short, balding man with a scruffy gray beard stepped out of the group of keepers. Ayla recognized him as soon as he spoke as the one with the raspy voice. "We will need time to consult the gods on this matter," he said lowly. "For now, I recommend you keep her under close watch and treat her as royalty just in case she brings us good fortune."

Prince Noland cleared his throat, "Keeper Nevin, I brought her to be a parlor maid or a serving girl, not a royal guest. Such a simple mind is not meant to be treated as an equal."

"Enough," the king's voice said. "Keeper Nevin's advice is good and we will take it. One cannot be too careful when dealing with signs from the gods. Stand up, Lady Ayla."

She stood and regarded the king. He seemed to look her up and down with great interest and then he nodded. "You will take the room in the west tower…"

She heard Prince Noland stifle a small laugh, and she wondered if perhaps it was not good to stay in the west tower. The prince was wearing a half smile, and his crossed arms and rigid stance spoke only disdain for the king's decision.

"I will have a seamstress bring you some dresses, and you will join us at the royal table for meals. Will all of this please you?"

"Yes, Sire," she said as quietly as she could muster.

"Since we are unsure of you, you will remain under guard at all times. You may wander about the grounds freely but not alone. Do you understand?"

She nodded and looked at her feet.

"Good," the king continued. "We will address you as a lady because we are unsure of your title. Keeper Nevin, how long will it take you to achieve a response from the gods on this matter?"

"Oh," the keeper replied. "The gods are unpredictable, but I will strive in my prayers and offer sacrifices to Feror, god of haste." He raised his arms with great show, closing his eyes and shaking, "No one shall eat! No one shall sleep! We will be sustained on our prayers alone!"

For a moment Ayla thought he was going to faint, and then the man opened his eyes wide and let out a great sigh.

"Very good," the king replied gravely. "This and prayers to appease Tione should be our highest priority. Now, Lady Ayla," the king turned back to her. "If it is decided that your coming is good luck, we will keep you here as a guest, and you will spend the rest of your days as a member of the royal household. If it is found you bring bad luck, may the gods have mercy on you."

Ayla noticed the king was very serious and it made her flinch. Her fate now seemed to rest in the hands of the man called Keeper Nevin. He had fiery eyes and an extravagant way of speaking strange things.

Ayla would never have trusted him.

CHAPTER 9

THE KING LEFT WITH RODERICK and the prince. Ayla heard them saying something about the full report of the war with Wadroland, losses, and an arms report. Keeper Nevin followed them but several of the other Keepers were assigned to stay with Ayla until a handmaiden could be sent to her.

Without the company of familiar faces, Ayla felt very alone. She kept her head down, hoping the Keepers would ignore her. They only shot her quick looks and talked amongst themselves about her simple nature. Others discussed the symbolic meaning of a raven and argued over whether it was a harbinger of death or of good luck. Each one seemed to take a turn reminding the others that answers had yet to be sought in the temple. At this, each one would nod gravely and then shoot Ayla a quick glance.

Ayla felt like a bug caught in jar by a curious boy. She did not like their looks and for some reason, the more they talked of the temple, the more twisted her insides became.

Finally, she caught the glimpse of someone else approaching from the castle. This was a girl in a dress a bit like Ayla's who was practically skipping her way to the pavilion. Her dust colored hair danced at her shoulders as she went, and even at this distance, Ayla could make out the smile on the girl's face. She was singing and her song hung in the air.

When the keepers saw her, they frowned and shook their heads. The closer she came, the more Ayla could make out the words in her song.

> *"Once there was a peddler,*
> *Fattest soul alive,*

> *Sold meat and apple cobbler*
> *For gold the count of five.*
> *He ate and ate his fill*
> *Till one day he couldn't walk.*
> *Stuffed bread into his mouth*
> *And then he couldn't talk!"*

She was only a few steps away when she stopped singing and tried to humbly carry herself into the pavilion, an insincere smirk on her face. She bobbed a small curtsy to them and kept her head turned to the floor, not looking at the men.

"You realize this is an important charge?" one of the Keepers said to her with an air of disdain for the child before him.

"Yes." The girl bobbed another curtsy, "Oh yes, sir, I do."

The Keepers seemed to let out a collective huff from their nostrils. "Good then. Take her to the west tower and wipe that ridiculous smirk from your face." They left the pavilion, talking amongst themselves about trouble and a black raven.

"Hallo!" The girl looked up and smiled broadly at Ayla, "I heard you was common so I don't bother with the airs. What luck you've had!"

"Excuse me?" Ayla said politely, "Luck?"

"Oh yes, miss. Landing in the palace and ordered propped up like a lady. There's nothing better than that right there. Nothing better."

Ayla could think of nothing to say so she just smiled and waited for the girl to speak again.

"I'm Brenia, but everyone calls me Bree." She stuck out a very dirty hand and Ayla took it, grateful for someone who wanted to be her friend and didn't know her in any way. "I'm from Kelvinor originally and it looks as if I'm going to be your servant until someone decides what to do with you."

"I'm Ayla. I guess I'm from Kelvinor, too." She looked at the statue, "And I'm not really sure what I am yet."

Bree looked at her quizzically, "You got a funny accent there to be from Kelvinor."

"Oh," Ayla said, "my mother had it. She died but I don't know where she was from."

The explanation seemed to work on the prince, and it also worked on Bree who just nodded and smiled again. "Well, I guess we'd better head off to your room."

"Oh. The west tower," Ayla said quietly. "Is it … an alright place?"

Bree gave her another puzzled look. "Of course! That's where the princess herself stays when she comes to visit. You didn't know that? They fly her flag when she's here and all. Fly it just above that tower."

Ayla now realized that the prince had scoffed not out of humor but out of disgust. She would be staying in his sister's room.

Bree turned back the way she came, and they followed a small, almost invisible, path in the grass towards the castle, the girl chatting as she went.

"I'll be fourteen in five days. I bet you're older than me. You look older than me. I work in the kitchen most of the time but got tossed out yesterday for throwing flour at one of the cooks. It weren't my fault. The man was joking about my mum but I didn't think it was that funny. He got a hair full of it, he did. I been wondering around looking for something to do since then. Don't think anybody wants my help. But you came along today and I think that's grand." She turned and gave Ayla another brilliant smile, "My other name besides Bree is 'trouble.' My mum says everywhere I go I'm trouble! That's why my hair's short. They cut your hair off an inch when you're bad. I been cut nearly six times this year but they won't get rid of me because my papa's the stable master and the best one, in fact. My mum's in the laundry and now, I'm with you! Maybe when I'm fourteen they'll let me be a real handmaiden. I'd like that. I'll be fourteen in five days. Do you think we can be friends, Ayla?"

The girl's question took her back. It came suddenly at the end of the girl's fast paced speech and Ayla wasn't ready for it. Ayla had never had a friend before, at least not in the way she suspected Bree meant. She saw the way the little girls in her town held hands and giggled together. They helped each other with school work and gave hugs to one another on bad days. They played games up and down the road in town and she had always watched them from the porch of her father's shop hoping to one day join in.

"Umm…" Ayla began, searching for the right words. "I have never been good at making friends…" Bree sighed and looked at her feet. "…But I should like it very much."

The girl's radiant smile returned, and she jumped towards Ayla with such enthusiasm that Ayla nearly fell over with surprise. Bree flung her arms out and embraced her new friend. Ayla felt awkward in the embrace, but she did not want to pull away. A part of her was as happy as Bree. She just wasn't sure how to show it.

"Good! Good! Oh, I'm so happy, Ayla. I haven't had a friend in such long time. It seems like forever!" She released Ayla from the hug and then pressed her finger to her lips and pulled her in closer so she could hear her hushed whisper. "But we have to keep pretending I'm your servant or they'll send me away and we couldn't see each other again. You're supposed to be treated all royal and everything. We'll be friends really, just in secret."

Ayla liked the girl's funny smile and her exciting way of doing things. Bree seemed to have an overflowing amount of enthusiasm at all times and a confidence Ayla admired. Bree would have had the courage to stand up to the rest of the children at the Matchmaking Ball, and she would have been clever enough to stay hidden from a passing entourage of soldiers.

As they returned to their walk, Bree climbed on top of a small stone wall and made her way balancing on top of it. The wall was not narrow in the very least but Bree seemed to enjoy making a great show of pretending to be on the verge of falling.

"Do you like it at the palace, Bree?" Ayla asked, uncomfortable with the sudden silence between them though it didn't seem to bother the other girl.

Bree shrugged, "We have more gold then we did before, and mum and papa seem happy. There aren't any other children around, though. None who are really children, anyway. There's a few who belong to those noble families, but they just walk around looking like little glass dolls most of the time. I asked my mom for a baby sister but she just laughed at me. What do you think that means?"

Ayla shook her head, "I don't know. Maybe handling you is enough?"

Bree stopped and looked down at her, the smile faded. "That was a right funny joke, now."

"Oh! I'm sorry."

Then Bree grinned. "I was beginning to think you were a bit boring!" She laughed merrily and then set out, this time running down the wall. "Come on, I'll race you!"

Ayla ran behind her, her legs and back screaming from her journey, but she didn't dare call for the girl to stop. A smile was forming on her lips and an even deeper one in her heart. For the first time, she felt she had a friend who was everything she imagined a friend might be.

Bree stopped just a few paces short of an old tree growing in a twisted knot beside the wall Bree had been walking on. Ayla could see as she approached that the short wall ended and just a few paces beyond that, white stone rose out of the earth to form the outer wall of the castle.

"I won! I won!" Bree declared, and then added as Ayla trotted up, "I bet you let me win, didn't you? Come on, the west tower is just on the other side of that wall. We'll have to enter through the side gate."

The side gate was a lot less grand than even the passages through the city walls. The gate was well guarded, but Ayla noticed that the only people passing through were dressed like Bree and herself. It was a servant's entrance.

"Come one! Come on!" Bree fell in beside her and whispered, "They told me to take you through the main gate but this way's shorter. Besides, they'll be looking for you there and when they don't see you ... they'll be in an entertaining tizzy!"

They passed through the west gate side by side and for a moment, Ayla thought no one would notice them. Then she heard Bree let out a muffled scream and the girl was suddenly jerked from her side. A guard had grabbed her by the collar and swung her around to face him.

"What's all this, little Bree. Aren't you supposed to be escorting a lady?"

Bree pulled out of his grasp and said curtly, "Already did or were your friends at the main gate not paying attention? She was a fine girl with a big fancy dress on and everything."

"I'm surprised the likes of you didn't push her in the mud." He nodded towards Ayla, "What's all this?"

"New pig girl is all. Here to tend the king's pigs."

The guard looked over Ayla and then turned back to Bree. "I didn't hear of a new pig girl?"

Bree's smile broadened and she tried to stifle a laugh. She looked from Ayla to the guard, then back to Ayla. Before the guard knew what was happening, Bree ran to Ayla and took her hand pulling her along. "Run, Ayla!"

Ayla would have been nervous as they ran along the stone street inside the palace walls but for Bree's laughter. The guard did not give chase but Ayla could hear him call out for them to stop.

Bree led her through a wooden door and into a kitchen area where they were greeted by the squawks of chickens and one angry cook. They ran down a corridor and up a set of stairs, through a fancy parlor where Bree had to stop a moment and look to see if anyone was there. They ran up another set of stairs and down another few long corridors. Bree finally stopped at another wooden door.

"Here we are," she said, gasping.

She flung open the door and took only a few steps up the stairs before collapsing on the broad steps into a heap of giggles. Ayla, grateful Bree had finally stopped running, sat down next to her and tried to catch her breath.

When Ayla next looked up, it was not the girl's satisfied smile that caught her attention first; it was the walls on either side of them. The white stone had been painted with a grand mural that covered the walls of the staircase. She followed it with her eyes and it continued up, twisting with the stairs to where she could not see.

"Oh," Bree said, following her gaze, "I forgot. It's quite wonderful to those who haven't seen it."

Ayla stood and walked to the wall, lightly tracing the outline of a horse and rider with her fingertips. The paint was slightly faded and chipped in a few places, but the thoughts the artist left behind were intact.

"What are they?" Ayla asked.

Bree stepped up beside her. "Can't you tell? It's all Kelvinor legend. See, this first one's of the beginning, how our whole world started."

She went to the bottom of the steps and pointed to the right hand wall. There, she saw the images of two men. Both stood in boats, their arms stretched above their heads. One figure held a blue stone above him that seemed to shine out over all the other boats. The other figure held a red stone but it was not glowing.

Ayla followed the mural, taking a few steps up the stairs. The boats had landed and Ayla saw a figure with a bow and arrow aimed at the sky painted in blue. She continued to follow the series of pictures and saw the arrow in the mouth of a white horse and the archer chasing him. Then the horse and archer were together in front of a painting Ayla recognized as Jade City. The towers rising out of the castle were unmistakable.

"Of course," Bree continued. "We aren't supposed to talk about Kelvinor legends anymore. It's all Talforland this and Talforland that. They say Lady Brista had this painted when her daughter Madlina was still a baby. The lords and ladies of Kelvinor used it ever since then to tell their children the stories." Bree sighed sadly before smiling again and gesturing to Ayla, "Come on, it's a long walk to your room."

They started up the stairs and Ayla found herself listening to Bree chatter again. "This tower used to be for all the children of the Lords and Ladies of Kelvinor. All of them lived together! Imagine that! Lord Kelvin started the tradition. My father said it was to stop the children from fighting wars with one another when they grew up. I don't know what living together has to do with any of that. Anyhow, when Talforland came, their Princess insisted on having the whole space to herself and it was turned into the cozy bedroom you're about to see. Her name's Kristlinadora and I've seen her … only once though and it was from far away. She's the oldest of the king's children but they don't let women really rule in Talforland. She just watches that kingdom while her father and brother are busy over here. It's because she's not married. If she were, they'd never let her do that. Can you imagine? She's nearly thirty and not married."

Ayla wanted to say she could imagine it very well but she held her tongue.

"Did you know Prince Noland is actually the youngest of the king's children?"

Ayla shook her head and Bree continued, eager to share what she knew. "Well, there were three brothers between Prince Noland and Princess Kristlinadora. One died during the war with Granland. Another was killed during the war with Kelvinor and the last disappeared when the king sent that troop to find the Freeland witch. Do you know that story?"

Ayla nodded, grateful to feel like she knew something next to this girl who seemed to know at least a part of everything.

"So now Prince Noland's on track to inherit the throne of the Talforland Empire.

He's a fool if you ask me, but don't tell anyone I said that. I could be burned alive just for saying that!"

When they reached the top of the stairs, there was another wooden door. It was plain and simple, not at all like the room it kept secret. As Bree opened the door for her, Ayla could see royal colors and fabric everywhere. It looked like something from a dream. The mattress stood at least a foot off the frame of the bed, and it was weighted with down blankets of a pleasant plum color. A gilded mirror adorned one wall above a beautifully carved chest which Ayla noted even her father would not have been able to make. There were paintings, a tall wardrobe, a bear skin rug, and curtains which flowed inward from the gentle breeze. It was bigger than the whole dwarf house she had lived in, and she could have stood there staring for quite a long time.

The room was truly astonishing, but what caught Ayla's attention the most was the tall, grey haired lady rising out of the rocking chair in the center of the room. Her hands went straight to her hips, and Bree let out such a gasp that Ayla thought the girl might choke.

"Well, Miss Brenia Sorrowheart, you've caused quite a stir downstairs. Quite a stir!"

Bree looked at her feet and stuttered, "I... I'm sorry, madam. I was just..."

"You were what? Having a bit of fun with our guest?" The tall lady looked absolutely frightening. "Do you know what the king's orders are regarding this girl? Royalty and no less! Now apologize this instant and away with yourself before you cause any more harm."

Bree was on the verge of tears. She turned to Ayla, still looking down. "Beg your pardon, My Lady. I do beg your pardon."

Bree turned and fled. Ayla could hear the girl's steps all the way down the staircase and her heart went out to her. Ayla reluctantly turned and looked towards the tall woman.

"Please excuse her, My Lady. She has not yet learned her place. My name is Madam Grayheart. I am the proprietress over the servants of the castle and former lady of the court. I also serve her Highness the princess Kristlinadora when she visits this palace." The woman gave Ayla a low and graceful curtsy and then popped back up to her full height with more vigor than Ayla would have imagined for a woman her age. She was marked with solemn wrinkles that made her frown look quite foreboding.

"Well, My Lady," the woman continued, "shall we dress you in something more becoming of your new station?"

Ayla just nodded and followed the woman to the wardrobe. When its doors were opened, she could see a row of fine dresses mostly the plum color of the bed sheets or a dark, royal blue.

"Now, I imagine you've never worn a dress such as this so we shall have to teach you to walk in it. Grace and fluidity, those are the two things to remember."

Madam Grayheart also pulled out a small pair of slippers and some white underclothes from a drawer. She looked Ayla up and down. "Yes, I think you're about the same size as the princess. You can wear these until the seamstress comes tomorrow." The woman gestured to a box in front of a standing mirror. "Just stand up there and I'll dress you. You've probably never been dressed before either, but I'll wager you won't know how to put this on by yourself."

Ayla was reminded of putting on the dress she now wore and shook her head, looking at her feet.

Madam Grayheart reached out and gently raised her head with the tip of her fingers. "You are a lady now. You must look down for no one and speak your answers."

"Yes. . .Madam." Ayla said, forcing herself not to look down again.

Madam Grayheart smiled and Ayla thought that if she smiled more, she might have a more pleasant face. "It's a start," was all she said before turning Ayla towards the box.

CHAPTER 10

MADAM GRAYHEART DRESSED Ayla quickly and efficiently. The clothes were loose on her, but she didn't mind. The cool, smooth fabric felt soft against her skin, and it was wonderful to be in clean, beautiful clothes.

When she was done dressing Ayla, Madam Grayheart had the girl walk the length of the room a hundred times.

"Glide across the floor. Hold your head high. Don't slouch!"

There was an endless stream of commands issued from the older woman's mouth, and Ayla tried quite hard to do everything right. There were so many things to remember. She tried to step right, but then she looked at her feet. Ayla tried to hold her head up, but then she would trip on the end of her skirt. Madam Grayheart finally seemed content when she was able to cross the room without stumbling. Her head was held up, but not too high. She could look down with her eyes and still see the hem of her skirt as it flicked in front of her.

Next, Madam Grayheart handed Ayla a book and commanded her to read from it. Ayla could read quite well, but when she opened the book, the symbols there were different from the dwarf runes she had grown up with.

"I…" She stuttered. "I can't read this but…"

Madam Grayheart's eyes narrowed on the girl, and Ayla stopped short. The woman's gaze was electric, and Ayla felt as if she might melt under her gaze. Her cheeks burned a crimson red.

"Well," the lady said curtly. "You will have to have lessons at once. We will get you a tutor. Is there anything you have studied?'

Ayla had studied a wide range of subjects, but everything had been related in some way to the dwarf way of living. She knew how to read and write…in rune. She knew a bit about herbs and how to use a small pen knife to shape wood, but none of that seemed useful here.

"No," she said and then corrected herself. "No, madam."

Madam Grayheart opened her mouth to speak again, but she was interrupted by a knock on the door and a voice calling to them. "Ladies, his majesty's herald at the door."

"You may enter," Madam Grayheart commanded in a stately voice.

The door opened, and a young lad stepped into the room very formally and offered them a low bow, taking his feathered hat off his head and waving it with a smooth flourish. The boy could not have been a day older than thirteen, but his manners were quite practiced.

"Lady Ayla," Madam Grayheart turned to her. "This will be a lesson for you on how a lady receives a messenger. First of all, you must always stand when a messenger enters the room. It is not so much for respect but so that your head is always higher than his. It shows your authority."

Ayla stood, for once remembering to keep her chin up.

"Now you must give him permission to speak."

Ayla cleared her throat, "You may speak."

The herald came up from his bow, "His Majesty requests the Lady Ayla's presence and the presence of her handmaiden for supper tonight in the great hall."

"Now, Lady Ayla, repeat after me," Madam Grayheart said, continuing with her lesson. "Thank you, Herald."

"Thank you, Herald." Ayla noticed that her voice lacked the older woman's authority.

"Inform the king that Madam Grayheart and the Lady Ayla will be delighted to join him for supper."

"Inform the king that Madam Grayheart and the Lady Ayla … will be delighted to join him for supper."

"Very good." Madam Grayheart smiled slightly, "Now you may dismiss him."

Ayla regarded the herald directly and noticed that the boy suddenly diverted his eyes to the floor. "You are dismissed," she said.

The boy bowed to each of the women and exited the room, closing the door gently behind him.

"No one should ever enter your room without knocking and announcing themselves first," Madam Grayheart said, looking after the messenger who had left. "And no one should ever exit without closing the door."

Because they had been invited to sup with the king, Madam Grayheart insisted Ayla wear a more formal dress. Ayla didn't see the point of changing again, but she didn't argue. The older lady pulled open the wardrobe again and removed a dark green gown, holding it up to Ayla. The dress was more than beautiful, but it had a strange simplicity to it. Blue leaves and flowers were embroidered into the fabric, wrapping their way across the chest and around the skirt.

"This will go perfectly with your eyes."

Madam Grayheart dressed her once more and sat her in front of another mirror brushing, twisting, and pulling at the girl's thick black hair. Ayla had rarely put it up. It seemed to prefer to hang free, wild and unmanageable. Girda often complained that Ayla's hair was the thickest she'd seen and wondered aloud if it might have been her human heritage that contributed to its unruly manner.

"Your thick locks!" Madam Grayheart lamented as Ayla bit her lip, holding back tears. "I've never seen such…" The madam stopped suddenly and shook her head.

"What is it?" Ayla ventured cautiously.

"It's nothing, my lady. I'll manage." Madam Grayheart ran the brush through a particularity nasty mass of tangles and Ayla winced. The next few minutes were painful.

"There," Madam Grayheart announced finally, and Ayla opened her eyes to see all of her hair wound tightly on the back of her head. A few tendrils hung fashionably around the front of her face. Ayla stared in wonder. In the dress and with her hair done, she was finally starting to believe she might be as pretty as the prince thought she was.

"Come along! Come along!" Madam Grayheart took her into the small adjacent wash room and set her hands in a dish of cold water. Taking a small brush, she began to scrub at the girl's fingers. Ayla watched as the dirt that was eternally wedged under her nails was rinsed away. Madam Grayheart finished by scraping the nails with a long file until they were rounded perfectly at the ends.

"A bit of powder and we'll hardly recognize you!" the woman said, heading back into the main room. The next thing Ayla knew, Madam Grayheart was tapping a small pillow across her face and shoulders. Ayla could not stifle a small sneeze as white power floated in the air around her.

"How will we know when to go to supper?" Ayla asked. She had eaten no midday meal and hunger was starting to creep up inside of her.

"Someone will fetch us," Madam Grayheart said, digging through a drawer of jewelry in the wardrobe. "Ah! Here it is. This will look perfect with that dress."

It was a silver necklace bearing a star shaped jewel. As Madam Grayheart fastened it around her neck, Ayla took the ornament in her hand. It was set with maybe a dozen blue stones that sparkled in the sunlight streaming through the windows. At its center was a single white diamond.

Madam Grayheart then placed two rings on her left hand. One was a simple silver ring with one blue stone and the other was a thick silver band. As Ayla took a closer look at it, she noticed the silver band was engraved with runes like what had been on the statue in the pavilion. The engravings shone a blue color, like that of the other jewelry.

"Madam," Ayla asked, "where did this ring come from?"

Madam Grayheart was pruning a few locks of her hair and looking her over. "The princess's jewelry box. She rarely wears these pieces. They're from the old kingdom and the princess dislikes foreign jewelry."

Ayla read the ring's inscription to herself.

Lady Lunara Joyinheart

She took the ring off and looked on the inside. Sure enough, she found some tiny runes engraved there.

From Mother and Father with love

Names were tumbling through her head now. The Lords and Ladies of Kelvinor, Lady Brista, Madlina, Kelvin, and now Lady Lunara Joyinheart. Who where they and what had happened here when Talforland came?

"Madam Grayheart," she ventured, "are you from Talforland?"

"Heavens, no,." the woman replied. "I was born and raised in Kelvinor."

Ayla found herself strangely relieved. "Can you tell me anything . . .about

Kelvinor?"

"Well, what would you like to know?"

Ayla thought for a moment, remembering everything she had learned so far. "I don't remember what it was like before Talforland came. I was a baby, then. I was wondering what it was like."

Madam Grayheart stopped playing with the girl's hair for a moment and smiled slightly. "Oh, they were good days, Lady Ayla. Not to say they didn't have problems, but everyone was happy…" She stopped herself and frowned again. "But you know we aren't allowed to speak of the old days."

Ayla would get no more out of Madam Grayheart tonight. The woman wanted to make sure her charge was well prepared to dine with the king and proceeded to lecture Ayla on proper table etiquette. Ayla tried to remember everything the woman told her, but there was so much to learn and no time to learn it. Ayla felt that Madam Grayheart had just gotten started when another messenger knocked at the door and upon entering, announced that the king was ready for them.

Madam Grayheart hustled her out of the tower and ushered her down the long staircase. Ayla tripped a few times on her skirt before she learned to hold it high enough in front of her. She felt Madam Grayheart's eyes on her, and she knew she might be practicing walking up and down the stairs in the morning.

When they reached the bottom of the staircase, the woman stepped in front of Ayla and led her down a long corridor.

"I shall announce you," she explained. "A lady is always announced."

She followed Madam Grayheart down several other long corridors, trying to remember to hold her head high and to walk with grace and fluidity. They passed several groups of people who all stopped and stared as she passed. A few even made slight bows or curtsies. Ayla was unsure of how to respond and afraid to ask Madam Grayheart so she just nodded slightly and then stared straight ahead, keeping her chin up.

Finally, they arrived at a pair of high wooden doors and Madam Grayheart stopped, turning toward her. "Now remember, it is a woman's prerogative to arrive last and her privilege to be served first. The men will not begin eating until your silver touches your plate, and they will remain standing as long as you remain standing.

Chin up, feet light!" With that, Madam Grayheart turned and opened the doors.

"Presenting Lady Ayla Ravenheart of Kelvinor."

Ayla stepped through the doorway and tried to remember to breathe. The name startled her, but she didn't have time to dwell on the comment. She had thought she would be dining with the king and the prince, but in front of her stood a whole table full of men, all standing. There were twenty at the very least. They were richly dressed, adorned with silver swords and jeweled emblems, and they were all looking at her. Every muscle in her body wanted to flee in terror.

"Lady Ayla." The king's deep voice greeted her, and she found him sitting at the head of the table, the farthest distance from the entrance. On his left hand side was the only free seat. "Come and sit by me."

Slowly and as gracefully as she could muster, she walked the length of the room to the empty seat. Her heart was pounding and every careful step seemed to take an eternity. At last she reached her seat and the gentleman sitting on her left side pulled the chair out, indicating she should sit.

"Thank you," she managed, and finally found herself seated. The men around the table sat and the great silence disappeared into multiple conversations and loud male voices. Ayla was relieved the attention had turned away from her.

The prince sat on the king's right side, looking bored. Roderick smiled at her from the next seat over. To her left sat the younger gentleman who had helped her with her chair. He was laughing with a rather portly man seated across the table.

She caught several tidbits of conversations. There was much talk about the war with Wadroland and of the Eastern Sea. Others chatted about things like home life and their wives. Once an older gentleman spouted to Roderick that he envied his ability to leave home so often.

"Must be grand to be in the thick of it!" he said, drinking from a large flask. "Fighting and riding around like heroes."

Roderick offered the man a polite smile but said nothing.

They talked and drank for a full hour before the food was brought out. There were two fat turkeys, mounds of hot potatoes, cakes, and puddings. Ayla thought she might be full just from looking at it. As Madam Grayheart had warned her, she was served first and no one lifted fork or spoon until Ayla took her first bite.

"Well, how is it, my lady?" the young gentleman next to her asked, smiling.

"Very good, thank you," she said quietly, knowing it would be polite to look up at him but being unable to do so.

The young man spoke again, this time even more friendly than before, "My name is Sir Jovan Lockheart of Talforland."

Ayla started and then turned to him. She remembered the name Landon had said. Was this the soldier she had been unable to see?

"Jovan?" She whispered, "Do I know you, sir?"

He smiled, "Perhaps. I was with the company that brought you here." It was then that Ayla could have sworn he winked at her before continuing, "My father is the Grand Duke of Talforland." He gestured to the portly gentleman sitting across the table. "I'm his youngest son and as such, had to join the king's army to earn any kind of name for myself."

The supper continued on for another two hours. Servants brought out another three courses and the men ate merrily. Ayla found she had eaten her fill after the first round of food. She could not keep her mind from straying to the children she had seen when entering the city. Their hallow, hungry eyes called to her from the back of her mind. It seemed unfair that the king and these men should eat in excess while they starved.

Ayla picked at the bones on her plate and scanned the men at the table until her eyes finally rested on the prince. His look had changed. He was staring intently at a wine glass on the table in front of him. As Ayla watched, the prince took the glass and filled it up with wine. As he sat the wine cask back on the table, his other hand passed carefully over the red liquid and Ayla noticed a few sprinkles of white powder fall into the glass and dissolve into the drink. Ayla blinked, unsure of what she was seeing.

The prince rose and handed the glass to his father. "A toast, Sire!"

"Ah, yes!" The king stood also, accepting the glass and raising it into the air.

The king gave a long toast to all manner of things. He toasted several gods and the war with Wadroland. He toasted his son and Roderick and all the other soldiers. He toasted Talforland and his daughter. Indeed, it took another thirty minutes for him to finish and for everyone to drink. Ayla watched as he wiped a trickle of the wine from his beard and dismissed them from the meal.

Before Ayla knew it, Madam Grayheart had appeared at her side and was asking, "Are you ready, Lady Ayla?"

She was still wondering about the king's drink, but before she could respond, Roderick was at her side.

"I beg your pardon, madam, but might I have the pleasure of a few words with the lady?"

Madam Grayheart frowned and looked the captain over. It was the same look Girda would give to any boy who tried to speak with one of the children under her care. "For a moment, Captain," she said curtly.

Roderick took Ayla's arm very formally and escorted her away from the others. "I need to look like I am talking pleasantries with you so keep smiling."

She did so and he continued, "I will come to you later tonight so do not sleep and keep a candle burning in your window. Can you do that?"

Ayla nodded, still smiling, and she noticed he too wore a very fake grin. "I can do that. What about the guards and Madam Grayheart?"

"Don't worry about them. I know this castle better than any guard or old handmaiden."

"Roderick, I must tell you something," she said, taking a breath. "I saw the prince put something in the king's glass. I think it was a powder."

Roderick narrowed his eyes slightly but did not remove his smile. "Are you sure?"

She nodded, "He did it right before the toast, when he poured the glass for his father."

"Alright," he said, looking across the hall to the handmaiden who was waiting with a scowl on her face. "We will speak of this later. For now, I must say goodnight."

He walked her back towards Madam Grayheart who was waiting at the hall entrance doors with her hands neatly folded in front of her.

Roderick made a great show of saying goodnight. He bowed and then rejoined the prince who was looking after them with scorn.

Madam Grayheart led her back down the corridor. The evening sunlight faded from the windows as they walked, and the castle was getting darker with each passing minute. A group of servants passed them, lighting torches that hung along the wall.

It gave the castle an eerie glow.

As they approached the tower, Madam Grayheart took a torch and led Ayla up the stairs once more. In the bedroom, the woman found a candle, lit it, and placed the torch on the wall just outside the door. She shut the glass paned windows and returned to the wardrobe, removing a long cotton night gown. For the third time that night, Ayla found herself on the box in front of the mirror being changed.

It was standing on that box again that Ayla realized how tired she was and remembered that Roderick had asked her to stay awake. It was going to be harder than she thought. The satin sheets and down comforter on the bed looked warm and inviting and all she had slept on for the last few nights was a hard, wooden floor.

Madam Grayheart turned down the bed covers for Ayla and set the candle on the small table next to the bed. Two guards knocked at the door and announced their arrival. Madam Grayheart took the liberty of greeting them on the other side of the door and then lecturing them on how they were not to disturb the Lady Ayla with their presence. Ayla found the whole thing quite amusing. When Madam Grayheart came back into the room, she insisted that Ayla get into bed.

"I'll wake you at first light and have a full day's agenda for you so don't take the liberty of making any plans," the woman said firmly. "If you have any problems, tell the soldiers in the hall and they will send for me. Is that understood, my lady?"

"Yes, madam," Ayla replied, eager for the woman's departure. She climbed into the bed and under the covers.

Madam Grayheart leaned down to blow out the candle.

"Wait!" Ayla stopped her and the woman looked up, startled. "I would like to keep the candle lit."

Madam Grayheart raised an eyebrow, "Whatever for?"

"I…" Ayla stuttered. "I'm afraid of the dark … and this is a new place and what if I have to go to the wash room during the night…and…"

"Alright," Madam Grayheart interrupted. "But I'll put it on the chest here so you don't turn it over as you sleep." She moved the candle and Ayla breathed a sigh of relief. "Goodnight, Lady Ayla."

"Goodnight, Madam Grayheart"

The door shut, leaving Ayla alone in the eerie glow of candlelight.

CHAPTER 11

AYLA WAITED A FEW PRECIOUS seconds until the sound of Madam Grayheart's footsteps faded on the stairs. She lay there, listening to her own breathing, wondering how well the guards could hear from outside the door. She hoped they would knock before they entered. Madam Grayheart's forceful lecture to them gave Ayla some courage.

Slowly, carefully, she pushed back the bed covering and stepped onto the rug. Her bare feet didn't make a sound. Tip-toeing across the room, she lifted the candle from the chest and placed it on the window sill. She tied back the curtains to keep them away from the flame and to make sure Roderick would be able to see the glow.

Ayla looked back to the bed with longing. She wanted nothing more than to crawl under its soft sheets and go straight to sleep, but that wasn't possible. Roderick had told her to stay awake and she would do her best.

Her feet were cold and she remembered what Roderick had said the last time he saw her without shoes and stockings. She opened one of the wardrobe doors. It made a small squeak, and she stopped, listening. There was no knock on the door, no sound from outside. She opened several drawers before finding some white stockings and soft slippers.

Now there was nothing to do but wait. She sat down on the box Madam Grayheart had her stand on when she was being dressed. Resting her head in her hands, she tried to think and to keep her eyes open.

She found both tasks near to impossible and finally stood and stretched. There had to be a better way of staying awake. Her eyes searched the room and fell on the book Madam Grayheart had handed her earlier. It was laying face down on the table by the bed.

Ayla took the book and opened it flat on the table, turning the pages rapidly for anything she might understand. She found a few interesting pictures: A woman sitting upright in a chair, a man and woman dancing, and a sketch of a woman curtsying to a very formal looking gentleman. There was nothing in the book worth serious study and she soon closed it, opting to pace the room instead.

She swung her arms to and fro, and stretched her shoulders and neck. She tried not to think about how much her legs and back ached. She traced the lines on the gilded mirror and studied every mark on the ornate chest. It seemed like she had been waiting for hours when she knew no more than a half hour had passed.

She finally laid straight back on the bed and stared at the ceiling, giving in to boredom and exhaustion. As Ayla focused her eyes upwards, she found an etching just above the canopy of the bed. It looked like writing and as she studied it, she realized she was looking at runes.

Ayla stood up, struggling to keep her balance on the soft mattress and straining to see the writing better. It was the same form of rune she was finding throughout the castle and her heart beat rapidly as she read.

Valkay Joyinheart

It was another name. The runes were roughly etched and it looked as though it might have been done by a child with a simple knife. She wondered if Valkay had lived in this room a long time ago. He carried the same last name as Lunara Joyinheart, the name on the ring. Her hand instinctively felt for the ring but Madam Grayheart had removed it.

She was just about to search inside the wardrobe for the jewelry when a soft clunk caught her attention. She started, looking around for its source. She saw nothing but heard the noise again and this time realized it was coming from the floor. She climbed down from the bed and saw that the bear skin rug was lifting ever so slightly at its center.

Ayla thought instantly of Roderick and she pulled at the edge of the rug only to realize it was fastened down at the corners. She lifted an edge and peered underneath. She saw that a small door had lifted out of the floor and someone was trying to climb through.

"Hello?" she whispered softly, fully expecting to hear Roderick's voice in reply.

But it was a youthful female voice that answered her. "Lady Ayla?! I can't see you!"

"I'm over here," Ayla said, half laughing at Bree.

The girl turned and Ayla could make out her face in the small opening. She posted an untypical frown when she caught sight of Ayla. "Oh! Lady Ayla, are you mad at me?"

"Not in the least!" Ayla reached her hand underneath the rug and the younger girl took it. With a great pull, she helped Bree slide under the rug and out into the room. The two girls sat on the floor quietly giggling for a moment.

"It's a secret passage!" Bree explained, "There's a lot in this place. Nobody knows about this one but me. I found it one day when I was hiding from the cook. He chased me into a closet and when I started moving things around to cover myself, I found this little ladder built into the back wall. I followed it and guess where it led me? Right here!"

The girls were still whispering, but Ayla wasn't going to take any chances on the guards outside hearing them. She took Bree by the arm and pulled her inside the small wash room.

"Bree, I'm so sorry that Madam Grayheart sent you away. I didn't want her to scold you like that just for being friendly."

Bree grinned, "But it's all a part of the game, you see? You have to act like a lady and I have to act like a servant. In secret, we'll be friends! That's what makes it fun."

Ayla wasn't sure how Roderick would react to finding Bree here but she didn't want the girl to leave, either. Besides keeping her awake, Bree was a wealth of information. The girl seemed to know a lot about Kelvinor and was more willing to talk than anyone she had met so far.

"Bree, can you read?"

Bree shrugged, "Well enough. Why?"

Ayla tip-toed to the table and brought back the book the madam had given her. "Do you know what this is?"

The girl took it and studied the words on the cover. "I think it's a ladies book. Something about being formal and such."

"You think?"

"I said well enough. I can read what I have to, and everything else is a little fuzzy. Can't you read?"

Ayla suddenly felt very stupid. "No."

"Oh." Bree gave her a sympathetic look and began to flip through the book. "There's a part about receiving guests. Something here about standing right… and I thought learning mathematics was pointless."

Ayla smiled. If there was anything she could do well, it was mathematics. Her father had taught her the subject and Ayla imagined that the language of numbers was probably universal.

"I bet they're going to make you learn to read, and you'll have to read this whole book and know it all by heart!"

Ayla laughed. "I hope not!"

"Well, it would be more fun than cleaning stables and watching chickens…" The girl sighed. "I wish we could just go out and play tomorrow."

The girl looked very sad and Ayla suddenly understood why she was so much trouble. No one ever gave Bree time to be a child.

"Bree," Ayla said, "my parents were very strict and never told me anything about the way Kelvinor used to be. Perhaps you'd like to tell me something?"

The girl smiled and sat up eagerly, "We're not supposed to talk about it but I'd love to tell you. Where to begin?"

"What about the mural outside? The two figures holding something? And the horse and the archer I saw."

"Oh," Bree nodded, "yes, that's a good place to start. That's the legend of the origin of Kelvinor. You see, a couple of hundred years ago a man named Kelvin came here with a small group of people from across the North Sea. They were survivors from an island somewhere in the ocean. It was completely destroyed by fire, but no one knows how or why. Anyway, Kelvin landed on the beach just north of here and decided they had better find a place to build a city. He was a really good archer so he decided to fire an arrow and wherever it landed, that's where they'd stay. So he fired and they all went to look for this arrow. They found it – but it had been picked up by a white horse. For three days they followed the horse until it dropped the arrow here and began to paw the earth. Then Kelvin built Jade City and a few years later became the first Lord of Kelvinor. People say he didn't want to be a lord but who wouldn't want to be a lord?"

"What about the people who already lived here?" Ayla asked

Bree shrugged. "There weren't any kingdoms or anything. Just a bunch of villages. Kelvinor brought everybody together. My papa says when the Lord Kelvin came, everyone from the Freeland Mountains to the Sunstone River started to work together."

"What about Talforland and Wadroland. . .Granland?"

"Oh, well, they were formed at the same time as Kelvinor," Bree said, matter-of-factly. "Kelvin, Talfor, Wadro, and Grandvor were all survivors of the same island; they just settled in different places. For a long time, all the kingdoms lived together in peace. Honestly, I'm surprised no one has ever told you any of this. I thought it was just common knowledge. Goes to show that Talforland really is taking over, I guess." Bree shook her head and frowned, "My papa still talks about how great things were before they came. Sure, there were problems but not like now. So many of the farmer's sons were off to war last spring that we didn't pull in half the crop we needed. There wasn't any food to be had and so many people starved or worse. It was terrible!"

"What does your papa say Kelvinor was like?" Ayla asked, pulling her knees up to her chest.

"Well, for starters, there weren't any wars. Papa says Kelvinor had a strict policy of peace. The lords and ladies also had some kind of council of people presiding over the land. They didn't just make decisions. The people had their say, too. Papa even told me that one winter when the crop had been bad, the lord and lady went out themselves to make sure everyone had something to eat!" Bree's eyes suddenly got big, "Oh yeah, and it was said that Kelvinor used to be the keeper of all the magic in the land!"

"Magic?" Ayla breathed. "All the magic?"

Bree nodded rapidly, "It's all a part of the legend. You see, on this island where Kelvin and the others were from, there were different people who protected different things. Kelvin was supposed to have been the protector of all things magical. He brought the island's magic with him when he came here."

"Where would the magic be now?" Ayla asked, finding herself caught up in the story.

Bree shrugged, "No one really knows. My papa said he doesn't remember it at all, but there are some older folks who claim to have seen glimpses of it."

"Magic," Ayla said again. "What did it look like?"

"Well," Bree held out her hands, "They say it sparkled at the tips of the lord's fingers when he used it." She laughed, "Imagine that! Sparkling finger tips! And…" Her eyes were big again and she spoke with drama, "Some say Kelvin brought magical creatures with him when he came here and that they held some of the magic."

"Like unicorns?" Ayla had heard that unicorns were magical and Otto had told her they once existed in the woods surrounding her town. No one had seen a unicorn recently though, and most of the younger generation doubted they had ever existed.

Bree nodded, "Unicorns and griffins, winged horses, fairies, nymphs . . . all of those things. Kelvin was supposed to have brought them with him from over the North Sea."

"What could have happened to them all?"

"My papa says they've slowly faded away." Bree returned to her matter-of-fact voice, "Some think that the Creator God never meant for them to escape the island."

Ayla sat all the way up. The dwarfs worshiped a Creator God. She didn't want to ask Bree outright if the people of Kelvinor worshiped one god or many. She imagined that the girl would have really thought her an idiot. Hoping to get her answer another way, she just said, "The people from Talforland worship so many gods."

Bree nodded, "You bet they do! They don't do anything before saying prayers to some stone thing. I'm glad for just one, thank you."

Ayla had her answer. The people of Kelvinor worshiped the same god as the dwarfs. "Bree, you said that Kelvin was supposed to have brought all sorts of magic things with him. What about dwarfs?"

The girl shrugged. "I guess so. What's so special about dwarfs?"

"Nothing." Ayla looked at the stone floor, lost in thought. "I was just curious."

Ayla heard the trap door shudder and was on her feet in a moment. Bree popped up as well and hid behind the taller girl, biting her lip.

"It's the madam, for sure," she whispered. "She'll skin me alive!"

Ayla silenced her with a wave of her hand. "I don't think it's Madam Grayheart, but you had best hide anyway."

Bree looked around franticly. "Where?"

Ayla's eyes fell on the ornate chest and she ran to it, pulling up the lid. It had a few blankets at its bottom but there was plenty of room for Bree. The girl squeezed in and Ayla shut the lid.

The rug was rising at its middle and Ayla ran to the spot where she had helped Bree climb into the room. Lifting the edge of the rug, she saw a bit of light shining through the trap door and Roderick's eyes looking back at her.

With a little help, he climbed into the room and out from under the rug. "Neat trick, huh?" he said with a small smile. "I'm glad I grew up here. I think I know about every passage in this place."

Ayla thought of Bree in the chest and wondered if she should tell Roderick the girl was there. Bree was her friend and seemed trustworthy enough to know anything she did but she was afraid Roderick would send her away. Or even worse, he would be angry with Ayla for having the girl there at all.

"I brought you some books," Roderick continued, "and if my suspicions are correct, I think you can read them."

Ayla noticed that he was carrying two books under one arm. He took one and handed it to her. The other he placed on the bedside table. There were runes on the cover.

"How did you know?"

"I saw the way you looked at the statue and I guessed. No one reads it anymore because even Kelvinor adopted the trade language, something of a mix between the rune language they used to speak and the language of the people who already lived here. We all still speak the same way but writing changed. It became a different way of communicating with sounds instead of symbols. I guess . . . the dwarfs kept using the runes?"

Ayla only nodded, reading the cover out loud, "Chronicles of Kelvinor: Part One."

"A scribe used to keep it. It's a monthly record of everything that occurred in Kelvinor between the years 286 to 368. Then there's part two." He pointed to the book he had laid on the table.

Ayla opened the book to the middle and read aloud again. "Second summer month, Calendar date 317…" She scanned the page. There was the death of an older noble, a note about some growing crops, and the announcement of a fall festival. Most of it seemed fairly unimportant. She looked back to Roderick. He was giving her an odd smile.

"What is it?" She asked.

"I have to tell you, Ayla." Roderick shook his head. "I had my doubts. Even when we were bringing you here, I thought that maybe you had learned the stories, knew who I was, and endeavored to fool me but this. . ." he pointed to the book. "This is proof. No one has been able to read this text for sixteen years. The people who did know were killed when you were a baby."

Ayla closed the book. "I don't understand. What could it mean?"

"Ayla," Roderick said, and she noted the air of excitement in his voice. "You're a direct descendant of Lord Kelvin and the legitimate heir to the throne of Kelvinor."

Ayla's heart beat faster as his words sank in. "What? How could that be?"

He picked up the second book from the bedside table and flipped it open to the very back, handing it to her. "I think you'll find the answer here. Look for the First Summer Month of 418."

Ayla found the page easily. The hand writing was different from the other book. This scribe wrote with long, more elaborate lettering. It made the runes somewhat harder to read. "First Summer Month, 418. Third year of Lord Valkay Joyinheart." She stopped for a moment, remembering the name carved in the corner of the ceiling before continuing. The first few sentences recorded the movements of Talforland armies and the loss of a battle 'along the southern road'. Then she saw another familiar name, "On the eighteenth day, the Lord Valkay and Lady Salisie celebrated the birth of their first child, Lunara Joyinheart." Ayla took a deep breath and kept reading. "The child was named for her great-great-great-great grandmother, Lady Luna, wife of Lord Kelvin."

Ayla stopped reading and looked up at Roderick. Could it be true?

"Six months later, Kelvinor was lost to Talforland." Roderick explained. "Lord Valkay was killed in the fighting. The scribes and learned men were put to death. Many of the nobility were killed. It was a bloodbath."

"And Lunara?" Ayla questioned, suspecting she already knew the answer.

"The baby was entrusted to a man named Brighton Strongheart. He and the child were never heard from again."

"Strongheart?"

Roderick nodded, "My grandfather. He was also a member of the nobility. My father took me and my mother into Halforton village where we pretended to be peasants when the army came. We saved a few of the books the scribes gave us." He gestured to the one she held in her hands. "That one and the other among them. Anything the scribes couldn't get out of the castle, they burned. It's one of the reasons why they were executed."

Ayla stared at the page in front of her. The possibility that any of this could be true stirred an unfamiliar feeling in her heart. She looked back up at Roderick. "What about Lady Salisie?"

Roderick crossed the room and sat on top of the chest where Bree was hiding. Ayla hoped the girl wouldn't make a sound. "Courtesy of war, you don't execute a former lady. She died very suddenly in the first year of her capture of what the king called an illness. Many of us, including myself, think that she was really poisoned."

"And they never looked for Lunara?"

Roderick shook his head, "Talforland never knew of her. Because they were so near to defeat when she. . or you. . .were born, they issued an order to the people for them to keep quiet about your birth. We did, for sixteen years."

"And no one from Kelvinor looked for her or Brighton?"

"We hoped you were safe." Roderick stood again. "We hoped you would come back some day knowing who you were. We hoped Brighton might still be with you, but in those early days of Talforland rule, it was difficult for anyone to travel without royal approval. We were afraid of being followed or of getting you killed."

He took a deep breath and started again. "Recently, the outer lands have been revolting and it worries the king. These people are tired of keeping your secret and a few have spoken about a lost heir. It makes the task before us more urgent. . ."

Ayla dropped the book on the table by the bed and sat down on its soft mattress. Her heart was racing with possibilities. "What if none of this is true? What if it's all just a coincidence?"

Roderick walked to the bed and stood right in front of her. She found herself unable to look at him, a wealth of sorrow suddenly pouring out of her. "I find it hard to believe after sixteen years of being nothing but odd and unusual that I would be something so grand as a princess!"

Roderick took her face in his heads and lifted it toward him. Looking in his eyes, she wanted nothing more than to tell him what had happened at the Matchmaking Ball and why she had gotten lost in the woods. She was a princess only in a child's cruel joke. None of this could be true.

"There is one way to be sure," Roderick said softly. "But it will take great courage and great risk."

Ayla nodded, a small tear streaking down her face. Roderick wiped it away.

"There is a prophecy that says an heir will return and claim the throne of Kelvinor. If the heir is true, then she will also be able to claim a certain power that is hidden in the temple on the palace grounds. The certain power lies in an old relic of Kelvinor, a blue pendant. If we can get you to the pendant, the whole kingdom might be saved, but we don't have much time."

"What do you mean?"

"The king is very ill," Roderick explained. "In fact, he's dieing. I've suspected for a long time that the prince might be poisoning him, slowly so no one will notice. What you saw tonight confirms it." He took a breath. "There is another power, a red pendant. It is cursed and evil and no one has been allowed to touch it for years. But if the king dies, I am sure the prince will seek it. He and an outcast priestess speak of it often. This priestess may even know its location."

"I don't understand," Ayla said, shaking her head. "What does that have to do with anything? How can a pendant determine who controls a kingdom?"

"It doesn't really. But the pendants are both very powerful and whoever controls one or both, will no doubt have the ability to destroy or create a kingdom." Roderick took a deep breath. "Ayla, do the dwarfs believe in magic?"

The dwarfs did indeed believe in magic, but from what she knew of these people and of the way Roderick spoke, she suspected he was talking about something different. The dwarfs believed that there was a kind of magic in everything. Under the Creator God's direction, trees grew, the seasons changed, the river always ran, the old died, and babies were born. It was all a sort of magic. No one endeavored to control it, they only whispered soft prayers over their farms and gave thanks when the magic seemed to favor them. What Roderick and Bree seemed to be talking about was the kind of magic people could harvest and control.

"Not in the way you're talking about," she finally answered. "But we do believe in magic."

"Talforland claims not to believe in any kind of magic," Roderick said with disdain. "In fact, they're quick to kill anyone suspected of being a magic-user."

"People who can use magic?" Ayla asked. "They exist?"

Roderick nodded, "They did though the memory of that has faded. Magic, in fact, was never native to this land."

Roderick repeated the story Ayla had heard from Bree about the founding of Kelvinor and the island the people had come from. Ayla listened patiently, not wanting to have to explain where she had heard the story before and wary of the girl hiding in the chest.

"Lord Kelvin was the Keeper of Magic and he brought it here in the blue pendant when he escaped the island," Roderick finished. "No one knows why the pendant is dead now. We only have the legend of how to bring the magic back."

He picked up the second chronicle of Kelvinor's history and flipped to a page, stretching it out to her. "I believe this is it written in rune."

Ayla read,

> *Blue jewel of creation*
> *That stores gift inside*
> *Will be stirred*
> *By a child's eye*
> *One touch can liven*
> *But the heir must beware*
> *For her blood could stir*
> *Sister's power elsewhere*
> *One other key*
> *May also hold*

The gift of power
For one so bold

Ayla wasn't sure she understood. "So if I am the heir that is meant to restore Kelvinor, I should be able to reawaken the blue pendant. But what about the ending?"

"We don't have the guidance of the scribe who wrote this so we don't know." Roderick looked down at the book. "Is there anything else on the page?"

She shook her head. "Just this and the date."

Roderick closed the book and sat it on the bed. "You understand now why it was important for me to get you to the castle. We have to get you to the pendant."

Ayla bit her lip. Her mind was swimming with thoughts. "Prince Noland doesn't seem to think I am any heir..."

"That's good," Roderick interrupted. "You're not a threat to him now. I hope he and the others do not realize that the sign for Kelvinor good luck is, in fact, a raven. The vision that was seen in the temple could very likely be real ... though I doubt it came from any one of the gods Talforland still worships..."

A small sneeze from the direction of the chest caused both their heads to turn.

"Oh, no," Ayla breathed as Roderick pulled his sword and walked to the chest.

CHAPTER 12

RODERICK PUSHED OPEN the lid with the edge of his blade revealing a rather sheepish looking Bree.

"Don't strike me, captain, please! I wasn't listening, I promise."

Roderick sheathed his sword and pulled her out of the chest by one arm. "Bree Sorrowheart!" he said forcefully. "Of all the people to find snooping around Lady Ayla's room. How much did you hear?"

"Nothing!" she said a little too loud, and Ayla silenced them both.

There was knocking at the door.

"Lady Ayla," a man's voice said. "Are you alright?"

"A bad dream," she called, thinking fast. "I'm alright."

"Shall we come inside?"

Ayla looked at Roderick. He shook his head. "No. I'm alright. I. . ." She looked back to Roderick and found herself smiling. "I haven't my stockings or my slippers on. I think you had best stay outside the door."

"Yes, Lady Ayla," the voice answered, sounding lighter and somewhat embarrassed.

Ayla looked back to Roderick who she noticed had looked toward her ankles. They were well covered, but he turned slightly red when she caught him.

"Alright, Bree," Roderick said very softly, letting the girl the go.

"I didn't hear nothing," she said again, looking from Ayla to Roderick rapidly. "Well, nothing important. Just a lot about Kelvinor and . . .Oh, Lady Ayla! Are you. . .Are you really. . .?" she looked back to Roderick and started, "But nothing, sir. Nothing."

Roderick sighed, "Did you know she was here?"

Ayla nodded, "I'm sorry. I told her to hide, because I thought you'd be angry with me. She came in the same way you did."

"I should have known." Roderick shook his head, "I should kill you right now, Bree, and save some poor head housemaid the trouble later."

Bree's eyes widened. "Oh, please, Captain. I won't tell no one what I heard. I promise. I'll not tell a single soul."

Roderick seemed to look to Ayla for an answer.

"I think we should trust her," Ayla said. "After all, it's my fault. I asked her to stay." Ayla smiled at Bree and the girl gave her a wide grin in reply which she quickly removed on catching the captain's gaze again.

"I should like to help," she said cautiously. "You're going to try and get the blue pendant, and I think I can help."

Roderick scoffed slightly, "I'm sorry, Bree, but the temple is well guarded, and you'll just get yourself into trouble."

Bree smiled, "I know it's well guarded, but I've been inside before and I can get inside again." She walked to Ayla's side and gave her a friendly nudge, "Didn't I tell you I knew all the passage ways in this place!"

Roderick raised an eyebrow, "Are you telling me there's a passage to the temple?"

Bree nodded, "By the black statue of Lord Kelvin where I met Ayla."

"But that one leads to the stables," Roderick's voice was solid. "Not to the temple."

"That it does," Bree said, her smile growing, "But there's a passage connecting to that passage that will take you to the temple basement, where they keep the wine."

From the way Bree said it, Ayla wondered if Bree hadn't gotten into the wine at some point.

"A passage inside a passage?" Roderick breathed. "Would you show me tomorrow night? I need to be sure."

Bree nodded, "Yes. But only if I'm in on all this and really in. I want to help."

Roderick opened his mouth to answer, but Ayla put a hand on Bree's shoulder. "You're in," she said lightly, looking to Roderick. "She can help us."

"Ayla," Roderick began, "This isn't a game. If we're discovered, all of us could be put to death. I don't want anyone involved that doesn't have to be."

Bree seemed to straighten herself up, "I'll be fourteen in a few days and that's grown up enough. I can help. Besides, they've never really punished me for doing anything, and I been caught plenty of times."

"That's right!" Ayla said with sudden inspiration. "Why couldn't we just send Bree to get the pendant? If she were caught, they would just think it was some childish mischief."

"I could go tomorrow!" Bree nearly clapped her hands with excitement.

Roderick held up his hand, "Hold on you two. Bree, do you even know where the pendant is?"

Bree blinked once before shaking her head.

"It's kept in a chest inside the altar of the sanctuary."

Bree looked at her feet. "Oh. Well, that makes things a bit difficult."

"The sanctuary has keepers in it at all times. Someone is always there praying to one of the gods," Roderick explained to Ayla. "Tomorrow is also a Sunday so we would have double the keepers to contend with. They will also be praying about you, Ayla Ravenheart."

"Is that what they are calling me. Ravenheart?"

Roderick nodded, "Derived from the vision, no doubt. And you two had better pray to the Creator God with all your might that those stone statues don't tell them that raven is bad news."

"But they don't really see visions, do they? They couldn't know who I am?"

Roderick just shrugged, "I don't believe in any other god but the one who creates. However, I do think there are forces that work against that God and pretend to have powers like His."

"Kal," Bree bit her lip, "the dark goddess."

"Not a goddess," Roderick corrected, "just a magical being who refused to be governed by good. She only masquerades as a goddess to gain followers... It was she who created the red pendant and filled it with the power to destroy."

Ayla had grown up hearing about a spirit the dwarfs called Kal. When crops failed or things were going wrong, people had often whispered about the dark spirit. Others just laughed, calling it superstition. It seemed reasonable to Ayla that if a benevolent Creator God could exist, an evil spirit could also be at work in the world. The thought made her shudder. It took her a few moments to realize that her companions were silent and looking to her.

"I'm alright," she managed a small smile. "What do we need to do now?"

"We wait," Roderick said. "In three days, the keepers will celebrate the official first day of spring. Sacrifices will be made on the temple steps and the sanctuary will be near to empty. Prince Noland will be preparing for his twentieth year soon and will doubtlessly resent my company. He'll send me away as soon as he is able, and I can use the passageway Bree will show me to get the pendant."

"Why not just let me sneak in there and take it?" Bree spoke up. "I'd be sure to be able to escape work that day!"

"Because Bree," Roderick answered, "you will be on your best behavior for the next few days…"

"Best behavior?" Bree frowned.

"So that when you ask to escort the prize calf to be sacrificed, they may indeed let you."

Bree's frown grew more intense, "And why would I want to do a silly thing like that?"

"Because," Roderick explained, a grin growing on his face, "the calf is going to mysteriously get away and you're going to fall down and hurt yourself so as to not be able to chase it."

"And the keepers will be doing cartwheels trying to catch that thing!"

"Yes," Roderick said, "and they'll call the other keepers out to give chase. It should give me plenty of time."

"I'll make sure they pick the roughest, meanest calf in the bunch!" Bree grinned. "I can't wait!"

Ayla had been listening with excitement. "What do I need to do?"

Roderick turned to her, "You'll be closely watched. Lady Ayla, I think it's best if you let the two of us retrieve the pendant and get it to you that night."

The plan would keep her out of danger, but Ayla found she was strangely disappointed. As unreal as it seemed for her to be a princess, she wanted to be one badly. She felt a growing sense of passion welling up inside of her. She felt like she should be doing something, anything to help.

"Can't I do anything?" she managed shyly.

Roderick nodded, "Do everything they ask you to do in the next three days. You have to be pleasing or the keepers will turn the vision against you."

She nodded lightly, remembering Madam Grayheart's hard lessons. It might not be easy to keep her patience over three days.

"Read these books when you can," Roderick continued. "They might tell us something we need to know. But be sure to keep them hidden and never let anyone know you can read the runes."

Roderick placed a hand on her shoulder, "I know you want to help, but right now, your learning about the old kingdom might help us more. Who knows what secrets that pendant contains?"

The thought of touching the pendant and feeling the throb of some magical power inside it made Ayla's heart beat faster. Would she know what to do with it? Would the power glow at her fingertips like Bree had told her? Three days seemed a world away and yet so frighteningly close.

"Will I see you in the next few days?" She looked up to Roderick.

He just nodded, "I won't come tomorrow, but perhaps the next night. I spend most of my days with the prince so when you see him, you will see me."

"And I'll come every night…" Bree began but Roderick cut her off.

"No, you won't! You will be on your best behavior, remember? And that means not doing anything that could get you in trouble if you were caught."

Bree looked disappointed, but just nodded sheepishly. "Oh, alright."

"We had better go," Roderick turned back to Ayla. "We both need to rest and me staying longer only increases the possibility of getting caught." He bowed to her, taking her hand briefly, "Goodnight, Lady Ayla."

She said goodnight and in a moment he had crawled under the rug and through the trap door.

"I guess I should say goodnight, too," Bree said when Roderick left. "You can tell me this before I go, though. Are you sweet on the captain? You seem to be sweet on the captain."

Ayla blushed. She had never really liked any boy in her life and Roderick was the first one who had paid any attention to her. He was a gentleman and was much older than she felt.

"He's very nice," was all she managed.

Bree smiled broadly. "You're sweet on him. I know it. Goodnight!"

The younger girl swung her arms around Ayla and hugged her almost as fiercely as she had earlier that day. Ayla could only smile and return the hug.

When Bree disappeared through the trap door, Ayla took the candle and placed it back on the chest. She almost blew it out before realizing that she had to hide the books Roderick had left her.

The wardrobe seemed like a bad idea as Madam Grayheart was always fishing through it. If anyone ever opened the chest, they would find the books in no time. Every hiding place seemed to be in plain sight.

She suddenly remembered hiding a bit of candy Girda had given her when she was a child. Otto would only let her eat a certain amount at certain times, and she was determined to be able to eat it whenever she wanted. She had wrapped the candy in a bit of fabric and placed it between the frame and the mattress of her bed. It remained there for weeks, undiscovered and long forgotten. Otto wondered what the sticky mess was when he finally turned her mattress some months later.

Ayla found a thin sheet in the chest and wrapped both books tightly. Careful of the fragile pages, she ducked her head under the bed and was able to sit the books just inside the frame of the lower mattress.

She smiled to herself as she blew out the candle and climbed into the bed. She wondered about Roderick and his family. She thought about where Bree might be sleeping this night. She wondered about the keepers and shuddered when she thought of Kal, the dark spirit, again. And as she thought, her head touched the pillow, and before she knew it, her eyes were closed. She found herself wanting to think some more, feeling the day needed more consideration. She tried to open her eyes again, but her mind was already drifting into the sweet abyss of sleep.

CHAPTER 13

Madam Grayheart kept her promise and woke Ayla at the first light of dawn. It was Sunday, the older woman told her, and the king had ordered them to come to the temple for a time of prayer. Madam Grayheart seemed quite excited about the invitation and dressed Ayla in a hurry, all the while telling the girl how she should behave in the sanctuary.

They were to pray silently for one hour before the keepers came and presented their own public prayers to the gods. Madam Grayheart told her it would be best to watch the king for her cues as to when to stand or kneel.

"And remember how to walk!" she reminded her. "Head high and with grace."

Once again Ayla found herself ushered out the door and down the staircase. The idea of going to the temple did not thrill Ayla. Thoughts of Kal made her wary. What if one of the stone gods had the eyes of the dark goddess and could see who she was? What if one of the keepers had a vision from the evil spirit? It was hard to remember to hold her head up as she walked.

Madam Grayheart led her through many corridors and grand rooms. There were many tapestries and fine paintings hanging on the walls. They even passed a few ornately carved statues but nothing bore runes and nothing looked familiar. Ayla didn't know in which direction they were headed. She had not seen this part of the castle before.

Ayla's mind was still racing with thoughts from the night before. It was hard to imagine that this could be her castle, that the fancy objects they were passing once belonged to her family. As Ayla followed Madam Grayheart, she suddenly realized that she was walking the same corridors that her mother and father had once passed through. It was a queer thought that made her head spin. She never imagined knowing anything about her mother and father.

She felt out of place as they passed a small group of servants taking up the torches from the night before. They gave her curious glances and bobbed curtsies exactly as they had done the day before. These were her people, Ayla thought.

Finally, the two women were making their way through a great expanse of gardens. Ayla was relived to be outside. The cool morning air made her feel steadier.

"This is the north side of the fortress, my lady," Madam Grayheart explained. "You entered through the southwest side when you arrived."

The north side of the castle was much grander, but Ayla found herself favoring the southern gardens. Her mind went back to the statue of Lord Kelvin. There were no ruins of old pavilions here, only beautiful trees and flowers. The ruins had given the southern gardens an interesting texture of old and new. This place was only pretty and had no feeling at all.

A neat stone path cut its way across the yard and about a quarter mile distance, right along the outside wall, Ayla could make out a tall stone building. She knew at once it must be the temple. People were flocking to its open doors in large groups. Ayla could make out the fancy dresses of the noblewomen even at this distance.

"Come, come!" Madam Grayheart chided her. "We're going to be late!"

The temple was surrounded by statues of people dressed in odd ways, and Ayla wondered if some of them might be the gods of Talforland. There was a tall man carrying a great staff. Another raised a stone sword to the sky. The tip was broken off from wear. On one side of the path, a woman held a basket of flowers and fruit and on the other a juvenile boy guarded a lamb. The figures were of men and women doing all manner of things. She stopped briefly to regard the menagerie as they passed, and her eyes fell on the stone figure of a woman kneeling.

She blinked, thinking she saw the woman move slightly.

In another moment she realized the woman was not a statue at all but a live person who merely had her back turned to them and was covered with a deep gray cloak. The woman turned and looked towards her and Madam Grayheart.

She was young and her hair was nearly as black as Ayla's but strangely speckled with white. Even at this distance her eyes reflected a startling blue and seemed too big for her delicate face. The look reminded Ayla of Keeper Nevin's gaze when he told them about the vision of the raven. Ayla quickly looked away.

Madam Grayheart's voice called for her to keep up a steady pace and soon they had passed the garden of stone statues and were approaching the front steps of the temple. The steps were broad and short, seeming to only be there for show. It gave the entrance a very regal feel. As they climbed the steps, Ayla watched very finely dressed nobility pass through the high wooden doors in front of them. Each one made a slight bow as they entered and then sat in rows of chairs which crossed the center of the room.

Ayla bowed slightly like the others as she entered and then let Madam Grayheart lead her to the very front row of chairs where she found the king and the prince. No one was speaking in the temple, and Ayla guessed that the time of their silent prayers had already begun. She offered a small curtsy to the king and prince who accepted her with a slight nod. Ayla took a seat in the chair adjacent to them.

She immediately looked for Roderick but didn't see him. The prince had more than likely sent the captain off on some pointless mission.

Everyone around her was sitting quietly in chairs with expressions that revealed a repressed boredom. No one talked or looked around and a few older gentlemen were falling asleep. The prince himself sighed loudly and let out an unapologetic yawn. The king and the keepers were perhaps the only ones with a look of urgent seriousness in their eyes. Or perhaps the king was tired. Ayla could see red veins protruding in his eyes and he looked pale and feverish. The prince's poison was doing its work.

Ayla used the hour of sitting to study the sanctuary and to wonder what it could have been when Kelvinor was still its own kingdom. The main altar was in front of them. There were a number of keepers there, all kneeling on the floor around a great golden platform with pained expressions on their faces. The statues inside the temple were similar to the ones she had seen outside. These seemed better taken care of and some even had flowers dropped at their feet.

There was one statue which seemed more ornately carved than the rest and more preserved. It was made to look as if it was wearing a robe and crown, but the keepers had placed a rich fabric over it as well and given the statue a ring of leaves and flowers. The figure had a sword, unsheathed and ready for battle. It was ornate; jewels sparkled from the hilt. The statue wore the fierce expression of a soldier going to war.

Its broad shoulders were inhuman, and Ayla imagined that if he were a real man, he might be rather beastly and proud.

The last person to enter the temple was the woman in the gray cloak Ayla had seen outside. She took a seat at the back of the room and bowed her head quite formally. Ayla could see that her clothes were clean and well cared for, but they did not in any way resemble the fine fabrics the other ladies wore. Her gray cloak also seemed to be a bit out of place for a lady. The look on her face reminded Ayla of a wolf, suspicious and solitary. The woman's massive blue eyes searched the room like a hunter and then stopped. Ayla found herself caught in the woman's gaze again. Ayla looked away, hoping the woman had not noticed. Even turned away, Ayla felt her stomach twist into a knot. She knew the woman was still watching her.

It seemed like they all sat there for ages staring straight ahead. By the time Keeper Nevin appeared and spoke, many of the older gentlemen around Ayla had clearly fallen asleep. Some were even snoring.

"All hail to the gods of Talforland!" Keeper Nevin shouted from the front of the sanctuary.

"All hail!" the people answered and Ayla jumped. They had spoken with one voice and the effect was quite chilling. It was enough to startle the older gentlemen awake as well.

"Alas, we have received many signs from the gods these past seven days. Some are good, some evil, and some remain yet to be determined."

Ayla's cheeks turned red as the keeper's eyes fell on her briefly before he continued. Keeper Nevin spoke of the prince's return and how it was foretold several days before a messenger brought word. He talked about the war god, Tione, gesturing to the great statue with the sword and robe and telling about how the god had predicted their victories in Wadroland.

"Indeed, has not the god of war led us to victory in all our trials? Talforland shall soon take complete control of Wadroland, and then, we can look to the heathen lands beyond the Eastern Sea."

Their armies will not stop, thought Ayla, *until they can claim every bit of land in the known world!*

The keepers began a chant together which praised different gods. Occasionally, the people would repeat something or would briefly chime in with their own words. At first, Ayla tried to follow along but the whole meaning of the chant was beyond her, and as hard as she tried, she couldn't keep up. She resigned herself to merely listening and hoped Madam Grayheart would forgive her for not following along.

When the chant ended, Keeper Nevin delivered a long, loud prayer to Tione. He was followed by another priest who offered a similar prayer to Feror, the God of Haste. The keepers continued like this for at least an hour. Each one rose and offered a different prayer to a different god all with the same loud and exalting voice. Some even went to the extremes of throwing themselves on their knees or raising their arms and waving them as if they might fly. If the men had not had such serious expressions on their faces, Ayla would have found it quite hard not to laugh out loud.

Finally, the last priest offered up his prayer and it was thankfully very short. When the man stepped back, Keeper Nevin came forward again and opened his mouth to speak.

He was interrupted by a dark female voice from the back of the room.

"All hail Kal, Goddess of Time and Destruction."

Ayla turned to look along with the rest of the people. It was the woman in the gray cloak that Ayla had seen outside. Ayla felt her whole body shudder when she heard the name the woman spoke and saw the hungry, powerful burning look in the woman's eyes.

"Priestess Maura, you know you and your followers are not allowed to offer prayers in this sacred chamber!" Keeper Nevin's face was turning red.

"I come not to grace you with a prayer in your temple of filth!" Her voice was filled with disdain. "My goddess wishes only to leave you with a command regarding the black haired girl who was brought to the palace yesterday." She raised a hand and pointed to where Ayla was sitting. Ayla suddenly felt the eyes of the people on her. She felt like she was among the dwarfs again, tall and ugly.

"That child will bring destruction to the Talforland Empire unless she is married to Prince Noland by the Spring Festival in three days." There was a rise of gasps and whispering as the woman continued, "If that can be arranged, Talforland is sure to rise as the greatest of empires the world has ever seen."

The king stood quite suddenly from his chair, his low voice echoing in the sanctuary, "Clear this chamber but for the keeper and this priestess. Prince Noland, you will stay with us as well."

The people filed out of the chamber with much low talk. Their eyes glanced from Ayla to the priestess. When the chamber doors were finally closed, Ayla felt some relief despite her circumstances. She wished Roderick were there.

"Your Highness," Keeper Nevin began in his raspy voice, "surely you do not put any value in this blasphemer's revelation?" The keeper walked down from the altar and came to the side of the king. The priestess was watching him with contempt. "Are we also to believe that the other gods are false and that only Kal deserves our devotion? We all know well these priestess's proclamations. If they were not noble daughters, they would have been hung from the outer gate and burned long ago!"

The priestess came forward in slow, solid steps, "Just because you scorn me, Nevin, doesn't mean what I say is false."

Her voice held a power that made Ayla cringe.

"Then tell me how this child could cause an empire to be laid to ruin?" Keeper Nevin spoke with mocking.

The priestess frowned and spoke in a low threatening voice. Her words seemed to surround them and Ayla felt an odd power swirl in the room. She wondered if the others felt it as well. "My goddess speaks of a lost treasure. It seems a god long thought dead favors this child." The woman's eyes suddenly locked on the prince and Ayla looked from one to the other.

Keeper Nevin sneered, "You speak of the God of Magic, the unnamed God of Kelvinor." He spat, "That god is dead, long bereft of followers and outcast from these lands. To say he may live is treason!"

"I do not say He lives," the woman seemed to growl back. "I say He is. He always was and always will be. Only Kal has the power to put Him in His place."

"Enough!" the king held up a hand. "Priestess, you say this child has power?"

The woman nodded and the king spoke again, "Power like that of magic?"

"Yes," the priestess nodded, "But I believe that if we hang her like we would a witch, the power will be lost to us. We should instead endeavor to control it. There is a prophesy...."

"Heresy!" Keeper Nevin spat again. "To attempt any form of magic is to invoke a curse from the gods!"

"Magic is the power of the gods!" The woman seemed to rise up in a righteous rage. She turned to the king, her voice seductive, "To have control over this magic would be to have control over the gods."

Keeper Nevin started to protest again but the king interrupted him, "Magic has been banned in Talforland for many ages. I respect your vision, priestess, but why should we not just kill the girl and destroy the dark power?"

"Because there is a prophecy based in old Kelvinor legend. It reads,

> *When blood of royal line*
> *Is united with its own,*
> *so shall Kingdoms build*
> *and Kingdoms fall*
> *with the light of ancient stone."*

The priestess paused and took a breath, "I believe this child to be Kelvin's heir and her marriage to the prince will awaken the blue stone which sits dormant in that altar." The woman bowed slightly, "The words of my goddess are shadowed in mystery. I know no more."

"Convenient!" Keeper Nevin stepped forward. "This woman is trying to take advantage of this girl and you, Your Highness."

"My king," the woman began respectfully, "Perhaps I should remind Keeper Nevin of the Kelvinor omens. Do you not remember the symbol for Kelvinor good fortune?"

"A raven," the man said quietly, "The black bird…"

The king scoffed, looking at Ayla, "Well, we now know the meaning of the vision. Why should we not just kill the girl and eliminate the threat?"

"No!" the priestess said forcefully. "Kill the girl and the powers of magic will be dead forever…"

"Magic is evil!" Keeper Nevin spat, "and forbidden. This girl should be killed!"

"Tell me about the magic, Priestess," the king said suspiciously.

"A great power, Your Majesty," the priestess's voice was alluring again, and

Ayla could almost see her spinning a web of deceit in the air. "Your family will be assured rule for generations, and you would have the power to take any kingdom you wanted."

"I must protest!" Keeper Nevin shouted above them.

The king stopped him, "Enough, Keeper. Power is the right of all kings. I see no harm in these … abilities … being in the hands of royalty. Prince Noland?"

The prince was still watching Priestess Maura closely, "I'll marry her, father. She's pretty and I have come to like her … in a way. If what the priestess says is not true, then we can kill the priestess for her treachery and it is no one's loss."

The boy was handsome, true enough, but his pride and arrogance made him ugly and malformed to Ayla. She could not imagine a life of games where she was made to feel like a fool. She would have no more instances like the Matchmaking Ball.

Ayla stood, suddenly finding some courage within her, "I will not marry him."

Her voice was quiet and lacked authority, but those present still turned to her. The king's eyes were sharp and hostile. "You will do whatever you are commanded to do. It is far more than you deserve."

Ayla felt the world around her begin to spin and she was forced to sit down. She should scream out what she knew, she thought. The prince is poisoning you! He's going to take everything from you! But no words came to her lips. Ayla felt that a power was stirring in the room, something that was quite happy to remain in the shadows for the time being. Her eyes fell on the priestess and she thought of the woman's persuasive voice. It had been irresistible, like being caught in the sight of the great emperor snake.

"Spring Festival, then," Priestess Maura smiled cruelly down at Ayla. "The ceremony must be done at the Spring Festival."

CHAPTER 14

AYLA WAS ESCORTED BACK to the west tower by a whole troop of guards. She saw no familiar faces among them, and she missed Roderick more than ever.

Everything around her felt frantic. Crowds of nobility had gathered around the temple whispering to each other. As the guards led her out, they pointed and shouted. Ayla did not care to hear what they said.

Priestess Maura walked with the troops step for step, her gray cloak blowing about her. She watched Ayla like the girl might break and run at any moment.

Indeed, Ayla was having a few desperate thoughts. If she had not known that Roderick would be looking after her, she might have tried something foolish. Her only comforting thought now was that the captain might come for her, and she would be saved. Somehow they would get to the pendant. Hopefully, it would be before she was married to the prince. The prophecy the priestess had quoted confused her. Would she have to be united with royal blood before the pendant's power would be restored or would only her touch bring it back? She remembered the writing Roderick had showed her.

> *One other key*
> *May also hold*
> *The gift of power*
> *For one so bold*

Perhaps marriage to royal blood was the final key. If that was the case, she had to find someone else. She would die and destroy the power forever before being joined to such a person as the prince for the rest of her life.

The guards let her walk into the grand room alone, but Priestess Maura followed her, letting the door shut behind them.

Ayla turned to face the woman, determined to be strong.

"Who are you?" the woman asked. Her voice was almost kind.

Ayla was taken aback. She was sure the priestess knew exactly who she was. "My name is Ayla."

"And what manner of creature are you, Ayla? And what was your purpose in coming here?"

Ayla didn't understand what the woman was asking her. Could it be that the priestess really wasn't sure who Ayla was?

"My name is Ayla. I'm. . .just a girl. I come from Halforton."

The priestess narrowed her eyes, her voice suddenly changing. It was alluring, persuasive, demanding truth, "You know nothing, then?"

Ayla shook the voice off, finding her strength in thoughts of Roderick. He would be here soon, she told herself.

"I suppose I know nothing," Ayla answered with as honest a voice as she could muster. "I've never heard of any power."

The woman seemed pleased. A smile spread across her face, and then she laughed, "Just as well. You should stay simple minded; it's for the best."

She turned to exit but Ayla stopped her, "Wait. . .I must ask you something."

The woman turned, "Yes, little raven?"

"I saw you kneeling in the yard outside the temple. . .Is there a statue of your goddess out there?"

The woman's eyes narrowed, "That is a very poor attempt to mock me."

Ayla shook her head, "I wasn't mocking."

The priestess took a few solid steps forward and stopped only a pace away from her. Ayla could feel her glare and had to look down to keep any nerve at all. The woman was ice cold. "I was kneeling where the statue of Kal used to be before her image was stricken down. All that is left is the statue's base and her feet."

"Why. . .why was it stricken down? Is Kal evil?" Ayla forced herself to look into the woman's eyes. The priestess needed her, she reasoned, and wouldn't harm her.

Priestess Maura reached out and took the girl's chin as if she was afraid the girl might look away again. "One thing you must realize, child. There is no good or evil. Power governs us all and whoever holds the power, decides what is good and what is evil."

The priestess turned and stalked toward the door before changing her mind and turning back to Ayla. "I think I shall keep you around when all this is done. Your simple mind may prove entertaining."

The door opened and to Ayla's relief, she saw the captain standing there. Her eyes instinctively lit up. The priestess gave her a hard look and Ayla quickly turned away, trying to look indifferent.

"The prince and the king wish for your company, Priestess," Roderick's voice echoed in the room.

"Captain," the woman said, raising an eyebrow. Her voice had changed and was almost girlish in its tone. "Know our little darling so well that you forgot to knock? Would I be so lucky as to have you come to my door unannounced." Maura grinned and stepped toward the door. Her body seemed to have changed as well. She moved slowly, casually and held the captain's gaze. "My dear Roderick, has the prince grown so tired of you that he sends you off to fetch a priestess? When is his twentieth birthday, anyway?"

"It's best not to keep the king waiting, Maura," Roderick's voice was flat and Ayla could read very little from it.

"It's amazing, isn't it, Ayla, to think of what a poor little stable boy could grow up to be in this kingdom." The priestess glided out of the room and Ayla turned immediately to the door. Roderick stood there for a moment, regarding her before he shut the door and left her alone in the room. She could read nothing from his expression and she found herself strangely hurt.

No one came to the room for a full hour. All Ayla felt she could do was sit on the bed and wait. Finally, a handmaiden entered, bowed slightly, and left her a plate of food and a goblet of water. For once she found it hard to eat and the food was cold before she finished the meal.

It wasn't until the second hour passed that Ayla remembered the books Roderick had left her and took them out of their hiding place, sitting down on the floor behind the bed. If anyone entered unexpectedly, she could slide the books under the bed without being seen. She found the first book and began to read.

It started with the first spring month of the year 286. The first entry was several pages long. It repeated the story Bree and Roderick had both told her about the creation of Kelvinor and added that the city and its white castle had simply risen from the ground where the white horse pawed. It also mentioned that the current lord was Kelvin Nobleheart and the lady was Luna Nobleheart. They had two children at the time of the entry, a boy named Jaran and a six-year old girl named Tova. The girl was the first child born in Jade City, the book mentioned.

She found the month where Lord Jaran Nobleheart took over for his father, Lord Kelvin. It was the first winter month of 309. It was also the same month of his son's birth, Jaran II. Ayla began to flip pages rapidly. She finally found where Lord Jaran II stepped in for his ill father, but there was nothing regarding the blue or the red pendant in any entry.

She flipped ahead again, finding that in 359 Lady Brista Clearheart was installed as the first ruling Lady of Kelvinor. She was Lord Jaran II's niece, the oldest daughter of his sister. Lord Jaran II had never married and as a consequence, had never produced an heir.

She was near the end of the first book and as far as she could tell, the remaining pages didn't record anything of interest. She flipped through them quickly until she reached the last page. It was the first summer month of the year 369 and the last recorded page in the first volume.

The entry seemed only to contain the usual notations about crop growth and the comings and goings of certain dignitaries. It ended like all the other entries, with the scribe's name and the exact date of its authorship. But when Ayla turned the page, she noticed that the entry was not over at all but rather something additional had been written.

A bit of writing was scrawled on the back of the last page. There was no title or explanation and the handwriting was unfamiliar. No scribe from the previous pages had written this.

I saw before me a Raven with a broken wing and yet it flew. It flew
to the temple of the Creator God and its wing was healed. It sang in the

temple with a mighty voice and all who heard it wept. "Woe to the war-makers!" cried the Raven. "For now is the time of their end."

A voice spoke in the heavens and it said, "Look for the Raven when four meets four minus one. She will restore all that has been lost."

"Great Lord!" I cried. "Show me the meaning of the bird if I am worthy to be your servant."

The voice answered, "Adorn your walls with the Raven. Speak of it often. Engrave it on your shields when you go into battle. Swear by it and paint it on the banner you hang from your towers. The meaning of the bird is good fortune."

Ayla read the passage over and over again. She had heard what the priestess said. The raven was a good sign for her people. This seemed to predict that a raven would bring an end to war when four meets four minus one. Could that be now?

Ayla ran her hand over the page. In the right hand corner, she felt something different and ran her fingers over the spot again. There was a small bump of sorts on the page as if something was hidden inside the jacket. She scraped at the spot with her fingernail until the backing tore. She pulled away at the small opening. Underneath was a small square of folded paper. She pulled it out and read the runes.

When blood of royal line
Is united with its own,
so shall kingdoms build
and kingdoms fall
with the light of ancient stone

It was the bit of prophecy the priestess had quoted only on this page there was something more. Ayla continued to read.

Good luck comes with the raven
Ancient power of love
Existing only in creation

Balance this with bear
Her claws bring destruction
She is never meant to rule
And must fall to the raven

Footsteps in the hallway caught her attention, and Ayla quickly slid the book back under the bed, hiding her new discovery in its folds.

CHAPTER 15

"I'VE COME TO SEE THE GIRL." She heard the familiar voice of Prince Noland in the hallway. Ayla fidgeted nervously, glancing down to make sure the book was properly hidden.

The door opened and the prince stepped inside. Ayla noticed he did not knock and wondered what Madam Grayheart would say. Perhaps princes did not need to announce their arrival.

Ayla forced herself not to look away as the door shut behind him, and he looked her up and down.

"So," he began, his tone nonchalant, "you're having a lucky few days."

She only stared at him as he waited for her to respond. Finally, he began again.

"Picked up by me and brought to live in the castle and now because of some silly prophecy, it looks like you're going to be my first wife."

"Is that lucky?" She could not hide her distaste.

He sneered. "I should say so. You're going to be a princess in a few days. Although, I suppose you will miss the good Captain Roderick?"

She finally looked away, her eyes moving to the floor.

"Oh, yes," the prince continued. "I see the way you look at him. It's a shame the man cares for no one. He's a slave to his duty. No, it's a soldier's life for him, I'm afraid. It's already done."

"What do you mean?"

"There is some advantage to me getting married." He was pacing the room now, coming closer to her and then moving away. "I'll be a man the day I marry you. Roderick will be reassigned. It's done, in fact. He leaves for his new post the very day of Spring Festival."

She looked up again, trying not to let her emotions show. She could feel the rhythm of her heart beating in her ears. "He leaves?"

Noland nodded. "For the Eastern Sea. He'll make a fine captain for a small army of reinforcements we're sending out."

Noland smiled and stepped right up to her. She closed her eyes so she wouldn't feel so near him. "I wouldn't want my new bride to be distracted by the likes of a former stable boy."

Ayla felt the rage building inside of her. She had never felt so sad and angry all at once. For a few brief hours, she had felt like she was special. She was important. She was meant to do things that were extraordinary. She had dared to hope, and now this prince and a priestess where ripping that hope away.

She opened her eyes and turned to look at the prince. "Is that why you came here? To tell me Roderick had been sent away and to make me look like a fool?"

"Something like that." He was smiling. "You need to know that I control your life now. I own you. No one can love you but me." He began to circle her like a prowling cat. "The priestess tells me you know nothing so your life after marrying me should be simple. You should be so lucky. I will be the most powerful man in the world."

Ayla clenched her fists. "I do not want you. And I will not marry you."

The prince slapped her with such force that she nearly lost her balance and fell. A hard, cold moment followed and then the prince began to laugh. He turned away from her, walking towards the door. Ayla felt some of her rage calm itself as he drew further from her.

"Well! You certainly have learned to act like a princess, haven't you?!" He laughed again as he opened the door and prepared to leave. "We'll see what happens in a few days, princess."

The guards shut the door after the prince left, and she heard it latch behind him.

Her face stung and her left eye teared. She willed herself not to cry. Lying on the bed, Ayla pressed her sore face against the cool silk pillows. Her head ached and she shut her eyes against the pain. She spiraled into an unwilling sleep for many hours.

The light was fading from the window when she opened her eyes again. Her dinner had been placed on the table by the bed. It was cold but she ate it, not caring. She thought about Roderick and wondered if she would ever see him again. She wondered if Bree had heard of her situation and if the girl would dare come that night.

She changed into the long night robe and left her stockings on just in case someone did decide to visit her. There was nothing to do but sit and wonder and watch the light fade from the sky. She did not feel like reading the histories again. Kelvinor had seemed so close only a few hours ago and now it was a distant dream.

Unable to sit in the bed any longer, she went to the window and pushed open the shutters. The courtyard was far below her. Green grass spread out across the great expanse from her tower to the temple and the inner wall. No one was about and she leaned on her elbow watching the sun fade from the sky.

A flicker, like a white flash caught her eye and in a moment she sat up again. There was something moving fast across the yard, headed from the temple straight toward the tower. She squinted against the darkness.

As the figure drew closer, she made out its form. It was a white horse. Not a speck of brown or tan could have been on its body. It had no bridle or saddle and Ayla could see no rider on the yard.

As the horse reached the tower, it stopped and shook its mane wildly. It rode twice around in a circle and then seemed to nod to her in a wild gesture.

Ayla remembered the mural and everything she had heard about a white horse and the founding of Kelvinor.

"What do you want?" she whispered, not really expecting anyone, much less the horse, to hear and understand her.

The daughter of Kelvinor.

The voice echoed in her mind and Ayla started. Could the horse really be talking to her?

"Have you come to see me?" she asked again.

I have come to bear you on my back and take you away from this place. Hope is waiting.

The horse snorted and nodded its head up and down again. Ayla wondered if she was dreaming. In any case, how was she supposed to get to the yard below her? She turned from the window for a moment and looked towards the carpet that covered the trap door. Maybe she could find a way.

She looked back to the horse only to discover it was gone. She looked out across the yard and saw no trace of it. The yard was completely empty and the sun was setting faster than she expected. She had no way of lighting her candle and found that the sudden thought of complete darkness unsettled her.

She went back to bed and buried herself under the covers. The image of the white horse burned in her mind. Had the vision been real?

Sleep did not come for a great while.

CHAPTER 16

WHEN AYLA FINALLY FELL asleep, her dreams started with a rush of wind and the pounding of hooves. She opened her eyes to find herself clinging tightly to the mane of a white horse riding across an open green pasture.

Be not afraid, the voice of the white horse echoed in her mind, I have come to carry you away as I promised.

I am dreaming, Ayla thought; this isn't real.

To her amazement, the horse's voice echoed in her mind again. You are dreaming but this is real. Dreams are only another reality we find ourselves in when we sleep.

"Can you hear my thoughts?" she asked the horse in her mind with some effort. "Are you a magic horse?"

Laughter followed and then the clear resounding snort of a happy horse. I am the messenger of the Creator God. I am his horse and I do His will. If His will calls for me to be a magic horse, then I am a magic horse.

"This is all quite wonderful," she thought, trying to clear her head of unwanted doubts. "Where are you taking me?"

To show you your past so that your future will be clear, the horse answered. Hold on tightly to my mane!

There was a blinding flash of light and Ayla shut her eyes, gripping the horse's mane with all her might. It felt as if they were suddenly flying into emptiness. She could no longer feel the rhythm of the horse's smooth running, but the wind was still blowing through her hair.

Hooves hit a marble floor, and when Ayla opened her eyes again, they were standing on the open pavilion where the statue of Lord Kelvin stood. But the statue was not as she remembered it and neither were the grounds around the pavilion.

The statue stood un-scorched and the path that had led her there when she first arrived was unbroken. Where littered marble ruins had once scarred the yard, grand statues and fountains stood. The walkway was covered with a well tended thatch roof and all of its stone columns were perfectly intact. Everything around Ayla seemed new or wonderfully cared for and she stared, amazed.

Lightning suddenly streaked across the sky and Ayla jumped, noticing for the first time that the sky above them was dark with the clouds of an approaching storm. Thunder rumbled in the air. Rain would follow it in short order.

Ayla heard footsteps and her attention turned to the covered walkway leading to the castle. A woman was coming toward them. She was heavily cloaked with a fine purple robe and was followed by a procession of young ladies dressed in black silk. They walked as if in a funeral procession toward the pavilion.

Listen. Watch. The horse's words intruded suddenly on her thoughts. This is but a shadow of what has already past. They will not see or hear us.

The lady in the heavy robe stopped in front of the statue of Lord Kelvin and looked toward the castle gates. She removed her hood revealing a solemn face and a cascade of hair the color of midnight. The other women circled around the lady. Some looked toward the gates while others hung their heads. All of them carried an air of sorrow with them, and from their red eyes Ayla could see that a few had been crying.

One of the women in black silk stepped toward the lady and spoke softly. Ayla was surprised she could hear their low voices. The words were clear, as though she were standing with them as they spoke.

"My lady, perhaps we should wait inside the castle?"

"No." The lady replied, not turning her eyes from the gate. "I will not meet them as a coward, hiding in a castle behind locked doors."

Ayla found herself staring at the young woman who had approached the lady. The face was too familiar for her not to recognize. Though younger and stronger in this vision, Madam Grayheart still had the same intense gaze and striking features. Ayla remembered that the madam had told her she was once a member of the court of Kelvinor. This vision was not an ancient one and Ayla's heart pounded as she guessed who the heavily robed woman might be.

"You would not meet them as a coward, but as a queen," the madam said strongly. "We will dress you in your finest robes, put your crown upon your head, and hang the royal pendant from your neck. They will see there is strength in Kelvinor yet."

The lady turned and looked at Madam Grayheart. Ayla could see a great sadness in her eyes. "You still don't understand, Priya. I am not a queen anymore. The day Lord Valkay died, that right passed to his daughter. I go back to the mere peasant I was born as and if I live to see the day Kelvinor is restored, I will serve my daughter as my queen." She turned her gaze back toward the gates. "They come."

A troop of heavily armed soldiers were passing through the gates. Their company was small, perhaps only twenty men, but they were armored in gold and silver not unlike what Ayla had seen the prince's soldiers wear. At their front, a soldier carried a standard embroidered with an all too familiar bear. They trotted slowly toward the pavilion. Some of the women held on to one another and a few began to sob.

The soldiers cantered right up to the pavilion and the lead rider removed his helmet. Ayla immediately recognized a younger, stronger King of Talforland.

"Lady Salisie." His voice was strong but contained a deep undertone of sympathy. "I did not expect to find you like this. Does Kelvinor normally greet conquering troops as it would any dignitary?"

The lady did not waver, holding her eyes firmly on the king. Ayla watched her, feeling as though her heart might explode. This was her mother! The king had said the name plainly and Ayla remembered it from the books Roderick had given her. Ayla gave into the tears as they began to pour from her eyes.

"I have come to greet you as there is nothing I can do to stop you. Just know that if you set up your idols and worship in this place, the wrath of the Creator God will fall upon you. That much has been written."

The king smiled slightly, "I do not believe in your god, my lady. Your prophecies are meaningless to me. If he is so powerful, why would he allow your defeat?"

"We lost His favor and now His wrath falls upon us. But it won't be forever, my lord." The lady's voice turned dark. "In this day you find victory, but your own blood will curse you long before your rule is ended."

"A dark prophecy from a queen bereft of power." The king shook his head. "Hardly potent, witch."

She curtsied slightly, letting her gaze fall on the marble floor. "Do what you will with me. I have done my duty in warning you. I know the time of my death is near."

"I will have no martyrs," the king said solemnly. "You and your attendants are ordered back to your room where you will remain to the end of your natural days."

"I will go." She looked up again, a fierce power in her stance. "But I will find my death at your hands before your curse is realized. Mark my words, Lord Donavan Proudheart."

With that, Lady Salisie turned on her heel and strode back towards the castle. Her attendants followed her, struggling to keep up with her strong pace.

The king's expression was sour as he watched the women leave. If her prophecies were true, the king really had killed her or had something to do with her untimely death.

The white horse turned under Ayla and rode across the yard again.

Do you understand the vision?

"Yes." Ayla replied in her mind, wiping the tears from her eyes and wishing that she could see more of the woman who looked so much like her. "That was my mother. Was she a prophetess?"

A very powerful prophetess of the Creator God. That is how she rose to be a Lady of Kelvinor. She was born a peasant.

"Will you show me my father, good horse? I would like to see him, too." Ayla hoped she was not being too forward in asking. Her heart was filled with longing.

No, the voice in her mind answered. He was a good man but we must not waste time on visions that serve no purpose. No, you must now meet another of your relatives, more distant and more powerful.

There was another great flash of light. This time they were standing in a dark stone chamber that Ayla did not recognize. A man was there, lying flat on his back in the center of the stone room and staring at the ceiling. He was wearing clothes which might once have been as rich as the king's, but now they were torn and dirty. A red robe bearing the familiar insignia of a bear was laid out beneath him. Until Ayla saw his eyes blink, she thought he might be dead. She was so taken by the man's strange appearance that she did not notice the other figure in the chamber until some moments later.

He was handsome and more plainly dressed in blue robes. Ayla thought he might be nobility from the formal way he carried himself, but his spirit was humble. When he spoke, Ayla felt a warm softness envelop the room.

"Keeper Talfor, you have been lying here almost three days. The power is lost and the mountain is beginning to burn. We must save the people we can and go."

The man shut his eyes and let out a moan that filled the room and sent chills crawling up Ayla's spine. For someone who was not dead, he made sounds like he might be a ghost.

"I have lost everything. My daughter is dead...everything is gone..."

"Yes," the other man said, his voice still strangely kind. "Your eldest daughter behaved like a fool and because of her loyalty to Kal has destroyed us all. Now you are being the fool."

Keeper Talfor opened his eyes and glared up at the other man from the floor. "You dare to call me a fool?"

"I dare to speak the truth!" The man in blue robes walked toward him. "You are a great man, a great keeper, and your people need you now. Too much has been lost already. We must go."

The man began to pull himself off the floor. As he did, he opened his fist revealing a silver chain. The charm hanging from its links held a single, bright red stone. The other man took a step back.

"That should have been destroyed!"

"No." Keeper Talfor shook his head and continued to rise from the floor. "I will pass it down to my family, my youngest daughter shall take it as a reminder..."

"No, Talfor. We must leave it on the island to be destroyed."

"No, Keeper Kelvin!" The man shouted and all at once Ayla realized what she was seeing. "The stone is mine! You can't take it from me. It belongs to me!"

"It belongs to Kal. It was made by Kal and is a contradiction of everything we believe." Kelvin shouted, his voice rising and powerful. Ayla saw Talfor shudder in his weakness. Then the man seemed to rise from the ashes. His whole manner changed as he strode the distance between them and tugged on a chain around Kelvin's neck.

Talfor pulled the chain's secret from beneath Kelvin's robes and Ayla could see a blue stone that looked exactly like the red one.

"And what has it proved?" Talfor yelled, madly. "The pendants are both dead of any power. Both Kal and the Creator God died on that mountain with my daughter."

"No!" Kelvin shoved Talfor away. "Some day our kingdom and the power of this pendant will be restored. That is the Creator God's promise to us. This one..." Kelvin reached forward and gripped the red pendant in his hand, "was never meant to be!"

A silence fell between the two, and Ayla whispered to the horse. She knew they could not hear her but it felt strange to talk outright.

"Can you tell me what happened on the mountain?"

Quiet. The horse replied, Listen!

Talfor and Kelvin released each other and the tension between them subsided. Finally, Kelvin spoke. "Take the pendant. We will decide what to do with it after our escape. We will consult the other keepers as well. Will you abide by their decision?"

Talfor just nodded, still gripping the red pendant around his neck.

"Good. Then let us go. Gather your people. The boats are waiting."

"How can I face them after what has happened?"

Kelvin shook his head, "Your people still trust you despite your daughter's treachery. Only time will tell us the future. We have the Creator God watching over us."

Talfor scoffed, "Had, don't you mean?"

"Dear keeper!" Kelvin exclaimed. "You can't believe that all of his love was contained in this pendant? The pendant was a blessing, a gift, entrusted to us. The gift has been lost, but the love of its giver remains."

Kelvin put one hand gently on the shoulder of the other keeper. "We must now rely on the Creator God more than ever. No object controlled by a mere mortal can help us now."

The two left the room slowly. Ayla wanted to call out to them. She wanted to know about Talfor's daughter and what happened on the mountain. What had the people done to lose the blessing of the Creator God?

I know what you are thinking, the horse invaded her thoughts. I did not show you this to satisfy your curiosity. I wanted you to see that the love of the Creator God is and always has been with this kingdom.

Ayla wanted to protest but the horse was off at a run again. She looked up just in time to see they were headed directly for a stone wall. She let out a scream and ducked her head into the horse's neck, convinced they were about to have a hard fall. No impact came, and when next she looked up, they were running once more across a green yard.

Open your eyes and look about you! The wind will show you what you need to see!

She looked around her, seeing nothing but an endless expanse of green. She felt the draft of a warm wind and in it, she heard whispers. She strained to hear and felt her eyes forced to focus on images that were real and yet distant, as if in a dream.

She saw many soldiers, like ghosts moving about the gardens of the castle in Jade City. They were breaking apart statues with hammers and setting fire to the thatched roofs over the walkways. Oil was being poured over the figure of Lord Kelvin and another soldier laughed as he set it aflame.

She saw soldiers in the street breaking down the doors of simple houses. They were pulling out men and woman and asking them questions. Somehow she knew they were searching for the noble families of Kelvinor. She saw them hang one woman by her ankles from the outer wall. Ayla screamed as they set fire to her dress and the crowd chanted "Witch! Witch!" over and over again.

Ayla saw the outer reaches of Jade City. There were well tended houses, and smiling villagers. They changed before her eyes to the rough, poorly kept homes she had seen when she rode into the city. She saw the people being robbed of their livestock and saw soldiers taking young boys away in carts to serve in the armies of Talforland.

It seemed as if she was watching the last sixteen years through many eyes in many places. She could feel the hunger of the starving children, the sorrow of a mother reaching out for her son, the burning hatred of the nobility against the foreign invaders. The images suddenly seemed to flash one after the other, overlapping. She shut her eyes but she could still see them. She could still feel the pain of each person, noble or peasant, as their lives changed forever.

She saw the King of Talforland laughing with his soldiers at a full banquet table, her mother praying in her grand room, tears rolling down her cheeks. She saw the temple being looted and idols of other gods erected. There was a child being put to death because he was somehow related to the royal line of Kelvinor. In the same moment, fine fabrics were being carried in for the royal ladies of Talforland. Through it all, the vision of the statue of Lord Kelvin in flames burned through her mind. Smoke rose into the sky around the castle as lightning flashed and rain began to pour down. And then there were faces. So many faces.

Her mother's face flashed in her mind and then Kelvin, Roderick, and Bree. Then faces she had not seen yet but knew she would come to know played in her head over and over again.

She felt herself start to shake against her will and she screamed in her mind and finally out loud, hoping the horse would hear her and take her to safety. She received no answer. She tried to make the visions stop, but they seemed beyond her control, replaying in her mind until all she knew was sorrow and the sound of hooves trotting on wet morning grass.

CHAPTER 17

AYLA DID NOT COME out of the dream slowly. In an instant she was awake and aware that something was wrong. She was afraid to sit up. Instead, she opened her eyes and glanced cautiously about the room. The soft moonlight cast a shadow across the bed and toward the door. She could make out the shadow of someone standing in the darkness.

Before she could manage a scream, the shadow was on her and her mouth was covered.

"Make any noise and you won't see morning!" the prince hissed in her ear.

He took his hand off her mouth, but pressed down on her shoulders sharply, straddling her. Her eyes were adjusting to the darkness and she could see him grinning. "I don't suppose it would matter anyway. I sent the guards away."

Ayla pushed against him but his hold was too strong. "What do you want?"

"I want you to know that I own you. I want you to learn your place." He reached behind him and pulled a dagger from his belt. "I'm going to mark you so that from now on, no one will think you are beautiful." He leaned in close, holding the dagger's cold blade against her cheek. "You'll be mine and mine alone."

Ayla turned her head away from him. "You're crazy!"

The prince only laughed. "What shall I cut off? An ear? Your nose?"

Ayla managed to free a hand and in a moment of panic, she tried to grab at the knife. The prince merely swatted her away. "Or maybe a finger? Is that what you're trying to tell me?"

With his free hand he brought his fist across her cheek. Ayla cried out despite the prince's threat. He put his hand around her throat. Her face throbbed as she choked out a desperate cough.

The next few seconds were a blur. She saw the prince's form pulled backward and heard the distinctive singing of a blade being drawn from its scabbard. When she regained her senses, Roderick stood facing the prince, his sword ready.

"Roderick! What are you doing?" the prince spat.

"Ayla, are you alright?" Roderick never took his eyes off the prince.

"I'm alright," she answered, her voice quavering slightly.

"Get up, get some clothes on. I'm taking you to safety."

Ayla obeyed, rolling out of the bed and quickly going to the wardrobe.

"Roderick, you'll be burned alive for this," the prince said through clenched teeth.

"Better burned as a traitor of Talforland than live as a servant to it."

"You're being foolish. Not that I care, but there are a million women in the world. Don't throw away your life for a pretty servant girl." The prince almost sounded as if he wanted to save Roderick, but Ayla knew it was a desperate lie. Prince Noland was scared for his life.

"There's more to it than you know."

The prince's voice turned hostile. "I'll hunt you down. You'll never be safe."

Roderick just nodded, "So be it."

He glanced at Ayla for a moment and the prince took the opportunity to lunge with his knife. Ayla screamed, but Roderick was ready. He parried the move and struck the prince on the back of the head with the pommel of his sword. The prince fell to the floor, unconscious.

They stood there a moment before Roderick sheathed his sword and looked at Ayla through the darkness. "Are you ready?"

She blushed. "I still need stockings and some boots."

He moved his gaze to the prince as she continued to prepare herself.

"Where are we going?"

"To safety. Just hurry."

She didn't ask any more questions. Quickly, she pulled on the lightest dress she could find, stockings and her boots. In one swift movement, she pulled the sheet off the bed and pulled the books from their hiding place. Wrapping them tightly in the linen, she fashioned a sort of makeshift strap and slung the burden over her shoulder.

Seconds later, she was following Roderick through the dimly lit corridors of the castle.

She was too nervous to recognize anything around her. The castle seemed unfamiliar during the day, but during the night it seemed even more foreign and distant. The torches glowed brilliantly at early dusk, but this was the dead of night. Their guiding flames had long since subsided. Only embers cast light on Ayla and Roderick's path.

Roderick took a sharp turn and for a moment Ayla lost him in the darkness. She gasped and took two quick steps forward, trying to catch him. As she did, she caught the hem of her dress and stumbled. Gripping at anything to keep her balance, she pulled at a small tapestry, sending its hanger to the floor with a loud clatter. Ayla held her breath.

She suddenly felt a hand grip her shoulder and she jumped, barely stifling her startled scream. Roderick was standing at her side.

He did not say anything but his look was tense. He nodded to her slightly and slowly she stepped away from the wall. He took her hand in his and the two of them began making their way down the corridor again.

A few moments later, Roderick pushed open a set of heavy wooden doors and Ayla felt the cold rush of the night air. Looking about her, she recognized the gate and courtyard Bree had led her through just two days earlier.

They made their way along an empty cobblestone street toward a wooden building just outside the servant's houses and storage shed. Behind the building, Ayla could see nothing but green pasture and horses. One candle burned in the window.

As they approached, the door swung open and out stepped a broad shouldered man Ayla had never met before. His expression was solemn and his demeanor so hard that Ayla could have never guessed what he might be thinking.

Roderick nodded to the man as the two of them entered. The door was quickly but quietly shut.

"I ran into some trouble," Roderick began at once. "We haven't a lot of time."

The broad shouldered man nodded and led them through another small wooden door. By the smell, Ayla knew at once that this was the stable.

Sure enough, there were at least twenty horses in their stalls asleep or quietly munching on oats. Ayla wondered for a moment if they were going to ride to their escape, but the broad shouldered man only opened an empty stall. He moved a few sacks of feed to reveal a small wooden door cut out of the flooring. With one swift move, he removed the door and was shuffling Ayla and Roderick inside.

"Bree will show you where the second path is." The broad shouldered man's booming voice seemed to fill up the air. "She's waiting for you in the tunnel."

"Thank you, Silas," Roderick said, accepting a small candle from the man.

Silas nodded, "Anything for the true heir." He turned to Ayla, "You've been a friend to my daughter, kind and gentler than any lady should be. May the Creator God keep you safe tonight! Blessings!"

Silas replaced the wooden door above them and she and Roderick made their way through a low tunnel on their hands and knees.

"How far are we going?" Ayla asked quietly.

"To the temple. But don't worry, the tunnel isn't this low the entire way."

Roderick was right. Only minutes later, the tunnel suddenly widened and dropped a few feet. They could walk comfortably in this part of the passage. The floors even gave the vague hint of having once been paved with stone.

"We have to retrieve the blue pendant tonight, Ayla." Roderick's voice echoed slightly in the tunnel. "Our situation has become desperate."

"Does this have to do with the prince marrying me?"

He nodded, "Yes. If he marries you, then blood fuses Talforland and Kelvinor. . .possibly forever. Your children would be the legitimate heirs to both lands and no one could contest that."

Ayla frowned. The thought of having children with the prince was much worse than the thought of being married to him. Still, there seemed to be a lot missing from Roderick's plan.

"But what about the prophecy I heard? About royal blood being needed to awaken the pendant?"

Roderick shook his head. "I only just heard the priestess and the prince discussing that. I don't know if it's legitimate."

"But won't there be keepers guarding the temple tonight?"

"Yes," Roderick said solemnly. "But we may be able to get to the pendant without a fight. From there. . .we will see what happens."

"And the prince?" Ayla said. "Why don't we just reveal that he's killing the king? Surely they must..."

Roderick stopped her before she could finish, "In our current circumstances, the prince is likely to blame us for the poisoning and there's no reason to believe our story over whatever the prince might say. Besides, that doesn't get us the pendant. Better to keep quiet for now."

A faint glow ahead of them illuminated the spot where Bree stood waiting. Her face lit up when she saw them.

"There you are! I was so worried. I'm so glad you're finally here. Come on, the passage is this way."

They followed a bit of the path until it ended, covered by twisted roots which crept through the ceiling of the tunnel.

"This passage only looks like it ends," Bree said with a chipper voice as she began pulling back the roots. "But if you keep digging, there's a rotted piece of wood. And if you pull it out..." She stopped for a moment and disappeared in the vines. Then her voice rang out again, "Ah, ha! There it is. A bit stuffy, but straight to the temple!"

Roderick climbed through the passage followed by Ayla. They followed Bree's voice and soon found the entrance to the narrow passage that led to the temple. It was, indeed, well hidden among the roots. Soon, Bree was leading them toward the temple, her voice echoing in the darkness and keeping them company.

"I've looked for the tree that grows above the entrance, and I think I found it. It's a great big oak tree that grows in the courtyard just a bit away from the castle wall. The path here twists around the castle and back towards the temple. Wonder what all the passages were for, anyway. Can't think of why anyone would need them. Especially in a place like Kelvinor! I mean, wasn't the kingdom supposed to be perfect and all? Why would you need secret tunnels?"

They seemed to walk forever, stooping in places, before finally stopping at a loose stone which Bree declared was the entrance to the temple's wine cellar. She pulled the stone out ever so slightly so Roderick could see through. Ayla peered over his shoulder.

The stone was a part of the very top of the cellar's ceiling. Still, the space had a low roof, and it would not be difficult for any of them to drop down. The cellar was filled with barrel upon barrel of wine, and it smelled of the fermenting grapes.

Roderick turned to Bree and whispered, "Are you ready?"

The girl smiled, "Been ready for a while now."

"Remember this isn't a game, Brenia. Alright?"

She just kept smiling. Roderick gave a nod and before Ayla knew it, the girl had dropped down into the wine cellar.

Roderick turned to Ayla, "Now it's our turn. Just follow me."

Roderick slid into the cellar first and then turned to help Ayla through. He took the bundle with the books first, setting it on the floor, and then raised his arms to Ayla. As she pushed her feet through the opening, he took her around the waist and lowered her gently to the floor. Their eyes met briefly and Ayla blushed before retrieving her books and following him up the stone steps to the short wooden door that must have been the temple's entrance into the cellar. With great care, he opened the door all the way and then lightly stepped back into the room, planting his back firmly against the right hand wall and drawing his sword. He motioned for Ayla to stand close at his side.

Bree was regarding them from across the chamber, poised for some mischievous action. Roderick took one more look around the chamber and nodded to her.

Bree began uncorking all the barrels she could reach. Ayla quickly looked to Roderick for direction, but he motioned for her to stay silent. Wine was pouring all over and around Bree, and she smiled with childlike glee. Finally after releasing more than a dozen barrels, Bree sat down in the middle of the chamber and began splashing about, singing at the top of her lungs.

> *"I'd pay a decent measure*
> *for a half a pint of beer*
> *But for wine as good as Kingies*
> *For that, I'd work all year!*
> *But I haven't any work*
> *And lo, I'm not a king*
> *So for my bar payment*
> *I'll just have to sing!"*

It wasn't long before angry voices were echoing in the corridor outside the cellar. Ayla held her breath as keepers stomped down the stairs.

"You silly, stupid servant girl! I'll have you whipped for this nonsense!"

He was too focused on the ruckus Bree was making to even notice Roderick and Ayla huddled close to the wall behind him. Soon enough, two more keepers were in the cellar lamenting the mess that Bree had made.

Roderick moved quickly, pummeling the first keeper with the back of his sword and knocking the second into the barrels of wine. The third got off a startled yell before Roderick knocked him out with a powerful blow to the face.

A moment passed in silence while Roderick sheathed his blade and both girls stared at the unconscious men on the floor.

The captain turned to Bree. "Thank you. Now do as we agreed."

The girl nodded and stood up from the floor ringing out her dress. "Good bye, Lady Ayla. But don't worry. I'll be seeing you soon enough."

She pushed a barrel to the corner of the room and went through the passage once again. Roderick took Ayla by the arm and cautiously led her up the short steps to the cellar door.

"But what about. . .?" She started to ask, but Roderick cut her off by shaking his head.

"There will be at least two more keepers in the sanctuary, guarding the altar. They will be armed so you need to stay behind me."

Ayla obeyed and followed Roderick as he made his way down two short hallways and through two sharp turns. At each corner, he would lean against the wall and peer around, making sure their path was clear. Then, he would signal Ayla to keep up.

Soon they were headed up a twisting, steep staircase. Ayla could see the first light of dawn from a window above them. They were above ground again.

At the top of the staircase, there was a long hallway with many windows. Across the expanse outside, Ayla could see the statues she remembered from the temple courtyard. They had to be very close to the sanctuary.

Suddenly, a shout rang out behind them, and Ayla and Roderick turned to see a very startled keeper at the opposite end of the corridor. He merely stared at them for a moment. Ayla wondered if news of Roderick's treachery had reached the temple.

The keeper finally dropped the heavy load of books he was caring and ran, shouting an alarm.

Roderick grabbed Ayla's arm. "We haven't much time."

They ran down the corridor and through the tall wooden doors. They burst into the sanctuary from just behind the great statue covered with flowers.

Roderick was in front of her, his sword drawn and ready. Five armed keepers stood against him. Slowly, he reached down to his belt and pulled out a dagger, holding it out to Ayla. She took it, glad for some way of defending herself. Her eyes drifted to the main altar, trying to figure out how it might open and she might retrieve the pendant inside.

The lead keeper spoke, "Surrender, Captain. We will not harm you or the girl." Ayla noticed that his voice wavered slightly. The keeper could not have been especially skilled with the sword. Perhaps he would lose his nerve.

Ayla let herself take a few slow steps around Roderick, toward the altar. Roderick moved to stay in front of her.

"I have no intention of surrendering myself or the Lady Ayla to the likes of you." Roderick's voice was strong, and Ayla noticed the keepers take a step back. She chanced another few steps toward the altar.

The thunder of hooves outside the temple startled her. Out the windows of the sanctuary, Ayla could see a troop of soldiers approaching.

The keepers had only a moment to look back at Roderick and sneer for the captain's blade was already thrusting towards them. "Ayla! Go!"

Ayla didn't think. She dropped her books and made a mad dash for the altar, hoping the priests would ignore her. She was wrong. As her hands gripped the altar's lid, a blade sliced the air above her, and she barely avoided having her throat cut. Quickly, she slid to the side of the golden box, using it as a shield against the oncoming keeper.

The keeper sent a thrust across the top of the altar and Ayla was forced to move again. Desperately, she slashed at the man with the dagger. The cut fell short and the keeper laughed, an eager smile upon his face.

Just a few paces away from her, Roderick was knocked back. He was parrying attacks from two different directions and another keeper was preparing to come at him from the side.

Ayla had no way of helping him. Her own attacker was coming at her again. She stumbled backward, away from the altar, and into the arms of another keeper. He trapped her arms and held her there, pulling his blade to her throat. "Stop this at once!"

The front doors of the sanctuary flew open and a whole regiment of soldiers entered. Ayla recognized certain faces, and she knew it must be the same group with whom she had traveled to Jade City.

At their lead was none other than Jovan. Ayla looked to him with desperation. She was trapped by two of the keepers, and three others faced off with the captain.

There were more hoof beats outside, and Ayla knew in her heart that at any moment the prince could be coming through the door. That would seal their fates if they could not get to the pendant first.

Ayla slammed her foot down on the ankle of the keeper holding her captive and he howled in pain, loosening his grip. She flung herself over the altar, pushing off the lid and knocking the heavy box over. Ayla and the objects inside the altar went skittering onto the stone floor.

Ayla looked up to see the gleam of a jewel on a chain just a few feet away from her. Her heart raced.

The doors of the temple burst open again, and the prince, followed by the king and several keepers, entered into the chamber. Noland took one quick look around and drew his sword, sneering at Roderick.

"What are you waiting for? Seize the captain!"

Roderick held his ground, shouting to the soldiers around him, "Men of Kelvinor, the time has come to stand against these invaders! The true heir has returned!" He pointed the tip of his sword at Ayla. She felt her heart beat even faster. She turned her gaze back to the pendant and inched herself forward.

Roderick continued his declaration. "Fight with me! Defend your queen!"

Jovan reached up to his left shoulder and pulled the insignia of the bear off his tunic. He stepped away from the soldiers and towards the keepers who were facing off with Roderick. Another figure also stepped out, repeating the gesture. It was Landon.

"Jovan!" The king growled, "You and your father will be punished for this treachery!" His voice was darker than Ayla would have ever imagined it could be.

Jovan just shook his head, "I am no traitor. My mother was of Kelvinor, and I love her kingdom more than that of my father's. It is not treachery to defend ones own country."

Landon nodded in agreement and as he did, four other soldiers stepped out of the group and moved towards Roderick.

Ayla's hand was inches from the pendant. She could now make out the runes engraved in the silver surrounding the gleaming blue jewel, but she could not take the time to read them. She was still glancing back and forth between the soldiers and her quarry.

"Foolishness," the prince shouted at the soldiers as they stepped away. "All those loyal to Talforland, seize these rebels!"

The chamber erupted in chaos. The sound of clanging swords and the shouts of men filled the room. Ayla launched herself towards the pendant and immediately felt herself pulled away. The keeper she had escaped earlier was now grasping her waist and trying to pick her up off the floor.

She screamed and kicked her feet, rolling on to her back. The man lost his grip and fell back slightly to avoid getting hit, but he was far from deterred. He was coming at her again, and this time, his blade was ready.

Ayla saw her salvation near her right hand. Roderick's dagger gleamed in the early morning light.

As the keeper brought his blade down on her, Ayla gripped the knife and brought it up, turning away as she felt the impact of the man's body against the blade. She let the handle loose and pushed herself back as the keeper fell.

She didn't have time to dwell on the man's blood seeping into the stone floor. She looked up to see the battle around her was not going well. Roderick and the men loyal to Kelvinor were fighting fiercely with the prince's soldiers, but they were outnumbered as much as three to one. A well placed thrust had caught Landon's thigh, and he was falling back, saved from a killing blow by another soldier but wounded, he would not be defendable long.

Ayla's eyes found the pendant and for once nothing was blocking her path. She hoped Roderick was right as she reached her hand toward the gleaming blue jewel.

The chain was ice cold as she touched it but when she pulled it to her chest, it turned hotter. Still, she gripped it, feeling the heat start to burn the inside of her hand.

As she held it close, she looked for Roderick across the hall. A sword was crashing down on him, and there was no way he would be able to counter its strike. Ayla felt her mouth open to let out a scream. Her cry seemed in-human as it echoed throughout the chamber.

The whole world slowed down in that moment, and just before the sword crashed down on Roderick, Ayla felt herself knocked backward into darkness.

CHAPTER 18

AYLA WOKE UP TO THE sound of crickets chirping and to the cool air of night resting gently on her skin. Slowly, she opened her eyes, struggling to remember where she had last been. Indeed, for a moment it seemed hard to even grasp her name. Her head was pounding.

The first thing she saw was the stretched out canvas of a tent. The flap was undone and blowing in the night air. It was illuminated by the flicker of a fire burning just outside. She was lying on a hammock of sorts that had been hung between the two posts of the tent. It was a sturdy structure. There were wooden posts holding up the four sides and the covering was braced with poles forming a triangular ceiling above her.

Ayla sat up and immediately felt something cold touch her chest. She reached down and pulled a pendant set with a single blue stone out of her tunic. She seemed to distantly recall that this had something to do with her last memory before waking up. She studied it intently for a moment, and then her eyes moved down her body. She was dressed in a man's tunic and pants that were slightly oversized. The pants had been tied off with a cloth belt and the tunic hung loosely over her shoulders. She pulled it closer, suddenly feeling a need for modesty though no one was around.

A shadow fell over the light from the fire, and Ayla looked up quickly. There were no voices and the shadow did not look like it belonged to a person. She looked around for some object with which to defend herself. Her eyes found a small dagger lying casually on a table next to her hammock. Carefully, she reached out, taking the knife.

The shadow moved closer to the tent at a casual pace, and Ayla found herself strangely resilient. She held the dagger out, ready for anything. As the shadow passed in front of the tent, the flap lifted and in came the head of a white horse. Ayla looked at him curiously. The horse seemed to stare back at her with laughing eyes. Memories flooded her mind like a whirlwind.

"Are you…?" She managed.

The horse shook out his mane and pawed the dirt letting out a soft huff. Ayla dared to imagine that maybe the white horse from her dream had come to carry her away. Slowly, she got up, lightly stepping out of the hammock and reaching out to the marvelous animal.

A sudden shout from outside the tent made her pull her hand away. She raised the dagger again, stepping back towards her hammock. The horse huffed once more but did not move away despite more shouting and the sound of many men making their way toward the tent.

Ayla saw two hands suddenly trying to push the horse out of the tent's entryway. "You unruly beast! Out of my way!"

She recognized the voice at once and it carried a vision with it of her last moments in the temple.

"Landon!" She cried, dropping the dagger and rushing forward.

Landon pushed his way past the horse just in time to catch Ayla in his arms. "Landon!" she sobbed. "Landon, where are we? What's going on?"

But Landon didn't answer her, calling over his shoulder instead, "She's awake! Come quickly! Jovan! Jovan!"

The horse was nipping at Ayla's loose tunic as if jealous of her attention toward Landon. She let the soldier go and took the horse's face in her hands. "Did he bring me here? Is he the Creator God's messenger?"

"My lady?" Landon asked, "Are you alright?"

She turned back to him, realizing that he was staring at the dagger she held. She dropped it abruptly, watching the blade as it fell to the earth. "The keeper…" She suddenly murmured, "Is he? Did I…?"

The dried blood on the daggers blade confirmed her returning memories. She looked to Landon for an answer, but he was unwilling to give her one.

A moment later, Jovan's happy face broke the tone within the tent. She did not have time to greet him for behind him there suddenly appeared a gathering of both soldiers and common people. They huddled around the tent's entryway, smiling to one another and staring at Ayla. They talked and whispered, all pushing to get into the tent. Landon and Jovan had to quickly turn their attention from Ayla to the gathering mob in order to restore order.

"Alright, alright, back up! Move back!" Landon began ushering them out of the tent. Satisfied that the crowd was under control, Jovan went to Ayla and quietly knelt at her feet.

Ayla didn't understand why he chose that gesture at that moment, but it triggered a series of bows and nods from the crowd as they were ushered away from the tent. She heard the hushed murmur of respectful titles. "My lady," they said and others, "Your Majesty."

"Jovan?" Ayla said, feeling his name spoken calmly from her lips and thinking her voice sounded strange. She began again, hoping to sound more sure. "Jovan, where are we?"

He did not stand up. "My lady, we are in the Stone Wood on the southern edge of what was once Kelvinor."

Ayla nodded, but she still did not understand where they were. She didn't know where the southern edge of Kelvinor had been nor had she ever heard of the Stone Wood.

"Please stand up, Jovan."

He obeyed.

"How did we get here?" she asked, slightly frustrated by his formality. "Please, tell me everything."

The tent flap was pushed all the way open again and Landon entered, kneeling before her. Unlike Jovan, he stood up again, and Ayla felt herself relieved.

"What do you remember, Your Highness?" Jovan asked.

Ayla shook her head as if trying to stir the memories, "I remember the fight in the temple and the keepers coming. I remember my books. . ." She looked around the tent and found the books on the table near where the knife had been. Someone must have retrieved them. "I remember that knife." She pointed the stained object on the ground. "Oh, and this." She touched the pendant that was now hanging loosely outside of the tunic. "I remember this."

Landon and Jovan looked at each other and then back to her.

"Your Majesty," Landon began, "we don't know what . . .this necklace?"

Ayla gripped the pendant. "Your captain? Did he tell you?"

Jovan immediately looked away, and Ayla's heart began to pound. "Is he alright?"

Jovan looked back to her. "You've been asleep in this tent, Your Highness, for nearly two weeks. For the same amount of time, the captain has been in a tent across the camp. He was wounded in the temple."

Jovan seemed unable to say more, and he looked to Landon.

"The captain's wound festers. It's infected." He shook his head. "Healers have come from the nearby village, but they haven't been able to help him."

Ayla didn't need anymore. She turned and pulled the blanket off the hammock, wrapping it around her shoulders. "Take me to him."

Jovan and Landon looked to each other again, but Ayla was resolute. If she was a queen now, she could certainly go where she pleased. "Take me to him," she repeated.

Jovan escorted her past the white horse and through the opening of the tent. "This way, Your Highness."

Landon followed behind them, giving the horse a frustrated push as they left. "Stupid horse," she heard Landon growl under his breath.

Ayla emerged from her tent into a forest lit by many campfires and torches. There were many people moving about, cooking, gathering wood, making shelter or weapons. Some were clearly soldiers but others were common folk: men, women, children, babies. All manner of people occupied this encampment. The light sound of voices was beginning to fill the darkness as more and more people rose from the tents and huts around her. The sky above the trees was slowly growing brighter. Morning lay just minutes from their grasp.

"Who are these people?" she asked Landon.

"These are the people loyal to Kelvinor," Landon answered matter-of-factly.

"And loyal to you, my lady," Jovan said. "They've come from all over the kingdom to support you."

"Me?" Ayla said.

Landon nodded, "The time of Kelvinor's redemption is at hand."

Ayla didn't ask anymore questions. She was distracted by the number of people who had noticed her walking through the trees. Men and women were bowing and stopping their chores to stare.

These are your people.

The familiar voice sounded clearly in her thoughts, and she looked back, stopping suddenly. The white horse was following casually behind them, nibbling on the grassy forest floor as he went.

"What?" She asked aloud softly, as she watched the horse approach.

"My lady?"

Jovan and Landon had turned as well and were watching her curiously.

"Whose horse is that?" Ayla asked, still wanting to see Roderick but unable to tear her gaze away from the animal.

"A stubborn beast," Landon answered. "We purchased him a day ago from a traveler who was passing through the woods. He listens to no man, and we haven't found a fence that can hold him."

"We were cheated," Jovan said angrily.

Ayla stared at the horse curiously. "Perhaps he is only meant to have one rider."

The horse was very close now, and Ayla stretched out her hand to him again.

"Be careful," Landon warned.

But Ayla was not afraid. Her hand touched the soft nose of the magnificent white horse, and he immediately bobbed his head up and down once with approval. Ayla smiled and stroked his mane and ears, letting her hands journey down his back.

"Landon, help me." She smiled and placed both hands on the horse's back, her intent on mounting him clear.

"Your Highness, I must really warn you that…"

"Landon," Ayla said, "everything will be fine. Help me up, please."

Jovan was shaking his head in disapproval as Landon stepped in to help Ayla. He knelt next to the horse, raising a knee so Ayla could use it as a step. She struggled for a moment, but soon found her footing and hoisted herself onto the horse's back. He did not move as she steadied herself on top of him. Ayla patted his back and smoothed the soft mane down onto the horse's neck.

"I need to see the captain, now," she said, as much for the two soldiers at her side as for the horse. She was still unsure as to how to direct the animal and could only trust he knew the way.

The horse obediently trotted forward with purpose, and Jovan and Landon had to quicken their steps to keep up with his sure pace. They did not have to guide the horse for he followed the path to where Roderick was being tended without wavering. The two soldiers did, however, keep a close watch for anything amiss, amazed by the animal's sudden change in attitude.

As they reached the captain's tent, Landon moved to help Ayla off the horse. But the beast would not have his help. He huffed and shook his head proudly at the intruding soldier.

"It's alright." Ayla stopped Landon and carefully slid off the horse's back. Landon shook his head and threw up his hands, walking away without a word. Ayla soothed the horse, patting his neck and whispering quietly into his ear, "Wait for me."

The three of them ducked inside Roderick's tent.

The light was low even with the sun beginning to rise over the trees. Roderick was laid out on a cot in the corner of the tent. Ayla went to him and knelt next to the makeshift bed.

"He's not been coherent for a few days," Landon said softly behind her. "There's not much time left."

The wound cut down Roderick's left shoulder and across the top of his chest. It was deep and smelled putrid, like rotting meat. Ayla could tell the wound had been stitched and cleaned soon after the injury occurred, but the foul odor and odd color of infection now spread over the wound and puss oozed out from under the crude stitching. The pillow beneath his thick black hair was soaked with sweat. Ayla touched his forehead. He was hotter than any ill person she had ever known. Ayla felt tears beginning to form in her eyes and she knelt down, hiding her face in her hands and letting the blanket that covered her shoulders drop to the floor.

"Please," she said to Jovan and Landon. "Leave me here awhile."

The soldiers obeyed and with short bows, they disappeared outside the tent.

There was a bucket of water and a rag sitting near Ayla's feet and she took it, mopping Roderick's forehead. As she leaned over him, the pendant fell forward, dangling from her neck.

The metal felt hot again when she leaned back, and she reached up, taking it in her hand. Had the power been restored to the pendant and could she use it to heal Roderick's wounds? She turned her gaze back to the captain. She didn't know how to use the pendant, and the only person who might offer a clue was not coherent enough to help her.

The only person, she thought.

She leaned in to Roderick. "I'll be back," she whispered. She got up and slid out of the tent into the early morning light.

To her left, Landon and Jovan were standing some distance away and were turned away from her. She didn't think they saw her exit. On her right, the horse's warm nose had come to rest on her shoulder. Ayla touched his nose and gently led him to the other side of the tent, hoping to stay out of sight for the time being.

"Please," she said to the animal. "I don't know how to talk to you. I need to know how to use the pendant and if it's awake."

She heard nothing from the horse.

"Please. I need to save someone's life. Roderick is dying..."

She cast her eyes down and let her hands stroke the side of the horse's head. There was only silence in the air and inside her mind. The tears she had been fighting ever since she first saw Roderick in the tent were rolling down her cheeks. Before she could think to breathe again, she was sobbing into the horse's mane.

He nudged her softly, pushing his nose into her shoulder. She started to take a step back, but found she couldn't. Looking down at her shoulder she discovered that the white horse had latched onto her tunic with his teeth. He was walking backwards, pulling her forward.

"What are you...?"

He took a sudden, fast step back and pulled her farther forward until she stumbled. He let go and moved to her back, still nudging her in the same direction with his nose.

"Alright. Okay. I'll go."

The horse kept nudging her forward until he seemed convinced that she would, indeed, follow him. Then, he trotted in front of her at a steady pace. She struggled to keep up with him, her feet only covered in thin stockings which didn't offer a lot of protection against the rocky ground.

She followed the horse beyond the tent, out of the encampment, and into the woods. Tears kept coming, but she managed to wipe them away without giving into the sobs. She didn't stop to think about where the horse might be leading her. She just followed, hoping and trusting.

After a few minutes, the horse stopped and snorted, shaking his mane and turning to look at Ayla. Curiously, she slid past him and looked ahead. The horse watched her.

The animal had stopped on the edge of a narrow road that cut through the woods. It would not have been wide enough for a wagon, but it was more paved than any footpath Ayla had encountered. She studied it for a moment and then looked up, stepping back in surprise.

An older man with a long white beard stood before her. He was smoking a pipe and seemed not at all surprised by her presence.

"Good day," he said and continued to smoke.

Ayla recognized him at once as the man who had claimed she was his daughter at the village of Halforton. Ayla looked from the man back to the horse. The horse whinnied in what almost seemed like a laugh, and Ayla turned back to face the man.

"You've been crying, girl. This is no time for tears."

Ayla instinctively wipped her eyes again. "I think I know you, sir."

"Indeed you do," he said. "I claimed you at Halforton." The man smiled, his lips barely showing through the scruffy mass of hair on his face. "And I'm the once owner of that proud beast that you followed. Although, I doubt anyone could really own him."

The white horse stepped up to Ayla's side and gently nudged her forward a few more paces, onto the path.

"He led me to you?" she said.

The man nodded. "And I imagine he had good reason to. What's your trouble?"

Ayla could not begin to imagine how to explain her predicament. Her hand instinctively gripped the pendant as she struggled desperately to find the words.

The man just shook his head. "Don't worry, child. I'm not a stranger to who you are. So, it's the pendant that troubles you?"

Ayla nodded, "How do you. . . .?"

But the man just waved her off. "I know a great deal more than you think. What s your question?"

Ayla could not imagine what the man knew, but she didn't see any harm in telling him her trouble. "Is the pendant awake, and if it is, how do I use it?"

"Oh! Well, that's two questions isn't it?" The man gave his beard a playful twirl. "The pendant is awake in a way. Your touch has stirred it as the prophecy says. However, it needs the union of two people of royal blood to be completely restored."

"So both prophecies are correct?" she asked.

He nodded. "They are from two different sources, but you are right; both are correct. And now I see you have another question burning in your eyes?"

Ayla looked down at the blue pendant. She was thinking of Roderick again and hoping he might live. "Can the pendant restore life?"

"It cannot restore life, I'm afraid." The man frowned. "Nor can it take life away. Once a soul is created, it cannot be created again. Once a soul is gone. . .it is gone. You are only given one lifetime. You will also find that the red pendant cannot take a life directly, though its destruction is true enough to kill."

Ayla looked away, back toward the encampment. Was there any hope for Roderick?

Suddenly the man spoke again as if he sensed what she was thinking. "But healing. Now, that's a different thing entirely. That is the most rudimentary of gifts from the Creator and even in its weakened state, the pendant can heal."

She turned back to the man, suddenly hopeful. "Sir, I need to know how to heal. I don't know how to use the pendant."

The man laughed, and Ayla thought at that moment that he really might just be a crazy man wondering in the woods. His clothes were tattered and worn, and he might have dirt on his body from decades ago. "That's very simple. The wearer of the pendant has only to ask the pendant to do its work! The jewel will comply however it sees fit."

"Just ask? That's all?"

He nodded. "Very simple. Just remember, the pendant can only create. It can only work in creation and can never destroy. If asked to destroy, the pendant's power could be lost."

Ayla thought for a moment. Was it really just a matter of asking?

The man took a step toward her, and Ayla resisted the urge to turn away.

"Just remember," he said. "Things happen in their own time. You may ask the pendant to create a fortified castle, but without strong backs and the will to build it nothing will happen. Magic exists on faith and will." He took a breath and gave her a wide grin. Several of his teeth were missing.

"How do you. . .?"

The man waved her off again and pointed to the horse. "His name is Sunfire. He is rumored to be a descendant of the white horse of Kelvinor. He certainly has the brains and the attitude for it." The man chuckled and then said in a low serious voice, "It's more than just a rumor. He will take good care of you."

Ayla looked from the man to the horse again. "But who are you?"

He bowed to her. "Just a traveler spouting good advice." When he rose, he smiled at her again and then nodded, looking over her shoulder and into the woods. "They'll be looking for you now."

Ayla heard the voice of Jovan and she turned at once.

"Lady Ayla!"

They were still some ways off, and she turned back toward the man. But he was gone. She looked all around the little road and saw nothing. She didn't hear so much as the sound of a footstep. This time Landon's voice called out to her and she turned and yelled to them. "Yes! I'm here!"

They came through the forest out of breath and sweating.

"My lady!" Jovan began, "We've been looking all over for you. What happened? Are you alright?"

"I'm fine," Ayla answered, stroking the horse's ears. "Our friend here led me into the woods a bit. I was just upset about the captain."

Landon shook his head, "Your Majesty, we were worried when we didn't find you in the tent and . . ."

"It's alright, Landon," Ayla interrupted. "I'm okay. I need to go back to the captain now. I think I may know of something that will help him."

"What, my lady?"

But she didn't say anything else. She simply walked past them, back towards the encampment. Strange encounters with poor forest dwellers were not something she wanted to share with the two. As much as she trusted them, they were still unaware of the pendant and its power. She needed answers from Roderick and she hoped she would have them soon.

CHAPTER 19

FROM THAT MORNING and into the next two days, Ayla hardly left the captain's side. She found that when she asked something of the pendant, it grew warm. It had been especially hot during the last several days. She clutched it in her palm and spoke the words of her request over and over again.

And Roderick began to recover.

The fever broke first, and then the infection began to subside. When the puss cleared away, Ayla helped a healer from the nearby village re-stitch the wound. Soon, it became clear that the captain would escape the cold clutches of death.

But Ayla's worries were not over. She had heard nothing of Bree. No one seemed to even heard of Bree and her family's involvement in Roderick's planned escape from the castle. Ayla had searched the camp to no avail. Bree was nowhere to be found. Hoping that perhaps Bree had gone elsewhere, playing some part in Roderick's scheme, Ayla waited as patiently as she could for him to awaken.

Landon and Jovan stayed ever present but were careful not to disturb Ayla. They asked her once about the pendant, but she wouldn't answer.

"When the captain wakes up, maybe then," she would say, and turn back to her tending of him.

It was the third morning after she had awakened. The early light of dawn was just beginning to fill Roderick's tent. Ayla was sitting by his cot as usual, gripping the pendant and waiting for Jovan to bring in bread and water. The bread and water came and still she sat, hoping. She was listening as she always did to his breathing and watching the soft rise and fall of his chest.

And then Roderick opened his eyes and blinked.

Ayla gasped as she watched.

"Roderick?" she whispered.

He turned his head toward her and looked around, scanning the room for something familiar. He tried to sit up, but Ayla stopped him.

"Take is slow, Captain. You've been ill."

He looked up at her. "Ayla?"

She smiled at the sound of her name. "Yes."

He leaned forward a little more until he could sit up. Ayla kept her hand on his shoulder to steady him. His eyes were still glazed, and he put his hand to his head, sweeping the tendrils of oily black hair from his eyes.

"Where are we?"

"In an encampment far from Jade City, a southern forest?"

He nodded slightly, his voice distant. "Stone Wood."

"Yes." Ayla reached for the water and handed it to Roderick. "Jovan and Landon are here and...others."

Roderick only nodded again. "I expect your supporters? Stone Wood...it lies near many small villages and they...they would still be rabid in their support of the old kingdom. Almost as faithful as Halforton...."

Ayla reached out for the food the soldiers had brought but Roderick shook his head, "I don't think I could stomach it."

"Should I tell the others you're awake?"

He shook his head again, "Not yet."

A moment of silence passed between them as Roderick sipped the water. Finally, Ayla began again.

"Roderick, I'm not sure what happened in the temple. I guess I...passed out. Do you remember how we got here?"

Roderick stopped sipping at the water. His gaze seemed far off, as if he was remembering something from a distant dream. "I remember a blade cutting down my chest, and falling onto the stone floor. From there, Landon broke through and pulled me out of the temple. I think one of the other soldiers managed to get you out." He turned his gaze toward her, "It seems after you fell that the soldiers with us fought with more strength and resilience than I have ever seen. It was as if some...power...came over them."

He reached up and touched the chain around her neck, pulling it out of the safety of her shirt. "The blue pendant?"

Ayla nodded.

"Do you. . .?" Roderick questioned and then stopped, starting again a moment later, "Have you learned to use it?"

Ayla shrugged. "I know that I must ask it to do things and that somehow you are well when all seemed lost a few days ago."

Roderick leaned back again, onto the bed. "It's a great power, no doubt. You have to master it." His eyes closed and Ayla could see he was drifting away again. No doubt he needed the rest, but Ayla was not ready for him to sleep just yet.

"Roderick, what about Bree? She's not here and. . ."

But Roderick had already fallen asleep.

Ayla wrapped her fist around the pendant. Her thoughts drifted from Roderick to the white horse, to the old man she had met in the woods. Somehow, it was all connected. She glanced at the entrance to the tent. Outside, she could make out the shadow of the horse. Sunfire snorted a bit. He always seemed to sense when she was looking at him.

It was a bright new day and the weather outside was perfect. A cool breeze broke through the normally stiff spring air and clouds rolled through the sky, easing the hot sun's breath against the earth. She knew that Roderick would recover. The pendant, or perhaps pure luck, had saved him, and any day now he would be strong enough to lead them again. Ayla counted on that.

Ayla left the water near Roderick's side in case he awoke again. She tucked a soft pillow under his head and slowly left the tent. For the first time in days, she felt relief and wondered if there might be something else she could do besides look after the captain. A new feeling filled her, one she could not identify. Perhaps it was sense of duty, the need to do something for her people.

Her people, she thought. They were all around her. They seemed to want her leadership but Ayla didn't know how to give it to them.

She walked briskly back to her own tent, her mind filled with the newfound feeling. Sunfire trotted gleefully behind her as he always did when she wasn't riding him. Since Ayla had awoken a few days ago and taken up with the animal, no one was bothered by the horse's free nature.

Some women from the encampment and surrounding villages had brought Ayla clothing, and she fished though the chest scattering bits of fabric about her. The dresses were not as nice as the ones from the castle, but that was the least of Ayla's cares. She needed something light, something she would be comfortable for riding.

She found a pair of boots, stockings, and a skirt that floated lightly in the air. A loose fitting white shirt and a bodice topped it off. She looked plain, like one of the women she had seen in the last few days, walking about the camp and starting the fires for the men. Still, she knew the people in the encampment would recognize her. They had seen her over the last few days, though rarely. When she did walk about camp, they seemed to not know what to do. Some would bow and others would stop and look at their feet. The younger children where usually corralled by their parents as she rode by and whispered to with urgency about proper respect. Ayla didn't know what to think of it all. She certainly didn't want to be treated poorly, but she didn't want to be feared either. She was a Princess of Kelvinor, not Talforland. Even in her little experience, Ayla knew there was a difference and the people would have to recognize that soon.

Jovan had given her a bridle and a saddle for Sunfire, and Ayla had quickly learned how to put it on the horse. He let her, though sometimes he huffed a bit and held his breath. She had no trouble with him today. He seemed ready, eager to ride.

She mounted him as steadily as she could though she still struggled. Sunfire didn't move as she pulled herself up. He was steady, patient. Pulling the reins into her hands more for show than anything else, she asked Sunfire in a quiet voice to take her through the encampment to the paved road that led to the villages. Sunfire nodded his head once, and began to trot happily forward.

They passed Jovan and Landon first who were startled to see her out of Roderick's tent.

"My lady!" Jovan called, running up to her. "We can escort you if you wish!"

But Ayla stopped him, "No, thank you, Jovan. I'm quite alright. The captain is doing much better, and I've decided I need a little air."

By now, Landon had caught up with them. "But where are you going?"

"Just through the encampment. I'll be back soon."

Sunfire trotted a bit faster, leaving the two soldiers behind and leading her into the part of the encampment where the common folk dwelled.

Just as Ayla expected, the people did everything from bow to look at their feet, to point and whisper. Ayla, like them, was not sure what to do. She wasn't even sure she wanted to be the person they all seemed to know she was. The world that Lunara Royinheart was supposed to have enjoyed seemed a long way off. She tried to look the people in the eyes as she passed, but that seemed too forward and yet, looking away seemed haughty and abrupt. So, she glanced here and there and occasionally made eye contact with people, only both parties quickly looked away.

As Ayla continued to glance around, she noticed a group of children playing who could not have been but a few years younger than herself. They were so engrossed in chasing one another that they didn't look toward her as she rode by.

But as Ayla grew closer, she could see that this was not a child's game but rather a petty teasing match. The children were chasing a smaller boy around their makeshift play yard and chanting at him, some throwing small sticks. They laughed as a bigger child pushed the boy to the ground, causing him to cry out. He rolled over on his back, revealing scraped and bleeding palms.

Ayla clenched her teeth with anger and told Sunfire to stop. When he didn't halt fast enough, she instinctively pulled on the reins and he jolted slightly, feeling her anger in the pull. The children were still laughing as she dismounted and walked briskly towards them.

The boy on the ground saw her first and his eyes went wide. He started scrambling, trying to get to his feet, but the bigger boy wouldn't let him get up. He was on the ground again in an instant.

Ayla took the bigger boy by the shoulder from behind and spun him around to face her. Her eyes were burning with fury.

"What gives you the right to hurt this boy?" she demanded as the child stood facing her in awed silence. Sensing he was too shocked to speak, she turned to the others standing in the circle. "What makes you think you are any different from this boy on the ground? What makes you think he deserves less?"

A tall girl with red hair answered softly, "We were just having a bit of fun."

"Oh?" Ayla replied. "And do you think it was fun for this boy?"

She gave them all a burning look and released the bigger boy from her grasp. She extended a hand to the boy on the ground and after a moment of consideration, he took it gratefully, careful to wipe the dirt and blood on his trousers first. She pulled him to his feet. "What's your name?"

"Yuri," he smiled, revealing a set of crooked teeth.

By now, some of the parents had appeared and were gathering their children to them, watching Ayla with interest. She turned to them, tears were now forming in her eyes from all the anger. Her voice was softer but still steady.

"Do you realize your children have acted in the way of Talforland? I haven't been in a position to know my own history for very long, but what I do know tells me that Talforland came here for no reason and took what they wanted. They tormented us like your children tormented this boy! If you want to be Kelvinor once again, you must act like it. Everyone must be treated with respect even if they're different."

She glanced to Yuri, giving him the biggest smile she could muster. She then turned and walked as fast as she could back to Sunfire, who seemed to be watching the whole scene with interest. Mounting him with more speed and efficiency than she had ever done before, she said simply, "Let's go." Their journey continued through the wood.

From that day on, the people in the encampment bowed slightly whenever Ayla passed by. They seemed more confident now and less afraid of her presence.

CHAPTER 20

THE NEXT DAY, AYLA WAS awakened by the sound of galloping hooves. Instinct sent her immediately to her feet. Pulling on the soft cotton clothes from the day before, she pushed aside the flap of the tent to discover Jovan running toward her. Behind him, the whole encampment of soldiers was on its feet, hands on swords. Many voices were shouting news and Ayla caught bits and pieces of the dialog floating in the air.

One of the king's messengers had appeared on the trail leading to the encampment. He'd been stopped by the lookouts and guards along the path. He bore a white flag and a message for the girl, Ayla.

Jovan came to a stop directly in front of her, "My lady. . ." He began, trying to catch his breath. She didn't let him finish.

"What's the message?"

"My lady," Jovan began again, "I don't know. They're bringing him to the encampment blindfolded so he won't know the way."

"Bring him to me when he gets here." She looked across the encampment to Roderick's tent. "I'll be with the captain."

"But my lady, it wouldn't be good for the enemy to see the captain in such a condition, and he may be carrying a weapon. You must be protected."

Ayla nodded, "Then you and Landon stay with me. Or others, as many as you want, but I will hear this news with the captain."

With that, she strode toward the tent where Roderick lay. After a few steps, her walk turned into a run. The familiar sound of trotting behind her assured Ayla that Sunfire was indeed following her again. He was never far from her side.

Ayla entered Roderick's tent and shook the captain lightly. He stirred but did not wake.

"Captain!" Ayla said urgently, and then, "Roderick! Please wake up."

The captain stirred and then blinked.

"There's a messenger coming from Jade City. He'll be here in a few minutes!"

Roderick seemed to shake himself awake. He rubbed his forehead. "Ayla? A messenger?"

She nodded. "You have to sit up. Please."

With her help, he slowly leaned forward, muttering, still half asleep. "Message. From Jade City…"

The tent flap opened and Ayla swiftly got to her feet careful to keep one hand on Roderick's shoulder. But it wasn't the messenger; it was Jovan and he wore an astonished expression on his face.

"Captain?" he said, regarding Roderick and then Ayla, "When did he wake up?"

"Yesterday morning. But he's not completely well, yet."

Roderick seemed to mutter something incoherent to assure him, if there was any doubt. Ayla steadied him. "Where's the messenger?"

"Outside. My lady, are you sure you…?"

"Bring him in." She interrupted him, still wanting Roderick, however delirious, to hear what was happening. "You and Landon may accompany him."

Jovan gave a small bow and disappeared for a brief moment outside the tent. He re-entered with Landon, and between them, they escorted a very young soldier dressed in the king's armor. The familiar sign of the bear seemed to glow from the breastplate.

He seemed confident though Ayla could sense a bit of fear in him. Both Landon and Jovan were larger and older than he. The messenger could not have been older than Ayla herself.

He gave a slight nod to her and then seemed to be waiting. After a moment, he looked at Jovan.

"Does the lady wish to hear the message?"

Courtly nonsense, Ayla realized and she took her cue. "You may speak your message."

The boy nodded and began. "The king's army is not two days ride from the

Stone Wood led by Prince Noland. Riding with him is the Priestess Maura. If you give yourself up, you will be treated fairly and will not be put to death for your treason. Although a long sentence surely awaits you…"

Ayla caught the mention of the priestess. She wondered why the woman would be riding with the king's army.

The messenger continued.

"Otherwise, you can fight and die. I have your surrender written out for you to sign." He held out a small length of parchment. "In order for it to be accepted, you must acknowledge, along with your surrender, that you are not the true heir of Kelvinor."

A moment slipped by as Ayla examined the document. She could not read it, but she already knew her answer.

"I will sign no such document."

The messenger nodded. "The prince thought you might reply this way."

Roderick's quavering voice interrupted the conversation unexpectedly. He was awake and aware, that much Ayla could tell, but he was still weak. "Tell Prince Noland this. He can come for us and we will be ready. We have more power than he could possibly imagine." Roderick glanced to Ayla and then back to the messenger. "Now go."

The messenger hesitated then nodded to them both. "By your leave."

He left the tent, followed closely by Landon and Jovan.

Roderick lay back down on the cot and shut his eyes briefly. Ayla watched him. Quite suddenly, he seemed to shake off the feeling of exhaustion and he sat up again, this time placing his feet on the floor and leaning over the cot. He reached up a hand to Ayla.

"Will you give me your hand?"

Ayla stretched out her hand and he took it. With a stiff pull, he came to his feet and she helped him over to where his tunic was.

"You shouldn't be here. Helping me like this. It's beneath you."

Ayla shook her head. "I owe you my life and so much more. How could helping you be beneath me?"

Roderick pulled the tunic over his shoulders, wincing as it touched the wound for the first time. "We're in the Stone Wood?"

Ayla nodded. "Somewhere near the border…"

"God knows how they knew. It should have taken them longer to find us. There should be three villages all within a day's ride of here. We need to gather support…"

"People from the villages are here already."

Roderick turned to her, "Do you know how many?"

Ayla shook her head.

Roderick took a few steps toward the door and faltered, holding onto the post by the entrance for support. Ayla was at his side in a moment.

"You still need to rest."

Roderick shook his head. "We don't have time for that."

Ayla let Roderick put his arm around her shoulder and she helped him outside of the tent. The encampment was bustling with activity, especially on the side where the villagers had set up their huts. People were going to fetch water at the nearby stream and others were cooking or washing linens. Ayla could hear the sound of children playing and men talking.

Roderick looked around, taking it all in. Ayla watched him with quiet interest. For so many days she had longed to hear him speak to her, longed to have him well. With his arm still around her shoulder, she felt an unfamiliar, dizzying sensation stirring in her stomach.

"More people than I expected." he finally breathed. "I need to see Landon and Jovan. They're the highest ranking of the men who would have followed us."

No sooner had he said it than Ayla saw the pair running towards them.

"Captain!" they each seemed to say in unison as they approached.

Roderick put up a hand to stop them and leaned a bit less on Ayla. "What are our armaments like? Horses? Bows?"

"Sir," Landon began, "we only have what we were able to bring with us when we left Jade City, and the villagers have tools, clubs and things of that nature."

Roderick nodded, a little disappointed. "Is there a blacksmith among them?"

Landon and Jovan looked at each other.

"Find one and send a group of soldiers out to gather as much metal as you can. Pots, excess armor, tools, anything that the villagers or we have. Has anyone ridden to the villages yet to gather reinforcements?"

Landon nodded. "And they've come in droves. More arrive every day. Unfortunately, most are women and children. They do have horses though; we could mount a massive cavalry, provided we had enough riders."

"We'll pray more men come." Roderick looked to Ayla. "And we'll arm the women as well."

"Sir?" Jovan questioned.

"The prince won't make a distinction between men or women when he comes here – he'll kill everyone who's joined us. . . most likely he'll burn every village along this border just for spite."

Ayla shook her head. "I don't know how to use a sword and . . .I doubt there's time for me or any other woman in this camp to learn."

Roderick gave her a still weak smile, "Don't worry, My Lady, I have something else in mind."

CHAPTER 21

WHILE LANDON, JOVAN, and Roderick spent the remainder of the day coming up with a battle plan, Ayla gathered all of the women together to hunt for anything metal that might be useful to the blacksmiths. She sent the younger girls off as well, but not to look for metals. They were instructed to find branches that would be good for making arrows and bows. They also needed thicker wood for making clubs. Even the youngest boys were put to work hunting heron and duck for not only food, but their feathers. Later, their task would be fletching the newly shaved arrow shafts. Even later, their task might be more gruesome; they might be stationed in the trees aiming bows at the king's men.

Ayla worked diligently to organize the effort and no one questioned her. As they worked, the white horse remained with her and followed her wherever she went. His presence encouraged her and she felt a sense of power when he was at her side. Whether Sunfire was the white horse of Kelvinor or not, Ayla treated him as such. As for the people, they had not missed the connection between the girl and horse. To them, it only solidified their belief that Ayla was the lost heir.

Once the women were sent off, Ayla was asked to come back to Roderick's tent. She wanted to help in any way she could, and she didn't mind taking orders from the captain. Her people saw her as a leader and following him seemed a wise way to find her own sense of leadership. As always, Sunfire continued to trot behind her.

There was one concern Ayla had yet to ask Roderick about, and as she made her way to his tent, her mind focused on Bree. The captain was just stepping out of the tent when Ayla approached.

"Roderick!" She called to him, picking up her pace. "The women have their orders. When I left them, they had already gathered their cooking pots."

Roderick nodded to her, "Very good. Now, there's more to be done…"

"Wait," she interrupted. "I've been meaning to ask you…about Bree and her family? Do you know what's happened to them? If they're safe?"

Roderick took a deep breath. "I don't know, Ayla."

Ayla shook her head. "But surely there must be some news…"

"No." He started again, "Ayla, Bree and her family were supposed to come here, but they never arrived. We don't know what's become of them, and we have no way of finding out." He stopped, letting the news sink in with her. "Unfortunately, there are bigger matters at hand."

Ayla nodded and looked away, toward where the women were still gathering metals. She thought of Bree's smile and her willingness to help. There were few braver in Ayla's mind. She thought of their first walk together. Bree would be fourteen by now, if she was still alive.

Ayla turned back to Roderick, determined to keep working despite her concern for Bree. She needed to believe that the girl was alright. "What else can I do?"

"You can follow me," he said and turned away, walking toward another part of the encampment.

Ayla followed Roderick through the tents. It didn't take her long to realize they were headed in the same direction that Sunfire had led her the first night she awoke in the Stone Wood. "Where are we going?"

"Where the fortifications are being built," Roderick answered. "Your presence there will encourage the men. We're headed east, away from the mountain range," Roderick explained. "This is a small valley sheltered by two ridges called the Dragon's Teeth by those who live here." Roderick pointed to the right and left of them, "See there, just over the tops of the trees."

For the first time, Ayla noticed the jagged points of the two cliffs sticking out over the trees on either side of them. The cliffs were a light color of gray compared to the green of the mountains behind them. Ayla thought that, indeed, they could have been teeth.

"This actually gives us one of the best defensive positions in the kingdom," Roderick continued. "Some supporters of Kelvinor have been encamped here for years without the king being able to root them out. Of course, he's never sent a full rmy before, only a small enforcement group. He's always underestimated them, and he ridges have always served them well."

"And you?" Ayla asked. "How did you come to support Kelvinor so fiercely?"

"Serving Kelvinor is in my blood. I was born for it." Roderick turned to her, "My amily was one of the few noble families to successfully hide within the common folk."

"But you became a captain in the king's army?" Ayla questioned.

Roderick nodded. "Yes. In order to serve Kelvinor, I decided to get as close to he enemy as possible. It served me well. I had the best training and . . .I found you."

The two walked for another few minutes, Sunfire still following a few yards ehind Ayla. Finally, they reached a clearing where she could see many men working. The ridges on both sides dropped straight down forming an entryway into that ection of the woods. The king's army would only be able to attack them from this lirection.

"The gap is a mere one hundred and fifty yards across. It will force the king's men nto a funnel as they attack, probably with horses."

Sunfire let out a short huff behind them, and they both glanced at the white east. Roderick wore a quizzical expression, "Do you always keep him with you?"

Ayla shrugged. "He follows me everywhere. I've never tried to tell him to go away."

Roderick's quizzical expression was now focused on her. "Tell him?"

"Well. . ." Ayla looked away, feeling rather foolish. Ahead of them, men were harpening large logs and planting them in the ground, forming a jagged slanted ne across the landscape. She pointed, eager to change the subject, "What are they loing?"

Roderick looked toward the men. "Setting up pikes to block the cavalry charge. He pointed toward the ridges on both sides. "We'll have archers up there as well. Mostly young boys. The height of the ridge will keep them relatively safe while they ive us cover."

At the edge of the forest, men were cutting down trees and shaving off the ranches. Others were making piles of branches according to size.

"They're building towers. The women who volunteer will be put there with large ats of boiling water and stones gathered from the mountainside. That will have to be repared later." He pointed to another pile of logs. "Those will be used to build more defenses on the ground. Walls for men to take shelter behind."

Ayla nodded, feeling a sickening feeling in her stomach. There would be much bloodshed here in just a few short days. "How many men do we have?"

"We don't know exactly," Roderick said. "We're working on a count. We think about a thousand or so. With the women, we may have a few hundred more fighting."

"And the king? How many soldiers will he send?"

Roderick took a deep breath. "From what I know, he has ten-thousand men that could march here in the time he has had to prepare. It wouldn't surprise me if he sent them all. The prince will no doubt ride with the force and may even fight in the battle." He looked her in the eyes. "He will be looking for you, Ayla."

She looked away from him and toward where the men were working. "I'll not leave."

Roderick shook his head, "I don't want you to. You're the reason these people are willing to fight. If you leave, what message does it send?" He took a deep breath "But I also want you safe."

Sunfire had trotted up and was nudging her shoulder affectionately. She patted his nose. "What do you suggest?"

Roderick also reached out and patted the horse. "Well, I think you need to be atop this fine animal. No doubt he'll help to defend you, and you'll be a glorious sight for our men, riding into battle for the Queen of Kelvinor." He looked toward the men building the defenses. "You'll have a guard around you. A few strong men who can be spared. If the battle begins to go the way of Talforland, you'll retreat with those men and head for safety along the coast. Gather another army there and fight again. You must continue to try until Kelvinor is regained."

"But what if the Talforland forces follow us to the coast?" Ayla questioned.

"They will." He turned back to her. "But the mountains will slow them down. They won't move as fast as a few horsemen on light mounts. You'll beat them by a week, at least."

Ayla nodded. "What about you?"

"My place is here, regardless of what happens."

Before she could respond, he turned and walked toward the men along what would be the front lines of the battle. She followed, along with Sunfire. She wanted to tell him that she cared too much about him to let him die here while she rode to safety. She wished she could find the words, but they did not come. He would surely think of her as foolish for having so much concern for him, a simple captain. She was a queen, after all.

They walked to the pikes and then along the gap between the two ridges. Ayla looked into the mud-stained faces of the men working. Many of them looked back, regarding her with curious, tired eyes. She had no urge to look away. Each set of eyes, each admiring and hopeful gaze, she met with a smile and encouraging nod.

It was time for Kelvinor to rise out of the ashes.

CHAPTER 22

THAT NIGHT, SLEEP ALLUDED AYLA.
         She could not shake thoughts of the battle yet to come. Even after the exhausting day was behind her, she could not close her eyes.

Sunfire was also restless. He pawed the ground outside of her tent, huffing and rolling in the dirt. He was agitated, nervous, and it made Ayla's heart stir to think he might be loosing his courage for the fight ahead.

Several hours of evening passed with Ayla continuously trying to quiet the horse as well as her mind. Finally, she slid off the cot and pulled on her day clothes. Lifting the flap of the tent, she went out to try to calm the horse one last time.

"What's wrong?" she whispered to Sunfire as she rubbed his back. "Are you worried about the battle, too?"

Sunfire took a sudden turn and pushed his nose into her back, causing her to stumble forward. When she turned back, he did it again. Remembering the night he had led her to meet the old man, Ayla took a few more steps forward and turned to see what Sunfire would do.

Happily, the horse trotted ahead of her and then stopped and looked back as if to say, "Are you coming?"

"I'm coming," she said and followed behind the horse as he led her into the woods again.

This route was different than ones she had taken before. They were making their way through the encampment and Ayla worried that they might wake the sleeping villagers. But the horse stepped softly between the tents and all Ayla could hear was the chirping of the night insects in the trees.

Finally, they passed through the tents and into the wilderness of the forest. With no path to follow, Ayla had to stay in the wake of the horse to avoid getting scraped by the thick branches. Some distance off, she heard the flow of water. It reminded her of her first adventure weeks ago on the river. Consumed by her new role, she had not thought of her dwarf father in some time. She wondered if she would ever see Otto again.

As they continued to travel, the sound of water grew closer until Ayla knew that they were approaching a river. Soon they emerged out of the trees onto a soft, sandy shore. Ayla looked down and could make out footprints. This must be the place the villagers came to gather water.

The river was wide, but even in the darkness of night, Ayla could tell it was not deep. The moon reflected off the water and Ayla could see the soft shine of stones beneath the glass-like flow.

Mountains rose up to meet the sky on the other side of the river and Ayla could make out the jagged cliffs called Dragon's Teeth stretching into the forest on either side of her.

Sunfire had stopped at the water's edge to drink. He didn't seem to have any intention of moving forward. Ayla patted his back and waited, whispering to the horse.

"Why did you bring me here?"

She stretched out and rubbed the top of his head. He closed his eyes and continued to drink, enjoying the bit of affection.

A splash shattered the sleepy sound of night and Ayla started.

She could hear her heart pounding in her ears as another soft splash followed and she realized the sound was coming from upstream and drawing closer to their shore. Sunfire huffed and took a step into the water.

Ayla tried to pull the horse back into the cover of the forest, but he wouldn't move. As the sound of splashing drew closer, she could stand to wait no longer, and she slipped into the brush along the shoreline, peeking out to watch the river.

After a moment, Ayla saw the soft outline of a thin boat moving through the water. Its captain was poised in its center, gently coaxing the craft along with the swift motions of a paddle.

The dwarfs made excellent fishing boats for the river, but Ayla had never seen a boat like this before. It was long and thin and glided across the top of the water rather than sinking into it. In a river so shallow, it was a perfect craft.

The figure in the boat turned toward the shore upon seeing the horse and Ayla ducked further into the brush.

"Hello!" a voice called out. "I know you're in there."

Ayla dared to peek out again. The boat was closer and the moonlight now seemed to reflect off a smiling face with a long white beard.

Ayla lost her fear instantly and stood up out of the brush. It was the older man she had met in the woods several days before.

She smiled, wondering why he was here again.

"Well, that's quite a different expression from when I saw you before." He hopped out of the boat and began to pull it to shore. "Can you lend me a hand with this, lass?"

Ayla obeyed and together they pulled the boat into the soft sand.

"A fine craft!" he continued. "Quick and never gets stuck on the rocks here. You see how the river's not so deep?"

Ayla nodded, but could think of nothing to say. The man turned to Sunfire and stroked his back. "How are you, my fine beast? Have you been taking care of this girl, here?"

"Yes!" Ayla piped up. "He has. He follows me everywhere."

The older man chuckled, "That might be difficult to do some day when you are parading around a palace."

"Sir," Ayla questioned, suddenly finding herself bold, "who are you?"

He only smiled and looked off into the woods. "I take it your young captain is feeling better?"

Ayla didn't have time to ask any more questions for at that moment, Roderick appeared out of the brush and swept Ayla behind him. His sword was drawn and ready.

Sunfire instantly placed himself between Roderick and the man and raised up on his front legs. He crashed back down and shook his head, preparing for battle.

"It's alright, Sunfire!" Ayla could hear the man calling over the chaos. "It's alright."

The horse reluctantly moved off but still grunted and glared at Roderick.

"Identify yourself, sir," Roderick said through clenched teeth.

Before the man could answer, Ayla tried to put Roderick at ease. "It's okay. He helped me. He's on our side, Roderick!"

"What are you doing here?" The captain wasn't backing down. "Your name, sir!"

The man took a deep bow, "Why, you know of me Captain Roderick Stronghear of Kelvinor. My name, I am certain is very familiar to you, though I am surprised you don't remember me as your helper in Halforton?"

Roderick's sword lowered slightly. "You're the peddler I met? You claimed Ayla."

He nodded. "And used the gold to buy this animal here from his captivity. You see, my name was once Baron Brighton Strongheart of Kelvinor."

Ayla knew the name as well. This was supposedly the man that carried her into the safety of the mountains sixteen years ago.

"Impossible," Roderick said forcefully. "Prove it."

The man gestured toward the boat, "If you'll permit me?"

Roderick nodded, and the man reached into the craft, pulling out an object wrapped soundly in brown cloth. He loosened its leather ties and let the wrapping fall, revealing a gleaming silver sword in its sheath.

"Lady Luna's sword, made especially for the Queens of Kelvinor."

Roderick's eyes widened as the man continued. "If you'll recall, grandson, no one but our family knew I took the sword." He gestured toward Sunfire, "Or that I knew where the two horses who became the parent of this one were housed after the war."

"Grandfather?" Roderick breathed and his sword slowly lowered.

The man nodded. "I have returned to continue my role in this drama."

Roderick suddenly dropped his sword and stepped forward, reaching out and embracing his grandfather. "I don't even remember you!"

Brighton just accepted the embrace and nodded. "I have been gone a long time."

When Roderick released his hold, Brighton stepped toward Ayla. "Now you know who I am." He held out the sword to her, "And this is yours. You're now old enough to use it. . .and you will use it."

Ayla took the sword, noticing the engraving of black birds on the blade and the runes along its hilt.

"The redemption of Kelvinor will come with the singing of this blad,." she read and looked up to the men for an explanation.

"The blade has always been called Redemption," Brighton explained. "It is a prophecy." He put a hand on her shoulder. "You, the words of your ancestors, this sword, Sunfire…they are all pieces. This is all meant to be."

CHAPTER 23

AYLA SLEPT WELL AFTER her encounter with Brighton Strongheart. She barely remembered climbing up on Sunfire and trotting back to camp, the two men staying close at her side. Roderick was speaking in low tones to Brighton and Ayla could not hear them. Her eyelids had closed while gripping Sunfire's mane, and she had leaned into the horses neck, Roderick's steadying hand on her back. She vaguely recalled the captain taking her in his arms and laying her on top of her soft cot.

The next thing she knew was light and the soft warmth of the morning sun touching her cheek. She opened her eyes and blinked, getting used to the day and letting the memories of the night before flood her mind.

Sitting up, she could see that the tent flap was opened. She instinctively looked for Sunfire, but his ever present shadow against the tent was missing from her view. She scanned the entire tiny room, but did not find it.

Neither did she find her familiar clothing.

Pulling the sheet around her, she got up and looked under the cot. Still, there was no clothing present. She did, however, find the boots and stockings and pulled them on. Pulling the sheet even closer around her, she peered outside of the tent.

Soldiers were milling about, preparing for the day. No one took notice of her and she looked around, finding her clothes hanging on a line a few yards away. They were dripping wet from presumably a recent wash.

Ayla frowned, not knowing exactly what she was going to do. She had no clothes and the day had started without her.

Quite suddenly, Ayla heard footsteps from the other side of the tent and before she could react, Brighton came whistling around the corner carrying a small bundle.

He looked different, mostly because he had shaved the long gray beard which once twisted down to his chest. It had been trimmed back to a simple beard and mustache. He wore a clean tunic with a white horse embroidered on the front and a belt with a massive, rather antique looking sword.

"Ah!" he said, seeing her. "I expect you'll be needing these." He held out the bundle and she took it, ducking back inside the tent and closing the flap.

"I'll just wait for you out here," Brighton continued. "Wouldn't want to intrude."

Ayla laid out the clothing on the bed and examined it. There was a tan tunic and belt with a place to keep her sword. On the center of the tunic was a white horse, much like the one she had seen on Brighton's tunic. But hers was far grander. The tunic was simple enough, but the horse was embroidered with fine silver thread. The shirt that was to go beneath the tunic was black and felt softer than cotton when she picked it up and pulled it over her shoulders. She put the tunic on next and then examined the breeches. She had never worn men's pants before and she was afraid they might make her feel a bit naked. Skirts covered up her legs well, but these pants hung in such a different way, revealing where her legs were. She pulled them on and tied them fast. Surprisingly, she found them to be much more comfortable than any skirt she had ever worn. The boots came next and soon enough she was pulling the tent flap back to greet Brighton.

She smoothed out the tunic as she stood before him.

"Wonderful!" she said, and spun around so he could see.

He handed her a ribbon, "Tie your hair back and you'll look like a true fighter."

She obeyed, pulling her unruly hair into a low ponytail. "What are we going to do today?"

"Be patient. You'll find out soon enough." His eyes glanced over her. "Your sword, girl?"

"Oh!" She suddenly realized it was still sitting beside her cot and she ducked back in to retrieve it. When she returned, she saw Sunfire trotting toward them gleefully.

"He knows it's your time, now." Brighton nodded to the horse as he approached, "Sunfire always seems to know the right thing to do, but you also must show him the way. It's not good to always follow. Sometimes you must lead."

Ayla patted Sunfire on the nose. "But what if he knows more than I do?"

"Then you must learn to know when to follow and when to lead." He chuckled,

Right now, you must follow. Come!"

Ayla followed Brighton into the encampment. It was still early morning and many of the children were just now getting their breakfast and preparing for the day. As they walked, a young girl stood up from the ground beside a campfire and ran forward.

"Lady Ayla! Lady Ayla!" she cried as she ran. "I have this for you!"

Brighton and Ayla stopped, waiting for the girl to reach them. When she stopped before them, she gave them a quick curtsy and then held out a small bundle of wildflowers.

"I picked them yesterday for you. My mum says their really weeds but I think they're pretty. What do you think, Lady Ayla?"

"They're beautiful," Ayla smiled at the girl, "like you!"

Ayla took one of the yellow flowers and placed it in the little girl's hair. She took another and tucked it behind her own ear. The little girl gave Ayla a broad smile and ran back toward her family's tent.

Brighton looked after the girl with his own smile. "I see you have earned the respect of your people. . ." He seemed to want to say more but stopped, playing with the whiskers on his face. Finally, he shook his head and gestured for them to continue.

They walked until they had passed through the village and into a small meadow where several boys were playing with sticks, knocking them against each other as if they were swords. Brighton stopped and gestured to the boys.

"They don't know it, but they have been training all their lives to be knights and swordsmen. This teaches them the basics even if they are only guessing at it. But you? You must learn to use your blade in a day."

Ayla shook her head, "But Roderick told me to stay away from the battle."

Brighton turned to her and took a deep breath, "I fear, Ayla, that the battle will come to you no matter how far you try to stay away. I can. . .see. . .you fighting."

Ayla looked into the man's deep, old blue eyes and they seemed to flicker with enchantment. She wondered how much he knew and what he wasn't telling her.

"Sir," she began, "are you a prophet?"

He chuckled, "Much is made of prophets!"

He shrugged and continued to make his way through the meadow. "I know things, Ayla. It is no more than that. I see them happening, and then they are."

"Then tell me what you see for the battle?"

Brighton frowned. "I see blood and tears." He turned to her. "And the rest you will see for yourself tomorrow."

He would say no more, and they continued to walk until Ayla spotted an old tree up ahead with many slashes cut into the trunk and the branches. As they got closer, Ayla could see the tree was dead and only held up by a bit of the cliff face that jutted up behind it. Brighton stopped in front of the tree, but Ayla seemed somehow drawn to it. She approached it cautiously and placed her hand on its trunk.

"This tree is dead. There's no life in it." She didn't know how she knew, she just did. It was the first time she thought she might understand what Brighton had been talking about when he mentioned being able to see things.

"That's why I brought you here," Brighton said behind her. "This is practice. Draw your sword."

Ayla obeyed. The ring of the sword's blade as she drew it from the scabbard sounded like singing, and she smiled. It was as if with the sword in her hand, she felt suddenly complete.

As she approached the tree, she heard Brighton say very softly, "Don't forget the pendant. Don't forget to ask it for help."

Ayla didn't forget and in the next moment, she felt her arm swinging the blade and felt an unknown power take over her mind. She led, finding the target with her eyes and letting the newfound strength and skill do the rest. With each swing she hit home, shattering bits of the tree until there was very little left to swing at.

Brighton had one eyebrow raised when she stopped and turned to him. "Good. Very good."

He drew his own antique sword. "Now for some practical swordplay."

Ayla didn't have to ask what that meant. In a moment, she was blocking blows from Brighton, amazed by her own speed and agility. She lost many times over the course of the next few hours, though, and as she did she grew more frustrated until finally, she stabbed her sword into the ground and collapsed.

"How am I supposed to fight tomorrow if I can't block anything?"

Brighton shook his head, "You're doing fine. Stand up."

"No," she said forcefully. "I'm loosing too much, and there won't be time to do it again tomorrow. I would be dead by now."

Brighton nodded, "Yes, you would. You forget one thing, Ayla, that I think you will have no trouble remembering tomorrow."

"And what is that?" she said, biting back.

"Tomorrow, the battle you fight will be to the death."

Brighton set his sword in the grass and kneeled next to her. "You're not really trying to kill me, and I'm not really trying to kill you. That gives me the advantage because I know how to check and pin a person without delivering a killing stroke. You don't know these things, and you don't have the desire to kill. It makes you weak."

The two were quiet for a moment as Ayla sat in the grass and thought. She never wanted to kill anyone, friend or foe. It seemed tragic and bloodthirsty.

"Brighton, sir," Ayla said softly. "The pendant is helping me. It gives me the strength to fight. . .but I know it can never destroy, only create. What if I kill while using the pendant?"

"That is a fine line," Brighton answered. "You must never ask the pendant to help you kill, only to give you courage to fight. You must find the will to take a life on your own." He shook his head, "War is the most tragic thing man invented."

Ayla sighed softly, suddenly feeling the weight of what she must accomplish in only a night. "So it's wrong to kill, but I must do it to save my kingdom?"

Brighton looked her in the eyes. "It is wrong to murder. But sometimes we must kill or be killed and there is nothing wrong with that."

Ayla nodded and lay back on the grass. "I don't know that I can practice anymore today."

Brighton examined the horizon, "The sun is going down. It's time to rest."

Ayla saw it, too. Just over the western ridge of the mountain, the sun was setting, letting the darkness slowly cover the terrain around them. They had been at practice all day. In the distance, Ayla heard the soft cry of a trumpet. She sat up, looking in the direction of the encampment.

"That would be the Talforland forces," Brighton sighed. "They'll be only a few miles off now."

"Will they attack?"

"Not until morning," Brighton explained. "They are confident they don't need the cover of darkness to win this battle." He turned to her. "Come. You need your rest."

Chapter 24

B UT AYLA DIDN'T REST that night. She could hear the soldiers getting ready for battle outside her tent, and the sound of metal armor banging and swords clanging into place would not let her forget the battle for sleep. It was even harder to sleep knowing Sunfire was not near by. She had grown so used to the horse's presence, but he now seemed content to stay in Brighton's shadow.

Finally, when she was convinced that no sleep would come, she pulled on her new tunic and pants. Placing her mother's sword on her belt, she lifted the tent flap with as much confidence as she could muster and stepped into the chaotic night.

She knew that most of the men would already be on the front lines, keeping an eye on the approaching army. Women were now heating pots of oil and water to be taken to the newly built towers, and the younger girls and boys were gathering the last few heavy stones.

Roderick and Brighton had both told her to wait here until she was needed. She needed to rest, they told her. She faced a long battle and possibly a long flight to the coast. But Ayla couldn't wait any longer. The battle was coming, and it was time to face it head on.

Placing one hand on the hilt of her sword and the other on the pendant around her neck, she set off through the woods, determined to do whatever she could to help prepare for the battle.

She had taken barely ten steps when the neigh of a horse caught her attention and looking up, she saw a streak of white pass through the trees ahead of her. A moment later, Sunfire was at her side, nudging her softly back toward camp. It was the first time she had seen him with a proper saddle, and he wore a warhorse's golden armor.

"No," she said to him. "I'm going, and you can either come with me or I'll go alone."

Sunfire nudged her again, harder, but Ayla did not fall back. Instead, she pushed past him and continued on her path to the front lines. Sunfire seemed to not know what to do. He trotted up along side her and huffed with frustration.

Ayla patted him but did not give in. After a moment, Sunfire seemed resigned to following her and Ayla pulled herself on his back.

"Don't get any ideas," she warned the horse. "We are going to the canyon, to the front lines."

Sunfire huffed again but obeyed.

As they turned the corner into the canyon, Ayla could see that something was not right. There were archers stationed on the tops of the cliffs and boys in the nearly complete towers the men had built over the last few days. Soldiers lined the front with pikes and stood at the ready, but every man's focus seemed turned in one direction – out toward the advancing army Ayla could not see.

Roderick stood in one of the raised towers. A shabby, hastily sewn, banner bearing a raven was propped up at his side, waving in the wind. Ayla could not hear what he was saying, but it was clear that he was shouting down to the open field below.

Ayla encouraged Sunfire into a steady trot and then, he edged into a run on his own. In a moment, they were galloping across the field toward the tower. As they approached, Landon ran out to stop them.

"Lady Ayla!" he said. "You can't be here! You were supposed to…"

Ayla jumped off Sunfire's back and ran for the tower without a word. She surprised herself by how easy the dismount had come. She suddenly felt herself fill with confidence and energy.

But Jovan was standing there, blocking the ladder of the tower. He put both his hands on her shoulders and held her fast. "Lady Ayla! You must stop!"

Ayla looked up to Roderick but he was too focused on the situation that lay before them to notice her. She strained to hear his voice.

"… Commander of this Army. You will deal with me and only me. Lady Ayla is…"

And then Ayla heard the familiar voice of the prince of Talforland, "What?

cared? Hiding? You produce the Lady to negotiate or I'll kill this girl and her
amily now."

Roderick was silent and Ayla could think of only one person the prince could be
eferring to. In one strong shove, she pushed the startled Jovan aside and climbed the
adder into the tower.

"Ayla! No!" Roderick looked down, noticing her for the first time, "You can't
ome up here."

As she climbed into the tower and turned toward the gap in the mountains, she
aw an army so vast that it looked like the ocean suddenly covered the field before
er. They were still some distance away, out of arrow shot, she reasoned, but their
resence nearly made her loose her balance. Roderick held her steady.

Looking down, she spotted the prince and his entourage bearing a white stan-
ard. They were just close enough to shout over the pike men below. With them
vas Bree, her hands tied and captive atop a horse. Even from a distance, Ayla could
ell her face was bruised, and there was blood on her lips. Her eyes did not hold their
sual playful spark.

"Well, well." Ayla could tell the prince was sneering. "Look at the Princess of
Kelvinor. How you've changed since I saw you last."

Ayla leaned on the front railing of the tower and shouted down to the prince;
ourage and anger filled her. "What do you want?"

The prince laughed. "That's a silly question, girl." He may have had a smile on his
ace, but his eyes shot daggers at her. "Surrender to us."

"No," Ayla said, drawing her sword from her belt. Ayla shot a quick look at
Roderick who only nodded to her.

Prince Noland laughed again, "Listen! She thinks this rabble army of theirs can
vin this fight. What lies have you been telling her, Roderick?"

The captain shook his head. "No lies. Just truths that have been long withheld
y you and yours. Talforland is the only place that keeps lies, and we are the people
f Kelvinor."

The shout that followed from the pike men below the tower gave Ayla more
ourage. The prince looked furious. He brought his horse up alongside Bree and held
knife to the girl's throat. Ayla could not stifle a small cry.

"Enough talk!" Prince Noland spat at them, "Surrender or this girl becomes th first victim among your supporters."

Ayla could find no words to reply, and she looked franticly to Roderick. The cap tain crossed his arms and leaned back, seeming indifferent. "No," he said. "You won kill this girl, not if you're smart." He turned his head to the side with an air of cockines "Of course, if you were smart, you wouldn't think that we would give up the kingdon for the life of one, even a friend. Kelvinor is much more valuable than that."

Ayla said Bree's name under her breath as her heart beat faster and faster. The gir had closed her eyes as the edge of the blade pressed tighter against her skin.

"And why," the prince began, "would I think the girl worthy enough not to kill?

Roderick uncrossed his arms and leaned against the railing in front of them. "No martyrs. You kill that child and word of her death will bring about such a will to figh in this land that you will never regain Kelvinor. Even in Jade City, the people will ris up against you! I doubt those of Kelvinor in your own army would remain loyal if you committed such an atrocity. No, you will not kill this child!"

The voices of the men around them rose again; they banged their shields in defi ance of the prince. Some of them raised blades in the air. Ayla could tell they wer eager for a fight. Even in her own heart, she felt a new feeling. She was eager for bloo in a way that that seemed almost holy. This fight would be bloody and tragic, but i was being fought for all the right reasons.

The prince spat on the ground and Ayla could see a wild look in his eyes, mucl like the look he had when he invaded her bedroom. "Will you surrender, or do I hav to kill you today, Roderick?"

Roderick was still looking at Ayla and she turned toward the battlefield, lookin at the endless expanse of the enemy.

"No," she said. "We will not surrender."

Prince Noland lowered the blade from Bree's throat and without another word the party spurred away toward their own troops.

Roderick put a hand on her shoulder, "You surprise me more every day."

She turned to him. "What now?"

"We prepare for the fight." He looked over the field in front of them, "They' come at any moment. Take Sunfire and ride for that ridge." He pointed to a plac where a band of archers had gathered. "They'll protect you if the battle goes badly, and they can get you to the coast and help you raise another army."

Ayla nodded and began her descent down the ladder. As she did, she could hear the sound of heavy marching feet.

"Hurry!" Roderick shouted down to her.

She hopped off the bottom rung and pulled herself onto Sunfire's back. Brighton topped them just a moment before they made a dash for the ridge.

"Here," he said, handing something up to her. "A cape so that you will look magnificent and radiant for all the soldiers to see."

Ayla took the cape without a word, and she and Sunfire ran for the ridge at full gallop, a pace that nearly unseated her.

Sunfire dodged in and out of trees and then up a steep trail in the rocks. He was confident, steady, and Ayla gave him barely any direction at all. Finally, his hoofs scraped the roof of the ridge, and lifted them to the safest place to view this bloody battle.

The troop of archers bowed at the sight of them.

"Please," Ayla said, "stand up."

They did so but Ayla said no more to them. She simply turned her attention to the battle below.

CHAPTER 25

RODERICK COULD SEE FOR at least a mile from the top of the tower, and all he could see was the advancing Talforland army. He had vastly underestimated their numbers, and he cursed himself for making the same mistake he thought his enemy might make. Moreover, the Talforland army was well equipped, its men well rested and fed. Numbers might not win a battle, but the situation was looking grim on all counts.

He looked for Ayla on the northern edge of the Dragon's Teeth ridge. She and Sunfire were just arriving and as he watched, she fastened a blue cape to the back of her tunic. She was looking every bit the rightful Queen of Kelvinor. The sight stirred all the hope that was left in him, and he drew his sword. The pike men below him immediately came to attention, ready to do their deadly duty.

"Landon!" Roderick shouted to the base of the tower and nodded to the soldier he had appointed archery captain. It was time.

Landon drew his sword and held it high, ready to give the order to fire. Roderick yelled to Jovan on his other side and the soldier took off for the forest. He had his own deadly orders to act out.

Roderick watched the enemy closely, hoping he had guessed their tactics right. He had fought alongside the prince in many battles, and he knew Talforland strategy well. The prince was bull-headed and predictable, especially when a battle was an almost certain victory. They were flaws Roderick had always cautioned him against, and now, the captain hoped to use them to his advantage.

The enemy's cavalry was moving into position. He had guessed right.

The prince knew they had pike men and infantry on the front lines. He could see them well enough. The prince could also see the bands of archers in the towers. It was a good, defensible position. Noland would know that sending in infantry was a mistake; archers could take out large numbers before they even reached the Kelvinor rebels. Cavalry was the better choice, and it was exactly the move Roderick was counting on.

The horses charged the front lines, ready to plow down the infantry and pike men waiting for them.

Landon dropped his sword and immediately the archers let loose their bowstrings, raining down arrows upon the enemy's heavy cavalry as it charged. They hardly slowed the enemy down, but Roderick saw a few riders fall. The prince had sent a thousand charging horsemen at them and a few hundred arrows did little good. Still, it was all they could do until the horses reached the Dragon's Teeth.

Roderick was yelling out orders to prepare for the impact, "Pikes to the front! Steady them in the ground!"

The men obeyed, putting the weight of two men on each pike, holding them firmly against the ground. Roderick could see the men sweating, and one pair of younger men, maybe only in their teens, struggling with their pike.

"Steady!" he called again as the sound of the horses hoofs beating the ground grew closer. "Steady!"

Roderick stole one last glance at Ayla on the ridge before the cavalry slammed into the pike men below. She was almost shining over them, and he could feel the power of her courage resonating on the field below.

Talforland's army crashed into the force of infantry and pike men and instantly the world turned upside down with the screams of horses and trampled men. Footsoldiers were fighting furiously among the dismounted horsemen, trying to avoid the blows of those still on horses. Pike men dropped their pikes and joined the fight.

Roderick pulled their shabby banner from the tower and waved it furiously. He looked toward the forest, knowing Jovan would see him even if he could not see the many horsemen hiding in the trees. The soldier would know it was time. Roderick dropped the banner and swung half way down the ladder of the tower, stabbing one cavalry officer as he rode past. "Don't let them pass the ridge!" he called over the heaving chaos around him.

He jumped down from the ladder and quickly found one of the many rider-less orses frantically rearing in the midst of the battle. He pulled himself into the saddle, nmediately facing several other horsemen. His sword rang true against the enemy nd in seconds, he had broken free of the fight and was riding even deeper into the attle.

The sound of more hoof beats caused many heads to turn and a few to be lost. Coderick bested his own opposition due to the distraction and chanced a glance oward the sound, already knowing what he would see.

Jovan was leading their own rush of cavalry toward the battle from the forest. His troops would trap the enemy in a deadly wedge between pike men, infantry and orsemen. The prince had underestimated them this time. Noland could not see the ebel cavalry, and had assumed them not a threat. The ambush would be a success, ut a small one.

Roderick let out a small cheer of victory and spurred his horse toward the nearst tower, hoping to get a look at battle from above. The captain leapt from his horse nd took hold of the ladder, hoisting himself up and over the rails. Above him, archers ere firing for the enemy, careful to avoid their own men.

Roderick put his hand on the last rung, only to find the footing below him suddenly give way. He looked down and saw a horseman coming around for another low. The enemy cavalry man's first strike had shattered all of the rungs below Loderick's feet to splinters.

Pulling with all his might, the captain managed to swing his feet up and avoid the nemy's sword as the horseman charged again. A hand caught his shoulder, and he ooked up to see one of the archers, a villager, hoisting him onto the top of the tower. As Roderick gained his footing, the same man notched an arrow and let it loose. The aptain's eyes followed it as it struck home, dismounting their attacker.

There was no time for deserved thanks, though the two men found a second to od at one another in gratitude.

Roderick surveyed the field below him as the archers continued to fire. He ould make out the prince's white mount still far from the battle. Beside him there as another grand rider. Roderick knew it wouldn't be the king. The king would ever leave Jade City because of his illness, but also because of the chance of rebelon within the city walls. This had to be the priestess.

The captain didn't have time to dwell on his thoughts. The prince was moving men forward, and as they drew closer, Roderick could make out the distinct insignia on their uniforms. These were archers, and they were almost in range.

Roderick looked across the tops of the towers and found Landon, still focused on the field directly below him. The captain slid his hand down the side of the tower and found the prearranged signal. He banged the small bucket over and over again against the wood keeping his eyes on Landon until the soldier turned.

Roderick pointed his sword toward the approaching archers and Landon saw them. In an instant he was calling orders to the men around him and the message was being carried all over the field. Bows were being turned toward the approaching threat. But now they were short of arms against the enemy below them and though the enemy horsemen were trapped, Roderick and his men were still outnumbered.

Worse still, the prince now had a force of infantry moving in behind the archers. They would be ready to rush the field at any time, with or without a hail of arrows reigning over them. The prince had men to spare and if some of them were killed by their own archers, it wouldn't matter. Life mattered very little to the prince in terms of war.

This was going to be a very brief, very bloody battle.

Jovan suddenly appeared below the tower. "Sir! The Lady Ayla!"

Roderick nodded. "Jovan, go!"

The man obeyed, spurring his horse toward the canyon where Ayla still looked out over the battle. Roderick took one last look at her and swung down from the tower, rejoining the battle below.

A moment later he heard a startled cry from the tower above him. It was the same archer who had helped him minutes before.

"Captain! They're using fire!"

Roderick looked at the sky about him, and just as he had expected, it was filled with a cloud of arrows. What he had not predicted was their burning tips.

"Take cover!" he yelled to those around him. "Shields at the ready!"

Roderick was not carrying a shield. He rolled just as the arrows were coming down and took cover in the small space underneath the tower. Others on the field were not so lucky. Roderick saw three men fall to burning arrows. He couldn't guess how many others had succumbed.

Smoke instantly filled the air. The defenses were burning along with the wooden towers. Men were leaping out to avoid the flames, but were now in the heat of the battle below them. For the villagers and young boys manning the towers, it would be slaughter.

But again, Roderick did not have time to dwell on his thoughts. The Talforland infantry had hit the front lines full force, completely overwhelming anyone in their path. Roderick was locking blows with soldier after soldier, his only hope for Ayla. Somehow she had to escape. Somehow Jovan had to get her to safety.

He stole glimpses of the ridge, waiting for Jovan to take their only hope away from the battlefield.

He dodged a strike to his shoulder, and thrust another stab at his attacker. The man went down, and he whirled around to face a new enemy. His blade blocked a swift swing to his head. As the two swords rang together, Roderick realized he was eye to eye with the Prince of Talforland. The Talforland men were moving away from them. This was a battle the prince wanted to fight alone.

Roderick attacked this time, but blow after blow was blocked. The prince had just entered the battle and his strength was fresh.

"Short of breath, Captain?" the prince sneered. "Need a rest?"

Four more strikes passed between them, and this time, Roderick had the upper hand, knocking Prince Noland to the ground. Before he could strike him, though, the prince rolled away. Noland wiped his lip, streaking blood down his face.

"You need more lessons," Roderick retorted. "Perhaps you need a keeper a bit longer, boy."

The prince thrust at him again, but Roderick dodged easily. Then came a shower of fierce attacks. The prince's blade was strong and solid. Exhausted, Roderick knew he couldn't stay in the fight much longer. His eyes found the ridge for a brief moment. There was Jovan, as he should be, but something was terribly wrong.

Ayla was screaming. Roderick could tell even though he could not hear her over the chaos of the battle. Jovan had just run through the last archer defending her and had turned to face Ayla, still atop Sunfire. Roderick's heart sank in his chest.

Jovan had betrayed them.

Roderick managed to push aside another blow from the prince and in a mad rage, the captain tackled him. Fists began to fly between to two men. Roderick was screaming, blinded by his own fury.

Hands grabbed the back of his tunic and despite his protest, hauled him back to his feet. The men around him were of Talforland, and he fought to escape their hold, pushing and punching, drawing blood wherever he could. His body was screaming in pain along with his heart as he fought until one of the men landed a sharp punch to his gut, and he toppled over.

In front of him, he could hear the prince laughing. "The Queen of Kelvinor indeed. Look!"

The men pulled him off the ground and turned him to face the ridge of the Dragon's Teeth.

Jovan had pulled Ayla off the horse. Her blade was still in her hand, waving wildly and fruitlessly in the air. Sunfire was rearing back, afraid to strike at Ayla's attacker in fear that he would hurt his beloved mistress.

It was then that Roderick saw a rider step out of the woods and onto the ridge. It was the priestess. Sunfire suddenly cowered and the rider reached down grabbing Ayla by the back of her tunic. One swift blow from the hilt of Jovan's sword, and Ayla fell into the dirt.

"No!" Roderick yelled in desperation, again struggling against his captors. It was futile. Talforland had Ayla and all around him, the men of Kelvinor were falling.

The prince strode up to him and punched him across the face. Roderick slumped again, his whole body burning with agony.

"Don't worry," the prince said in his mocking tone. "She'll be well taken care of."

But a second later, all turned to chaos again, and Roderick suddenly realized he was free. Looking up from the ground, he saw Landon atop a horse locking blades with the prince. The soldiers around him were distracted.

Roderick pulled his knife from his boot and planted it in the side of one of the men as he rose. A well placed punch toppled another one as he drew the blade from the fallen man's side.

Landon managed to break free of the prince and gallop to Roderick's side, pulling him up onto the horse.

"Captain, you're hurt!" he called as they galloped away from the battle.

Roderick shook his head, "No time for that! Get to the ridge. Ayla's in trouble."

Landon urged the horse faster. They would cross paths at any moment with the priestess and Jovan. Roderick could not believe the young soldier had betrayed them.

He could see them in the distance, and he leapt from the back of the horse, rolling to safety and rushing at Jovan.

"Traitor!" he called to the man, their two blades locking against one another.

He suddenly felt a great force overwhelm him, and he was knocked back, falling in the dirt a few feet away. Jovan laughed and Roderick looked up, eye to eye with a rider on a black horse.

"Priestess Maura!"

She smiled, a dark look spreading across her face. Where once there had been a hallow beauty, there was now only darkness and power.

"Hello, Roderick," she spat, "or shall I address you as a duke now that your rebels are determined to bring back the old kingdom?"

She raised her hand again, and the tree above him and Landon began to sway furiously. Branches cracked and fell around them until finally the tree itself gave way, missing Roderick by inches as it crashed to the ground. Landon was thrown from his horse as it panicked, and was caught up in some of the tree's branches. The young soldier broke free a second later, wielding his sword with anger.

"Well," Maura's voice seemed to mimic the prince's tone, "I don't seem to quite have the hang of it yet, but I'm sure I'll manage."

She un-tucked the red pendant from her robes and held it out for them to see.

"Oh, and now you're confused," she teased. "I'll enlighten you. Kal, not to be undone by the Creator God, made this pendant as you know, but it was thought lost. I have had it in my possession ever since, passed down from the cursed daughter of Talfor. I am its heir, the heir to her line, and the only one who can control it. Unfortunately, the blue pendant must be fully restored before this one will regain all of its power." She sneered, "But now, that one has stirred and as a consequence so has this one. Now I have both."

Roderick shook his head. "You'll never have both. The Creator's pendant can only be used by the heir of Kelvinor. The true heir."

The priestess laughed. "The prince will be the true heir after he marries this girl. When she dies suddenly and tragically afterwards, he will have control of the pendant. And as the prophecy foretells, the pendant will reawaken completely when it is aligned with another royal blood line. Or did you not understand that part?

> *When blood of royal line*
> *united with its own,*
> *so shall Kingdoms build*
> *and Kingdoms fall*
> *with the light of ancient stone.*

This has been scrawled across the altar in the fallen temple of Kal for years! It was scrawled there by the prophets of Kelvinor. This girl was always meant to reawaken the stones completely by marrying into the line of Talfor! Until that time, both pendants will be of little strength." She sneered, still fingering the red pendant. "This one can only destroy."

She raised her hand again, and Landon gasped, feeling the life begin to escape him. She twisted her hand around as if choking the soldier as Roderick looked on in horror.

Landon fell to his knees and Roderick fell with him, holding the soldier as he gagged, searching for air.

"Stop this!" Roderick looked up at the priestess, but she was unrelenting. "Jovan!" he pleaded. "Whatever loyalties you have to the prince... this is your friend!"

Jovan turned his head away from the dying man and said nothing.

Roderick looked desperately for anything he could use against the priestess and her power, but all he found was a rock. He quickly had it in his hand and sent in flying through the air. It bounced helplessly away from the priestess, and she laughed again.

"Sticks and stones! Really, Roderick!"

But it wasn't sticks and stones that stopped her. The brutal lunge of an old soldier out of the branches of the fallen tree nearly dismounted the woman. She managed to hold on to her horse as it twisted and bucked against the weight of the attacking man, ut her attention was turned away from Landon and he coughed, trying to recover.

Brighton had hit the ground hard after leaping on the woman's horse and now he drew his sword, yelling with an aggression far deeper than his age. "Stand down you she-devil! I'll have the whole of you!"

Maura whirled her black beast around and held the pendant tightly in her grasp. Brighton cringed at the sight of it. Seconds later he was knocked backwards, into the trees.

Roderick took the few precious seconds to pull Landon to his feet and the two took cover in the woods. As Maura turned her horse toward them once more, she found only the forest staring back at her. She wouldn't have time to search.

Hoof beats sounded nearby and Roderick and Landon knelt down, trying their best to stay out of view.

"Priestess!" Roderick heard the soldiers calling to the group. "The prince calls you. Have you retrieved the girl?"

"Yes. We'll report." Her voice was not nearly as impish, "What of the rebels?"

"They're in retreat. The battle is won. The prince will leave a small regiment to track down the survivors."

"Excellent." Roderick could almost feel her eyes scanning the woods around them as she spoke. "Tell them to search this area twice as hard. And search it soon! The enemy captain and his companions may be hiding here."

Roderick heard hoof beats again as the priestess and riders rode away.

Roderick looked at Landon and gestured for him to follow. Slowly and carefully they made their way through the forest to where Brighton had been thrown by Kal's pendant.

They found him lying on his back in the brush of the forest floor. His arm was bent at an odd angle and a horrible gash stretched across the back of his head. Blood was already soaking into the earth, and his eyes were closed.

"Grandfather," Roderick whispered to the old man as they sat by his side.

Brighton opened his eyes and let out a ragged breath. "I am dead."

Roderick shook his head. "No, Grandfather."

Brighton choked out a small chuckle, and Roderick saw flecks of blood appear on his lips. "But I will be soon. You must listen."

"No," Roderick said again. "We'll take you…"

"Oh, be quiet," the old man said, suddenly stretching up his uninjured arm and taking his grandson by the shoulder. "There isn't much time. You must listen!"

Roderick took his grandfather's hand and placed it gently on his chest. "Alrigh We'll listen."

Brighton took another short breath. "There is a prophecy the priestesses of Ka claims is about the red pendant. The Pendant of Destruction."

Roderick nodded. "Maura told us."

Brighton smiled despite his pain. "It is incomplete. She only uses the part she ca claim. The rest says that creation will always defeat destruction and the raven will ris above the bear. You understand this?"

Roderick nodded.

"Good. Now, you must let the pendants regain their power…"

Roderick shook his head. "No! Let Ayla marry that pig?"

Brighton stopped him. "There is another way…but first I must tell you that yo are not alone. The people of Halforton are still loyal and…they will help you fight th prince. Though I fear that is not the only power you must go against."

Roderick listened as the sad, wet nose of Sunfire suddenly brushed the side o his face.

"It was by their blades and mine that the legend of the Freeland witch was cre ated to protect the heir of Kelvinor. They above all people will believe you and figh with you. Go to them now!"

"And the other way to help Lady Ayla?" Roderick asked. "How must I do that?

Brighton chuckled and more blood flecked his lips and beard. "The answer lie in your heart…"

Chapter 26

AYLA WAS FRIGHTENED.

Jovan was supposed to be taking her to safety, but instead he had ruthlessly slaughtered the archers protecting her, and was now raising his blade against her. She pulled her sword, still unable to comprehend what was happening.

Ayla blocked the first strike, but she struggled to find the will to fight against one who was her friend.

"Jovan!" she cried. "What are you doing?!"

Jovan gave no reply and took another swing at the Queen of Kelvinor. Sunfire took a few unsteady steps and reared in protest. Ayla raised the silver sword against Jovan again, but suddenly found it limp in her hand. She couldn't control the weapon.

She only caught a glimpse of the lady rider on the black horse as she stepped from the woods. Power radiated from her like heat from the sun.

And then the world went black.

She vaguely remembered Roderick's voice and faces passing before her. She felt the pounding of hoofs underneath her, and caught a glimpse of the plains rushing by. Time seemed a plaything. She knew days were passing and yet, there were only minutes and seconds she was aware of. Those times her mind was screaming for answers. Where was Sunfire? Where was Roderick? What had become of the rebellion? Was he even still alive?

Ayla sat up suddenly, her heart racing and her mind filled with fear. Visions of Roderick fighting in the battle filled her head and the darkness around her gave her no relief. She could see nothing in the room and felt only a hard, cold floor beneath her.

Her hands started to search, finding only more stone. She could feel the ridges of the bricks but nothing else. There was no sound to give her any idea of where she was, only horrible, deafening silence.

"Hello?" she said, just to make sure she was awake and alive. Her voice echoed in the small stone room, but there was no response.

Then, out of the darkness, she heard the echo of footsteps. She felt her way toward the sound and discovered a small opening guarded by iron bars. A second later she heard doors opening, and a light peeked into the tiny room. She shielded her eyes, letting them adjust to the brightness as the footsteps continued toward her.

When she opened her eyes again, a fierce gaze greeted her, illuminated by the light of a bright lantern.

"Well, well. My Lady Ayla, haven't we earned quite a name for ourselves?"

Ayla recognized the voice of Priestess Maura at once. "It was you on the black horse!?"

The priestess narrowed her eyes on the girl. "Yes. I had to come and get you before you spoiled my plans. It was very convenient, though, that you did manage to retrieve the pendant."

"Convenient?"

The priestess nodded, holding up a red stone, letting the light reflect off of it. It was identical to the blue pendant except in color.

Ayla immediately grasped at her neck, looking for the familiar stone. There was nothing there.

"Oh, I couldn't let you keep it. You'll be marrying the prince tomorrow and then the pendant will regain its full strength. So will this one. Its twin, if you will."

Maura let out a long laugh, her eyes flashing wildly. Ayla noticed that the pendant's red stone seemed to pulse as the priestess held it, clutched tightly in her hand. No doubt the red pendant was leaking its own evil intentions into Maura's blood. Where the Pendant of the Creator had given Ayla strength and courage, this one seemed to be giving Maura a taste of ambition and greed.

A sudden shuffle and small groan made them both turn.

"Must be your friend waking up," Maura said. "I'm sure you'll have a lot to talk about."

The priestess smiled at her again, turning with a great flourish and returning to the entrance of the prison. Ayla listened as doors opened and Maura's footsteps grew quiet. She looked into the black for a long time after her, wondering about the power of the red pendant and what new power a marriage might bring. Ayla touched her face in the darkness. She was alive, at least. As long as she was alive, there was hope for Kelvinor.

A tiny voice rose from the cell directly across from her. "Hello?"

Ayla recognized Bree's voice at once.

"Bree! It's me, Ayla!"

"Oh!" Ayla could hear the girl moving around, and her voice was suddenly closer. "Lady Ayla, I'm so glad it's you. You being alive and all. I thought we was both dead out on that field. I'm so glad it's you."

Ayla reached her arm through the bars, "Can you reach me?"

A second later she felt Bree's hand in hers. The girl took it and held it to her face. "Oh, lady Ayla, what are we going to do? No one knows we're here and there's no way out. No passages or anything. . ."

Ayla knew that if there had been a way to escape, Bree surely would have found it. "Are you alright, Bree? Is your family down here somewhere?"

"They're dead." Ayla could hear the tears in the girl's voice. "The prince killed them."

"I'm sorry." Ayla thought about the man she had met only once who had given his life to help her. "Truly. I am sorry."

Silence followed for what seemed like a long while. Bree held on to Ayla's hand a wept with both joy and a deep sorrow. Her family was dead, but here was her friend to help her. Maybe there was some hope left.

"Bree," Ayla said finally. "Your family was very strong. You're strong, too. We'll get out of here somehow. When I am queen, we'll build a monument in the courtyard to honor your family, and they'll be celebrated as heroes."

Doors opened again in the darkness and shut quickly. Fast footsteps returned and Ayla made out a small light coming toward them.

"Oh goodness!" Bree cried. "Who's it now?"

Ayla held Bree's hand tightly as the figure approached. She could see the outline of a woman's long dress. She held her breath, hoping the priestess had not returned.

Bree let out a small cry as Madam Grayheart appeared in dim candlelight. She held a small candle in one hand and raised the other, holding a finger to her lips.

"Quiet!" she commanded sharply, "We can't be discovered. I'm here to help you."

Ayla heard the distinctive song of keys dancing in Madam Grayheart's hand as she fumbled to unlock the cell door. She reluctantly pulled her hand back from Bree's and felt her way to the door.

"That foolish, fat grounds keeper in the temple." Ayla saw the woman's hands turning the key as she spoke. "He'll believe any woman who shows him a bit of attention! Ha! I told him I'd lost my master set of keys. Imagine! I've never even had a master set of keys, but if I did, I'd certainly never lose them."

The door was unlocked. Ayla pushed it open as Madam Grayheart turned, taking the light with her to Bree's cell. Ayla stepped into the passage and waited, Bree's quivering voice calling to her.

"I don't trust her, Lady Ayla. She's a right hard one."

Ayla remembered how Bree had feared the madam, but now, they didn't seem to have a choice but to trust her. She also remembered her dream. Madam Grayheart had once served her mother, and it was very likely that she was still loyal to the line of Kelvinor.

"Quiet, girl!" Madam Grayheart spoke. "Do you think I would be freeing you if I were not here to help?"

"She's right," Ayla whispered as the woman swung open Bree's cell door. "Come on. We have to trust her."

For the first time since the battle, Ayla saw Bree. She stepped into the candlelight from the dark cell, filthy and bruised. The fierce, rebellious girl Ayla had known was gone and there stood a skinny, quivering child, completely afraid of whatever her future might hold.

Ayla took her hand once more, smiling in an attempt to rekindle the girl's hope. She was desperate to find the spark in Bree's eyes she once knew. "Let's go."

Ayla and Bree followed Madam Grayheart down the corridor.

"We'll have to go out a different way. The entrance is heavily guarded," Madam Grayheart explained as they passed two heavy wooden doors.

"They'll know you helped us?" Ayla said as they walked. "They saw you come in?"

She nodded, "There was no other way."

Ayla did not argue. She was grateful for the madam's help and knew that the hope of many people rested on her success. "Where are we?"

"In the temple dungeons. But this passage leads to a hidden staircase that will take us to the stone gardens outside the temple walls."

Ayla remembered the place. It was where all the discarded, magical gods of Alforland had been placed after their worship was no longer necessary. It was where the statue of Kal now rested.

Madam Grayheart quickened their pace, and Bree and Ayla had to almost run to keep up with her long stride. She turned a corner and for a second Ayla lost the candlelight. She gripped Bree's hand even harder and pulled the girl to follow faster.

Finally, Madam Grayheart slowed and shined her light along the right side of them, feeling the stones with her hand. "Quick! Run your hands along these stones and see if you feel one that's different. It should pull outwards."

"You mean you don't know exactly where it is?" Bree said, her voice frightened.

The madam sighed, "It's been a long time since I've been sneaking around the grounds, Brenia."

"Yes, I bet you got into tons of trouble," Bree said under her breath and Ayla was relieved to hear a bit of old sarcasm in her voice.

"Believe it or not, child," Madam Grayheart answered, still running her fingers along the wall, "I was once as mischief-filled as you."

"Really…" Bree said with interest and then cried out, "I think I found it!"

Ayla turned and looked at Bree just as she was pulling a stone from the wall. The wall began to slide out and all three stepped back. The wall continued to move, sliding to one side, revealing a winding staircase.

"Go ahead." Madam Grayheart pushed them forward, handing Ayla the candle. "I'll close the wall behind us."

Ayla mounted the steps first with Bree following closely. The steps were steeper than they looked, and it took a few seconds for their feet to get used to the climb. Holding on to the walls, they climbed up four steps and waited.

Ayla could hear the wall sliding shut, but she didn't see Madam Grayheart. Then a voice shouted out of the darkness.

"Go! Run!"

Bree and Ayla looked at each other, fear in both their eyes. As the wall slid completely shut, Ayla swore she heard the sound of many footsteps coming down the corridor. The two girls turned and began to climb the stairs as fast as they could finally dropping on their hands and knees. The stairs had become so steep that no one could possibly climb them standing up. A few more feet, and Ayla felt like she was climbing a wall, not a set of stairs. She could barely hold the candle and still make her way upwards.

"Madam Grayheart could never have climbed these steps!" Bree called up to her.

The girl was right. The older woman would never have been able to make the climb. Maybe she had tricked them into going alone.

Finally, Ayla's free hand hit a wooden roof below a small platform above the steps. She set down the candle and pulled herself into the short space. She then turned to help Bree.

"How do we get out?" Bree asked as Ayla hoisted her upward.

"I don't know. How do most of the passages open up?"

Bree pushed on the wood panels above them. They seemed to move, but didn't give way. "There's got to be a latch or something holding it down. Feel along the edges."

The two girls did and in no time found two iron clasps holding the wooden planks in place. They released them and both pushed up on the door above them. It gave way and they held it above their heads, peering out over the stone garden beside the temple. Moonlight shone down brightly all around them.

Bree quickly ducked back down, leaving Ayla standing with the wooden door. A few feet away from them were the long robes and heels of a priestess.

Ayla could tell she had her back turned and the woman was whispering, almost chanting. Ayla held her breath and listened. Suddenly, the voice changed and rose into the air. Ayla realized at once the priestess was Maura.

"Kal, Goddess of Time, I am here as your servant!"

Ayla was startled when she heard the second voice, deep and resounding yet still feminine. It seemed to whisper, breaking in and out. It was coming from the broken statue.

"Servant, what news do you bring to me?"

"Much," Maura answered. "The wedding will take place tomorrow, and then the two pendants will be restored. Your power will be restored as well."

"Excellent," the voice came again. "And the Creator's Pendant?"

"I have brought it for you." Ayla could see Maura lift something out of her robes. She thought she heard the statue breath heavily for a second.

"Place it at my feet. Its power will make me whole once more."

Maura obeyed, carefully kneeling and placing the Creator's pendant at the statue's feet. Ayla could see it sparkling in the moonlight.

"My Goddess," Maura said quietly. "The pendants are not yet powerful enough to create…"

"The pendant has power like yours. Weak. But it still can…make…me…grow." The ground rumbled slightly and Ayla gripped the wooden panel. The statue laughed darkly. "By this time tomorrow, my image will be restored and with the power of the red pendant, I will be ready to take back what is rightfully mine. Go now. Leave the Creator's pendant with me."

Ayla pulled the panel back down over her head and waited. A few seconds later she heard footsteps above her head. Maura was leaving.

Ayla turned and looked at Bree. The girl was biting her lip and holding her knees tightly. "We have to go up there, Bree."

She shook her head. "They'll catch us."

Ayla nodded, "Maybe. But if we stay here, we don't accomplish anything. This kingdom needs saving!" She extended her hand, "Come on."

Bree took her hand, and Ayla pulled her up, towards the panel. Slowly, the two girls lifted the wooden board up and peered out again. There was no one in the garden, and the only sound was the chirping of crickets.

Ayla pushed the panel aside and crawled out onto the wet grass. She looked immediately for the pendant as Bree made her way out behind her. She found the pendant on a small stone platform. The only thing left of the statue that had been there was a pair of ornately carved woman's feet. The pendants chain was wrapped around the feet and the blue stone was glowing dimly. Ayla slowly crawled toward the platform and extended her hand.

The voice came - the same as she remembered when it spoke to the priestess "Daring, little girl." It whispered into the night air.

Bree jumped and looked around. "Ayla?"

Ayla hushed her sharply and continued toward the statue. It spoke again.

"I may not have eyes to see you, but I know you are there."

Ayla's fingers touched the stone. It was warm, as it always was when it was working.

"This pendant is weak. It works slowly yet it is the only one that creates. Mine works fast, and is more powerful than you can imagine."

Ayla took the pendant and placed it around her neck. She looked into the air and whispered. "You are only the trifling remains of an old statue. I'm not afraid of you."

She stood up and turned to Bree, helping the girl off the ground. Nothing more came from the statue as they made their way across the temple grounds.

"Ayla! That statue, it..."

Ayla hushed the girl again. "We need to decide where to go from here."

Bree shook her head, "I don't know..."

Ayla and Bree made their way along the wall of the temple and across the empty field toward the outer wall. The outer wall would offer the cover of trees and long grass, but they would still have to cross a field with nowhere to hide or duck for cover. They heard no one following them and began to run. Ayla had no trouble keeping a good pace in her tunic and pants, but Bree's dress held her back. She was reminded of their first meeting when they raced like two little girls along the inner wall of the castle.

Ayla reached the wall first. Bree came in a few seconds behind her, breathing heavily from exhaustion. They now had cover and moved through the trees and the grass along the wall as fast as they could.

"There should be a ladder around here somewhere," Bree said. "I think I remember it. Haven't used it in forever 'cause I got caught on it once. They still use it sometimes but not too often. It's all overgrown and such with vines."

Ayla nodded and they continued to fight through the foliage, struggling to stay concealed. They could both hear guards marching along the wall above them. There was shouting, though it was too far away to make out what was said. Ayla could only guess that their escape had been discovered.

Finally, Ayla's hand brushed the wooden rungs of an old ladder, carefully built onto the wall. She looked up to see several guards passing above them in a steady march. They continued along the wall, leaving the two girls and the ladder behind.

"The shifts are about three minutes apart," Bree whispered quietly behind her. "I remember from when I stole this chicken and. . . ."

Ayla nodded, not letting the girl finish, and began to climb, trusting Bree to follow. The wall was at least sixty feet high, and once they passed the tops of the trees, they would be in clear view of the guards. She stopped half-way up and just below the foliage. Ayla turned to Bree, putting a finger to her lips.

"We wait," she said to the girl quietly. Bree nodded.

Another guard passed overhead a few minutes later. Bree was right about the timing between patrols. Now was their chance.

Ayla continued their climb as fast as she could, hand over hand, until she could pull herself easily over the top of the stone wall. She immediately ducked down, pressing herself against the stones and hoping to stay out of sight. Bree was right behind her and followed suit. The two stayed down, ducking along the wall and looking desperately for cover. They didn't have long until the next patrol passed by.

But on the other side of the wall, toward the city where Ayla had seen the homes of the nobles, they could hear screams and the sounds of chaos below. Fresh fire licked the sky and through the darkness, Ayla could see smoke rising. The two girls were unable to resist and slowly made their way across the narrow walking path on top of the wall. They peered over the edge, amazed.

The city below them was indeed in chaos. Troops of armed peasants darted in and out of the city streets bearing flaming torches. Soldiers were being struck down and nobility ran for their lives, struggling to fight with useless ornamental swords. Down the wall some distance, a band of peasants were hauling a large wooden log against the gates to the palace. Others held wood flats that looked like pieces of roofing above their heads to avoid the arrows of soldiers stationed above them. Looking out above Jade City, Ayla could see smoke rising everywhere and in the distance, she made out an advancing group of soldiers.

"The city's in rebellion!" Bree cried above the noise.

Ayla now faced a desperate decision. They could escape the castle and risk being killed in the chaos below, or they could turn back and risk captivity. Neither seemed like a good choice. And they didn't have long to make a decision. At any moment, soldiers would be on patrol along this part of the wall.

"Come on!" Ayla grabbed Bree by the shoulder and pulled her to the left, in the opposite direction of the gate.

"Where are we going?!"

"I don't know," she admitted, "But away from the soldiers seems like a good idea. Maybe we can find a safe place to crawl over the wall and into the city. Somewhere where the rebellion isn't so rampant?"

Bree nodded, trusting and following her.

After a few moments of crouching along the wall, making their way slowly, Ayla could see the tops of the soldiers' heads as they made their way toward them around a sharp curve. She looked over the wall for any hope. There, a few feet away, was a small path of stones leading down the wall. Bree saw it, too.

"Do you think we can make it?"

Ayla nodded, "We have to. I don't see that we have a choice."

Bree pushed past her and stepped over the side. "Here, I'll go first. Don't want you to break your royal neck."

But Bree was slow going down the wall and the soldiers were moving faster now it seemed. Ayla stepped over the wall to follow just as they turned the corner and saw the two girls.

The soldiers made a dash for them, and both girls hurried to climb down the wall. Ayla was only a few feet down when her foot slipped on the stones and she was left hanging there, trying to get a better grip.

"Bree, run!" she called as an armored hand reached over the side of the wall. "Go! Just go!"

She looked down as the hand caught her wrist and began to heave her back onto the top of the wall. Bree was still standing there, looking up in desperation. "Go, Bree! Find help!"

Bree hesitated once more before nodding and darting into the chaos of the city.

The hand tossed Ayla down on the stones and an instant later she was looking up at a whole troop of soldiers. It was reminiscent of her first encounter with the prince and Roderick in the woods.

From out of nowhere, one of the soldiers lifted her up and struck her hard across the face. A second later, she saw only darkness.

CHAPTER 27

AYLA AWOKE WITH A SHARP sense of pain across her cheek. She was instantly aware of being slapped, and she blinked several times as her eyes opened, feeling unwanted tears start to form.

A hand grabbed her chin and lifted her head up. She was staring into the blank, formless eyes of Priestess Maura.

She instantly tried to step back, but found that her arms were held fast by two soldiers. They were in the temple, and it was decorated ceremoniously. Incense burned on the altar and fresh flowers had been placed everywhere. Her tattered tunic had been taken away as well. She was wearing a red gown, but she could still feel her own boots on her feet. How strange it seemed to have had them through her entire new life, the only remnant of her life among the dwarfs.

Maura was dressed differently as well. She wore robes embroidered with the image of a bear and of flames. Her black hair was pulled up behind her head, and she carried a long staff topped with a red jewel.

"Well, well, well… thought you could escape, did you?" Maura spat at her.

Ayla glanced down, searching for the Creator's pendant.

"Oh, don't worry," the priestess sneered. "The pendant's right where it belongs."

She stepped back and pointed to the altar with her staff. Both pendants were there, sitting atop the golden box like beacons of good and evil. "All we need now is a groom and we can start."

"No!" Ayla fought against the guards, pulling left and right wildly.

Maura slapped her again, and Ayla tasted blood on her lip.

"Better stop that," the priestess said darkly. "Wouldn't want to ruin that pretty face on your wedding day."

The doors opened behind them, and Ayla looked back. The prince was entering with an entourage of soldiers and the king at his side. The older man looked weaker than she remembered, and Prince Noland looked sickeningly stronger. He strode toward the altar like a bird of prey, his beak-like nose only highlighting the sneer on his face.

"My lady," he said, giving her a mocking bow. He turned to the priestess. "Are we ready, then?"

She nodded and pulled a small knife from within her robes. Ayla struggled again Maura gave her a threatening glare.

"Both must extend palms. This union will be made with blood."

One of the soldiers took Ayla's hand and thrust it forward, holding it tightly in place. The prince extended his hand willingly.

"With blood will we consummate this marriage," Maura began in a very dry, ceremonial tone. "The blood of this prince and princess shall flow forth and touch the ground of this land, the land to which they will pledge their work for all the days of their lives."

The priestess reached out and slashed open the palm of Ayla's hand. The girl screamed and gasped as a searing pain shot up her arm. The prince made no complaints except for a small flinch as the priestess slashed his palm open. Ayla thought she heard a small cry from the entourage behind them, but she was too focused on her own pain to give it much notice.

"The blood will touch the feet of the gods and the floor of the temple, the spirit they will commit their souls to for all of their lives."

Never will I serve the gods of Talforland, Ayla told herself. *Never will I serve Kal.*

"And now, may these two hands come together so that these two hearts may be joined. In blood, these two will commit their hearts to each other for all the days of their lives."

The prince extended his hand towards her, and the soldier gripping her wrist forced her hand toward his. There was nothing she could do but watch in horror as the two hands came closer and closer together.

The next few seconds were a blur. She felt herself being knocked backward. The soldier let go of her wrist, and she pulled it away only to feel another grab her hand

She heard the priestess scream over the clanging of swords as she was pulled away. When the world stopped spinning, she looked up to see it was Roderick holding her bleeding hand and leading her away from the small skirmish that was taking place in the temple.

"Roderick?!" She let go of his hand and flung her arms around him. "What are you doing here? What happened?"

He shook his head and pulled her off of him, "No time to explain. Look." He held out the hand that had pulled her away. It bore a cut similar to the one the priestess had made on her and Prince Noland.

"I don't understand."

Roderick took a deep breath. "Ayla, you and I are from the same royal bloodline. I was a noble, descendant of Kelvin just like you. If we.. .if our..."

Ayla suddenly understood. She turned away from him and looked out toward the temple altar. "Oh, no..."

She could see the two stones pulsing with light and out of the corner of her eye, saw that the priestess was beginning to notice as well.

Ayla ran to the altar, her hand gripping the Creator's pendant just as Maura gripped Kal's pendant. Both had flung the jewels around their necks in an instant.

Ayla was immediately struck by an overwhelming sense of power, but she also felt courage, loyalty, and love. She held up her hands to see blue light dancing between her fingertips. She looked toward Roderick to find that he was staring at her with amazement. Her jet black hair was standing on end and the red dress she was wearing turned a deep shade of blue.

Dark laughter filled the air. Ayla turned towards Maura. Only she wasn't Maura any longer. A dark cloud was dissipating around the priestess. Her hair had turned completely white and her eyes were black, only dark soulless wells stared out at the world. This new form immediately turned its attention toward Ayla.

The battle between Roderick's small force and the prince's men had stopped to stare in wonder at the transformations of the two women.

"So, a servant of the Creator God!" The unmistakable voice that had come from the statue filled the room. Only this time it was not empty and hallow, it was filled with power. "He sends a child to conquer me?!"

Every hair on Ayla's neck stood on end. "Kaliarta?"

She nodded. "Foolish Priestess. I am the only one who can use this power properly." She turned her attention to the prince and his entourage. "And foolish, pitiful royalty. Did you really think I would give any power to you after you scorned me for so many years? Did you really think this union could save you?!"

She flicked her hand at them and the entire force was knocked back, excluding the prince and the king. They looked absolutely horrified as she walked slowly toward them.

"Did you know, King of Talforland, that your son has been slowly poisoning you for years?"

The king looked at his son.

"He was going to kill you as soon as he wed this girl. He had your final meal all planned."

"Don't believe her, father!" The prince shouted, his sword still raised from the skirmish. "Why should you believe this witch?!"

Kal was still approaching them, taking each slow step like a snake slithering toward its prey. "Why do you think the healers could find no cause for your illness? Why do you think the prince insisted that your meals be made in a separate kitchen? And why do you think he rushed so willingly into marriage? Would that not make him an adult able to take the throne from a dead king?"

Kal stared at the two of them, and a few seconds passed in tumultuous silence. Ayla could almost see the evil whispers of Kal floating in the air. However truthful her statements, she was poisoning the minds of both men with revenge and hatred.

Without warning, the king suddenly lifted his blade against his son and brought it down hard, "You lying traitor of a son!!!"

"No, father!" The prince blocked and the two began trading blows, Noland obviously faster and more skilled, but trying simply to dodge his father's angry blows. "I don't want to kill you!"

"You've been trying to for years." The king made another thrust, "Why not do it now where all can see?"

Ayla continued to hear the clanging of their swords as Kal turned back to her. "Human minds are so fragile." She smiled and began her slithering walk towards Ayla.

You are, after all, only human yourself, Ayla. Give up now, and I'll spare you and your friends."

Ayla began to feel the Creator's pendant working, and she realized that it was reflecting some sort of magic from Kal. She could see the red pendant glowing round the demon's neck.

"That pendant can only destroy?" Ayla said simply. "But this one creates. I understand now. They're opposites."

"Very good," Kal said sarcastically. "What of it?"

"You need both of them to be all powerful. Otherwise, your power can always be canceled out."

Kal narrowed her eyes. "And I shall have both of them."

She waved her hand at Ayla, but the force did nothing. She waved again and the blue pendant only glowed in response. Kal gritted her teeth and suddenly rushed at the girl. She tripped a few seconds later. A pair of vines had grown out of the earth under the marble flooring and wrapped around her ankles.

Ayla had barely thought about vines tripping the demon before they were there, doing exactly what they were asked to do. The power startled her, but she was feeling the will to use it grow with each passing second.

Kal touched the vines and they disappeared in flames. "Anything you create, I can destroy!" she spat and a second later, stones were falling from the temple ceiling above her.

Ayla dove for cover behind the stone columns, getting hit by some of the falling rocks. She crawled away from the rubble and found herself at the feet of the statue of Tione, the Talforland God of War. Ayla touched the feet of the statue and thought about creating life.

A second later, she ducked down as a mighty roar filled the temple hall and the armored statue stepped down from his platform as a full flesh and blood man.

"Very good!" Kal laughed as the warrior shook the dust from his new body, "but can you control something that is worshiped to destroy?"

The statue turned on Ayla with uncontrolled fury and raised his enormous blade. With no time to escape, all Ayla could do was cover her eyes as the blade came crashing down.

But the killing blow did not come. Roderick was there. He blocked the massive sword and made a quick swipe to the beast's ankles, cutting them both. The beast fell back.

"The bigger they are, the slower they move. I've got this one!" Roderick jumped forward to take on the statue again as Ayla turned back toward Kal.

The demon was infuriated. She sent a long stretch of flame ripping toward Ayla as she crawled up from the floor.

Rain, Ayla thought, and seconds later, thunder rolled through the hall and storm clouds appeared on the ceiling sending a blast of water down on them all.

With this new display of power, the prince's entourage got up from the floor and fled into the night. Roderick's men were clapping and cheering.

"Very clever!" Kal retorted. "Guess we'll have to do this in an older way." She picked up a sword from the ground.

Ayla backed up, looking around desperately for a weapon.

"My lady!"

Across the hall, Ayla spotted Landon holding up her gleaming silver sword.

"Sunfire saved this for you!" He gave it a toss and she caught it lightly and perfectly, feeling the pendant's power already taking over the blade.

When Kal came at her, she was ready, blocking every blow swiftly and accurately. Her mother's sword did its job well. One thrust and then another, the blades rang against each other for several minutes. Finally, Ayla's sword struck home and nicked the demon on the shoulder. Kal stumbled back in pain and shock.

"What?!"

Ayla nodded to the wound. "Did you forget how it felt to be in a mortal body…"

But Ayla stopped short. The demon had once lived in a statue and then had wanted the statue to be restored, even slowly. Kal's power must be contained in the remains of that image.

"What happened, Kal?" Ayla pried, knowing that she must tread carefully. "Needed even a mortal body to become whole again? Willing to take the first thing that came your way?"

Kal growled back at her, "After being trapped in that ruined statue for ages, I had no choice."

"I thought your power was contained in the pendant?"

She nodded. "Power, yes. My infinite power. But my spirit, my will, was cursed to ʈay in the statue by your Lord Kelvin. He then had it destroyed." She laughed. "But ʈe feet remained and I stayed quiet all these years."

She thrust at Ayla again and the girl dodged, answering with a blow of her own. ʈe feet, Ayla thought, if they destroyed the feet it was possible Kal would be killed.

Ayla delivered several strong blows, Kal barely holding her back. The two were ʈangerously close. Suddenly, the demon leapt forward, dropping her own sword and ʈlutching at Ayla's throat.

Ayla leaned back and tried to escape, but Kal was too close and her sword swung ʈselessly away. Kal's fingers grasped the pendant around Ayla's neck and pulled. Ayla ʈould think of nothing to do, but reach out and take the demon's pendant in her hand ʈs well.

The two fell on the floor in a heap, Ayla's sword clattering across the floor. Each ʈeld the others pendant in her grasp. They pulled and struggled against each other ʈke two children, rolling right and left on at the marble floor. Ayla had worked for ʈears helping her dwarf father shave down wood for furniture. Her hands and arms ʈere strong.

Still grasping at Kal's pendant, Ayla drove a hard punch to the woman's stomach. ʈhe coughed, letting go of the girl and struggling to get away. But Ayla had locked ʈer fingers around the red pendant's chain like a harness.

In one hand, Ayla pulled the demon and in the other she picked up her sword. ʈcross the hall, she found Roderick and the rest of the men putting the living statue ʈf Tione to rest. They cheered when they saw her.

"We haven't won yet. Follow me."

They followed Ayla out of the temple to the courtyard where the ruins of the ʈncient statues were standing. Ayla found the one of Kal easily, two stone feet standʈg atop a short pedestal.

"No! No!" Kal was screeching as she raised her blade.

It took the sword of Kelvinor only one strike to shatter the ancient stone to ʈieces.

Kal screamed, but the screaming quickly turned to laughter.

Ayla jumped back, letting the demon go as she felt the woman's skin grow ho
The demon broke away and stood in front of the ruined statue.

"Foolish girl! I knew you would take my bait! Forbid this statue be rebuilt. . .
was my prison! Lord Kelvin put me in there, and only a sword of Kelvinor could eve
set me free."

She let out a long stream of laughter as her skin began to boil. The woman wa
beginning to change shape in a hideous way.

"Now I am free to roam in whatever form I see fit. Now I am not restricted by th
confines of this mortal body!"

They all watched in horror as what was once a woman, twisted and grew int
a horrible shape. The red pendant seemed to stretch with it, forming a sort of colla
around what was the woman's neck. Finally, the shape formed together in the dark
ness and the huddled group of rebels saw what they were facing.

An enormous black dragon stood above them.

CHAPTER 28

THE WORLD AROUND THEM became blazingly hot, and Ayla felt the ground shaking. Large cracks opened up in the earth and threatened to swallow them whole. The group hung on to the fallen statues for dear life, trying to keep their balance.

Flames erupted from the cracks around Ayla, separating her from the rest of the group.

"Roderick!" she cried out as the shaking earth knocked her on her back and into a circle of fire. The dragon roared above her, raising its terrible wings and lifting itself into the air. She could see nothing as the beast rose into the black night above her. Nothing but the hideous glow of yellow eyes and the red pendant pulsing with power around the dragon's neck.

The flames burned hotter with each passing second. Ayla could see the magnificent blue dress starting to burn in places. An ominous crevice split the ground beneath her, and by the light of the fire, she could see that something was moving inside of it. She managed to crawl a few feet away, but the flames prevented her escape. Inside the crevice, she could see ghastly figures, like men with charred skin and claws for hands. They stretched out, reaching for her ankles.

She slashed willfully with her sword and one of the creatures screamed as the blade split its charred skin. It sank back into the crevice, but another and then another were reaching out to her. She stabbed and slashed at them, holding them back.

She heard the flapping of wings coming down on her and she looked up. The dragon was descending, sending an evil stream of fire toward her. Ayla dropped her sword and held her hands up, thinking of the water.

This time, she felt liquid bubble up from her hands and spring forward into the flames. As the dragon swooped down on her, a waterfall shot up from her hands, forming a protective hallo around her. Steam filled the air as the two forces collided. Ayla continued to hold her hands up as the water poured down around her. The water seeped into the earth and the horrible creatures sank, screaming, back into the crevices, their skin smoldering.

When the dragon lifted back into the sky, Ayla turned her attention to the flames around her, letting the water do its work. Soon the fire was gone and she stepped over the crevices, rejoining her companions.

Far above her, the dragon was turning for another pass.

"Roderick!" she fell into him, holding him tightly. "I have an idea. I need you to go. Take cover in the temple."

He shook his head. "My place is here."

Ayla let him go and looked up toward the dragon. It had turned its attention elsewhere. She followed its gaze across the vast field and found the front gate where, even from this distance, she could see the wood cracking.

Suddenly, the gate fell in and a flood of peasants and rebels emerged onto the castle grounds. The dragon flew toward them, eager for blood.

"Oh, God," Roderick whispered under his breath. "It will be a slaughter."

Ayla turned back to him. "Go to them!"

She didn't have time to hear his response. Her feet were already carrying her across the palace gardens toward the small stone courtyard where she had met the king for the first time. Her own wind blew at her back, pushing her forward.

She reached the courtyard and slid on the stones, her feet giving way beneath her. She fell in a heap, but didn't take time to worry about the searing pain that shot through her legs. Her hands felt the shapes carved into the marble floor. A dragon, unicorns, fairies, a dwarf. Then she found it. The image of the three griffins fighting against the dragon. She didn't know if it was a prophecy, but she knew she could give the image life.

Her hands touched the three beasts in succession, and the marble floor began to shake around her as they began to emerge from the images.

It was like watching a chick hatch from its shell. The marble stone cracked and the stone griffins rose out of the cravings. As they did, the stone turned to flesh, and ney began to shake off dust and debris. As they regarded one another, their beaks issued shrieks that filled the air, and Ayla had to cover her ears. It sounded like the cry of an eagle, only each shrill scream ended with a roar.

The beasts regarded the sky and cried to each other again as their eyes found the dragon. They looked fiercely toward Ayla, and she crawled backward a few feet, hoping she was right. The feathers on the griffin's necks rose and ruffled as they looked from one to another, again. The biggest of the three stepped toward Ayla and cocked his eagle-like head. His lion's tail flicked behind him and he raised his wings out to his side. He then bent his front leg and made the unmistakable gesture of a bow. Ayla nodded her head in reply. The moment seemed to last for an eternity before the three creatures lifted themselves into the sky and made for the dragon.

As they flew, Ayla looked into the crowd of peasants and rebels for Roderick. Everyone seemed to be staring in shock at the dragon above them and as it let out a streak of fire, they scattered in all directions, seeking cover in the darkness.

As the crowd dispersed, Ayla found Roderick among a small group of determined soldiers, ready to fight the enemy. They raised steel shields and held their weapons high.

Ayla started down the hill toward the fight, ready to join the battle once more. She sheathed her sword, running faster and faster, listening to the griffins' cries above her head. She watched as they shot toward the dragon, their claws extended in terrible fury.

The dragon turned and sent a stream of fire toward its new threat. The griffins spun and twirled away from the flames in an elegant spiral. They looked like bees swarming around the giant beast, tearing into its flesh as they dove in and out. The dragon bent and turned wildly in the sky, shooting strands of fire and biting at the creatures.

The dragon caught one of the griffins in its jaws and shook it relentlessly. Another of the griffins landed on the dragon's neck and drove its claws deep into the demon's flesh. The jaws of the great creature relented and sent its prize spiraling helplessly through the air. The wounded griffin landed with a shriek and rolled across the ground toward the small band of soldiers. Ayla watched as they scrambled to get out of the way.

The two griffins in the air screamed with fury and came down on the dragon's back. The demon wasn't able to hold the burden and stay aloft as the creatures' claws tore through the web-like flesh of its wings. Slowly, it began to sink out of the sky as the griffins continued their assault.

The dragon caught another of the griffins in a stream of flame as its heavy body landed on the field below and shook the earth. It snapped out, trying to catch the beast in its mouth. But the other griffin was there, bearing its claws and sinking its sharp beak into the dragon's nostrils. The demon cried out in pain and shook the griffin off its face.

The one remaining griffin landed on the ground in front of the dragon and shrieked wildly. The soldiers took their positions around the creature, holding it in a small circle with their swords. It threw fire around the circle, pushing some of the men back, but their steel shields held most of the soldiers fast. Ayla joined the circle, crouching behind Roderick's shield and redrawing her sword.

The great beast reared, raising its front claws in the air. It brought them back down, sending a thundering earthquake throughout the ground and shaking some of the men off their feet. The griffin lifted back into the air to avoid the blow.

Hunched over, the dragon began to whip its long scaly tail in and out of the circle. Men went flying through the air. Ayla watched as Landon prepared to take on the blow. As the tail swept toward him, he stuck out his blade and impaled the beast's tail; it caught him and threw him through the air.

Landon's sword barely seemed to irritate the creature even though Ayla could see streams of blood ebbing out of its tail. The circle began to break, and a few men fled toward the temple. Roderick moved himself and Ayla back, away from the danger.

She gripped the Creator's pendant around her neck and ducked down, planting both hands on the ground. She focused all of her energy on what she wanted to do.

Roderick looked up in surprise to see thunderclouds forming in the air above them. On the ground, he watched as large roots seemed to spring up from the earth and fly toward the dragon. Hail began to fall from the sky.

Roderick raised his shield over his head and took cover as the hail began to come down. He tried to cover Ayla but she stopped him. "Don't worry about me. Get the dragon!"

He looked up to see the dragon charging toward them and realized that it was coming for Ayla. The griffin was there, but would not be able to hold off its blazing anger. Roderick stepped out in front of Ayla and raised his blade, preparing for anything.

The dragon did not stop. Roderick could see dark acid dripping from its teeth as flames streaked toward him. He held up his shield, forcing back the flames.

The roots were now growing out of the ground, ripping up the earth around them and twisting around the dragon's clawed feet, holding it in place. The dragon fell forward only a few yards from Ayla and Roderick. It quickly lifted its front claws off the ground and began to tear at the roots growing up its body. The griffin came down, planting its claws in the dragon's back and tearing at its flesh with its sharp beak

Roderick leapt forward, slicing his blade into the dragon's stomach. He tried to pull it back but found it stuck fast in the dragon's hide. The dragon howled in pain and twisted back toward him, turning its attention away from the roots that were gripping its body. It roared, lifting itself up as high as it could muster.

Ayla stood up from the ground and held one hand toward the sky. Lightening came down from the clouds and struck the dragon's heavy jaw. It twisted and shook with pain, but the beast's heavy scales seemed only singed by the strike.

Roderick turned to her. "Do you still have a plan?"

"Plan?" Ayla shrugged, "Slay the dragon?"

The dragon broke free of the growing roots and moved swiftly, swinging its tail again. Roderick and Ayla were directly in its path, and there was no way to avoid taking the blow. They were knocked backwards; Ayla's sword flew free of her hands, and Roderick's blade was still stuck fast in the dragon's stomach.

Roderick recovered quickly, but he was without a shield or sword. He was now weaponless except for a small knife. He pulled it, grateful to have something in his hands.

Ayla landed hard on her back. She gritted her teeth against the pain and sat up on her knees. A few feet away she could see a discarded sword lying in the dirt. Her hands reached for it.

The dragon whirled around and snapped at Roderick. He barely avoided the

230 ~ *K. A. Thomas*

strike, ducking under the jaw as it passed dangerously overhead.

A second later, Roderick sidestepped the dragon again as its head came crashing down, jaws open, ready to devour. He swung the knife just in time and caught the dragon just above its eye. The creature reared, shaking its head wildly at the sting.

Ayla took the blade in her hand as she watched the dragon go for Roderick again.

"Roderick!" she yelled, catching his attention and leaping to her feet. Wind, she thought, sending the blade soaring through the air gracefully. He caught it, pulling it out of wind's grip. Ayla turned for her own blade, now some distance away. The wind again would pull it to her. She thrust out her hand and in a moment, found the hilt in the air.

As she turned toward the dragon, she saw Roderick lifting his blade again and again toward the dragon, holding it back. The griffin had lifted in the air and was preparing to come down on the dragon's back once more. But the dragon was batting at it with its tail, keeping the creature at bay.

Ayla held the sword tightly in her hand and summoning the wind for a third time, pulled her arm back and sent the blade spinning through the air.

The dragon's jaws were coming down on Roderick when the blade struck with unearthly speed and implanted in its forehead to the hilt. It roared, rearing back and twisting in agony. Ayla could see blood streaming down onto the earth as the dragon's skin began to twist and shrink, bubbling on its surface.

The griffin swooped down onto the dragon's neck, biting into its flesh and pulling free the red pendant. It shrieked at its victory and flew across the field to Ayla, Kal's pendant locked tightly in its beak.

She watched as the griffin flew over her, dropping the glowing red pendant from its mouth. It fell toward the earth, its light slowly fading.

Ayla caught the jewel out of the sky and opened her palm, regarding its stone. As she did, the glow subsided completely and Ayla felt that for the time being, the jewel was quiet.

She looked across the gardens to where the dragon had been. She saw only the griffin circling above a bloody figure on the ground. Roderick was making his way toward the spot and Ayla followed, catching up to him just as they approached.

In the grass lay the bloody body of Priestess Maura, her blank eyes staring up into the sky. A few feet away, Ayla found her mother's blade and picked it up.

Maura suddenly took a breath and her eyes moved over to Ayla.

"You won't destroy Kal. Her spirit will live forever no matter what you do to me."

Ayla said nothing. She opened her palm and looked at the red pendant. It was warm and glowing ever so slightly. Ayla kneeled beside the priestess. As Roderick watched, she placed Kal's pendant in the dirt next to Maura's battered body. Vines began to grow out of the ground and surround the evil object.

Ayla took her own stone in her hand and stood.

"The pendant of Kal will be taken deep into the earth and buried so that her power will never be discovered by any of her servants ever again."

The priestess gritted her teeth and glared up at the girl. Ayla knelt down next to Maura and touched her forehead, speaking softly. "Since you love Kal so much, your body will hold her spirit in captivity for the rest of the ages."

Ayla thought of the stones from the mountain and the broken statues all around her. She thought of the rain, of creation, and she let the power of the Creator's pendant flow through her hands and into the priestess. Slowly, Maura's skin turned a shade of gray, and as she opened her mouth for one last protest, stone closed in over her. Soon she was nothing but a statue lying in the grass, her life and soul concealed in marble.

Ayla turned to Roderick, still speaking softly. "We'll bury her deep in the earth as well and build a new temple above her, a temple that celebrates creation."

Roderick nodded, still taking in all the events of the evening.

Ayla turned and looked back toward the temple. She saw a figure highlighted by the moonlight swaggering toward them, a drawn sword in its hand. As it drew closer, Ayla saw the prince emerging out of the darkness. There was blood on his sword, and he wore a crazed grin on his face.

"Bow down, subjects! The king is dead. Long live the king! Long live the king!" He laughed and then stopped short, catching sight of the remaining griffin as it landed near Roderick and Ayla.

"You!" he pointed to Ayla. "Witch!"

She shook her head, watching as others emerged from hiding in the temple. "I pity you, sir."

"You pity me?" he roared at her. "Why would you pity me? I am the king! I am King of Talforland!" He laughed manically, never taking his eyes off Roderick and Ayla. "And you are traitors! Kill them. Strike them down! I'll have the whole world when they are dead."

The prince spun around and yelled at the people emerging from the night around him. "Take them down. I command you. I am your new king now!"

But the people were now moving toward Roderick and Ayla. Even the prince's men who were coming out of their hiding places were not moving to support him. Instead, they began to encircle the prince as he yelled at them, cutting him off from their captain and new queen.

"What are you doing!?" he shouted at them. "I am your king. Kill the traitors! Kill the traitors!"

Landon appeared in the circle of figures, holding his arm. Ayla could see the bone jutting out and the young soldier was growing pale as the blood dripped down his tunic and armor. With his uninjured hand, he drew his blade. "No man or woman can rule without the support of his people," and he pointed to Ayla with his blade. "I serve the Lady Ayla! She is the Queen of Kelvinor."

A shout of support went around the circle of men and the prince swatted at them wildly with his sword as they closed in around him. Suddenly, he broke and ran at one of the men, knocking him over and punching him repeatedly.

"Traitor! Traitor!" he cried, dropping his sword and drawing back his fist again to deliver another punch. Landon ran over to free the man and then pulled back.

"Jovan!" he cried.

"Help me! Please!" Jovan yelled, trying to knock the crazed prince off of him.

Landon hesitated and then charged forward again, grabbing the prince from behind and throwing him off of Jovan. He then hauled the man to his feet and pushed him away from the circle.

"You're not welcome here!" Landon shouted in anger at the soldier who had once been his friend.

But Landon could not see the prince recovering behind him. Noland pulled a knife from his belt and stood, glaring at Landon's back.

"Landon! Watch out!" Ayla shouted, but it was too late. The prince ran at andon, the knife lifted high in the air. Landon turned around just in time to see the

rince charging.

Jovan leaped forward, pushing Landon away and taking the full force of the knife

low in the center of his chest.

Ayla cried out as the prince pulled the blade back and then struck Jovan across

he face, sending the injured and bleeding soldier to his back once more. Landon

ulled his blade with his good arm.

The griffin left the side of Ayla and Roderick and flew toward the prince. Noland

creamed as the creature dropped down on him, knocking the knife from his hand

nd carrying him into the air, its massive claws gripping the back of his armor.

The griffin shrieked, causing everyone to cover their ears. The deafening roar

hat followed echoed through the valley as the griffin circled the group of men and

hen flew back to Ayla and Roderick, dropping the crazed prince in front of them.

The griffin let out a short shriek as it landed and regarded Ayla with its giant, hawk-

ike eyes. The message was clear. The fate of the prince was up to her.

Prince Noland was muttering to himself about Talforland and Kelvinor as he lay

prawled on the ground. Insanity was clearly taking over his mind; the power of Kal's

pendant had assured that and there was very little Ayla could do even if she really

wanted to save him.

She turned to the men now gathering to support her. "Take him to the dungeons

below the ruined temple. We will be sending him back to his sister in the coming

weeks with a message to keep far from our borders."

The men obeyed, grabbing the crazed man by the arms and dragging him toward

the temple. A groan lifted up from the grass and Roderick and Ayla ran toward where

Landon was kneeling. Jovan was staring up at the sky.

"Don't worry about me, Lady Ayla. I would rather die than face your wrath." He

smiled, blood appearing on his lips. He looked to Landon and Roderick. "Perhaps I

have redeemed myself?"

"I'm sorry you had to," Landon whispered to him, "but I'm glad you did."

Jovan leaned back, closing his eyes against the cold night. One last anguished

breath filled his lungs and then stopped short.

Landon took his friend's hand. "His heart has stopped."

Ayla felt tears in her eyes. She turned and walked away from them, not sure where she was going or what to do next. She just walked, step after step across the field.

Roderick chased after her. "Wait! Where are you going?"

She shook her head, "I don't know."

She looked up seeing the smoke rising into the air from the direction of the walls. She could hear shouts and chaos still coming from the city.

"There's so much to do." She stopped, regarding the broken gates.

Roderick came up behind her and put an arm around her shoulder. "Don't worry. We'll do it together." She looked down at his hand, remembering the identical slash she had seen there.

She turned and looked up at him. "Does that cut mean we're married?"

He took a deep breathe and nodded. "It was the only way to save you from being joined to the prince and to empower the pendants."

"Oh," she said, her cheeks turning red.

"But only you have the power to rule, Ayla." He turned to her, taking both her hands and kneeling. "And I will follow you, my queen, for as long as I live."

Ayla couldn't help but smile at his seriousness. She pulled him up and laughed slightly, throwing her arms around his neck and letting him lift her into the air. When her feet hit the ground again, they were in an embrace that Ayla never wanted to end.

"Promise me this," she said.

"Anything."

"When all this is over, can we have a real wedding?"

He laughed and nodded, "Yes."

CHAPTER 29

B RENIA MADE HER WAY UP the long spiral staircase, careful to lift her skirts free of the steps. It was her fifteenth birthday, and the Lady Ayla was waiting for her in the royal chambers. It had been a long month since their last audience together. It seemed that the Lady of Kelvinor was always busy with someone or something. New trade routes had to be discussed, a parliament had to be set up, and orphanages needed caretakers and gold coins. It seemed the queen's work never came to an end.

Brenia was exhausted as well. The long line of nobles and representatives that had come from all of the surrounding lands in the last year had to be greeted and entertained by someone, and Brenia had set herself up in the role of head greeter. Lady Ayla's first priority was always her own people, and many times the delegates were waiting for many hours to see the Queen of Kelvinor. Brenia had learned from Madam Grayheart to serve them tea and biscuits and to speak politely without her commonly accent. She had learned this so well after a few months that when Ayla's dwarf father arrived from the mountain with an entourage of company and greeted everyone with strong hugs, Brenia was quite taken aback at the lack of formality.

But Brenia quickly relaxed around the people whom she'd always regarded as a myth. Now, she saw Otto almost more than the Queen herself and had developed a special friendship with Girda who loved to make dresses from the soft fabrics now available to her skilled hands. All the other dwarfs had returned home with assurances that the Kingdom of Kelvinor would leave them be. The mountain would be a protected region for as long and Ayla and her descendents reigned.

Brenia knocked softly on the door of the queen's room, remembering with a smile that just a year ago, she had entered this very same room through a trap door in the floor beneath the rug. The Lady Ayla had not sealed it.

"Who calls?" came a soft voice through the heavy wooden door.

"Bree. May I come in?"

But the Lady beat her to the door, throwing it open.

"I should have known!" she said, embracing her friend, "It's only you that forget all the proper greetings."

"Oh," Bree caught herself, "I'm sorry."

"Don't apologize." Lady Ayla took her arm and led her through the doorway. "You are going to be my first maid at my wedding. Surely you can forget some of the formalities. Remember, we promised to be friends and only pretend when people are looking."

"This is true." Bree grinned and let go of the queen's arm, giving her a grand bow and getting a good look at her for the first time. Lady Ayla seemed exhausted and sadder than usual. Roderick had been gone for two months helping to restore the Kingdom of Granland, and Brenia knew his absence had taken a toll on the young queen. "So, Your Majesty, you called?"

"Yes," the queen smiled, "but I'm afraid it's not a joking matter. I have a birthday present for you of sorts ... an adventure I need you to undertake for me and for your kingdom."

"What sort of adventure?" Brenia stood and moved to the bed, sitting on the soft coverlet.

"I have received word from Talforland's queen." The queen unfolded a bit of parchment Brenia did not realize had been in her hand. Lady Ayla handed it to her.

> To the Lady Ayla Lunara Joyinheart, Queen of Kelvinor:
>
> I have received your message regarding the defeat of my brother and father in those parts of Talforland which have now been abandoned, and I do recognize your claim to the throne of Kelvinor. You have given me my own kingdom and I will hold no dispute with you. The Prince of Talforland now finds himself captive in his own kingdom and can bring you no harm.
>
> However, my kingdom contains a treasure which we both can share.

A box lies in our temple locked with the Key of Mazi. Fire and pressure can not open the box, only the key which is lost to us. My father thought it might be in your kingdom; however, he found no trace of it.

Should you have such a key, an inscription on the box reads that all the treasures of the world are locked in the box. We can share these treasures, you and I. Send your most trusted representative to me and we will meet on neutral ground.

"The letter is signed, Queen Kristlinadora of Talforland," Lady Ayla said as Brenia finished the letter. "I've sent her a message which should arrive in three days time. She will meet you at the only bridge that crosses the river dividing our two lands on the evening of the full moon. That should give you two weeks to find the key and get to the meeting spot. You'll take Sunfire, Landon, and a small battalion of men with you."

"You want me to go?" Brenia stared at her in disbelief. "Why? I'm not a fighter or..."

"But you are my most trusted friend," the queen interrupted, "and you know the power that the red pendant produced. That, like this box, is a treasure of Talforland. The contents of that box cannot be trusted to aid Kelvinor or any other land."

Brenia nodded. "And the key?"

The Lady Ayla retrieved a book from her working desk nearby. Brenia smiled a little to see it so piled high with papers. Messages were coming in from every part of the country, every day. She marveled how Ayla could possibly read and respond to them all. The Madam Grayheart, however, was a good teacher. Brenia knew that firsthand. Lady Ayla had learned to read and write the trade language much faster than anyone had expected.

Lady Ayla flipped the book open on the bed and turned to a marked page. "This entry in the History of Kelvinor tells of a golden key filled with the magic of opening many doors. Supposedly, it could turn any lock, no matter the size or shape."

"Does it say where it is?" Brenia squinted her eyes trying to decipher the runes. Lady Ayla had only taught her a few of the symbols.

"No. The last mention of the key states that it was with a great man, Diesis, sent in a boat to explore the open sea. The boat never returned and it's believed to have crashed in a great storm."

Brenia nodded, "I remember it from my father's old bedtime tales. Not the key though. All my father said was that Diesis was a great warrior who lost faith in the Creator God and was claimed by the sea demon, Rahab. He was punished for his pride, thinking he could sail through any storm."

"I think the story is at least partly true." Lady Ayla closed the book, "And I think that you should go looking for that key."

"Lady Ayla, that key is at the bottom of the ocean, if it even exists!" Brenia just stared at her in disbelief.

"Bree, I have faith that if you go out on the water looking for that key, it will find you." Ayla put her hand on Brenia's shoulder. "Take a boat out on the water and just have faith."

"Alright." Brenia took a deep breath. "When do I leave?"

"In the morning," Ayla answered, standing up from the bed and going to her wardrobe. She fished through a small drawer until she found a silver band. Lady Ayla took it and placed it on Brenia's hand. "My parents had this made for me long before I could even wear it. Take it with you for luck."

Brenia threw her arms around Ayla, "It's not a common birthday present, I suppose. But thank you! Thank you for my adventure!"

Ayla said her goodbye's to Bree and the girl left. As the door closed behind the girl, the queen's face fell to a worried frown. She walked slowly back to the book sitting on the bed and flipped through the pages until she reached a passage she had not shown Brenia.

The prophecy on the page was quite clear. It was Brenia's turn to make her mark on the history of Kelvinor.

Printed in the United States
132148LV00002B/11/P

9 780980 205152